ALMOST Human
CAT MARSTERS

ELLORA'S CAVE
ROMANTICA PUBLISHING

*W*hat the critics are saying...

ഇ

"Oh, wow! Almost Human is exactly why Ms. Marsters is one of my new favorite authors. Her previous work was great, but this book goes above and beyond your usual erotic romance. […] Almost Human took every aspect I could want in an erotic romance, and made it perfect." ~ *Erotic Escapades*

"Almost Human is a fast paced story that really puts the "E" in erotic. […] Ms. Marsters had me in her grip from the beginning and I read this book well into the night to finish it in one sitting. Every time I tried to put Almost Human down, I kept thinking just one more page until there weren't any pages left. I think that says it all—don't you?" ~ *Joyfully Reviewed*

"ALMOST HUMAN is an epic novel. It will take you on a wild ride through many realms, introduce you to many intriguing people and creatures, and most importantly will get your heart pumping enough to love every page." ~ *Cupid's Library Reviews*

"Almost Human is a really hot story that all fans of paranormal stories will love and this reviewer can really recommend the book." ~ *Loves Romances*

An Ellora's Cave Romantica Publication

www.ellorascave.com

Content Advisory:

S – ENSUOUS
E – ROTIC
X – TREME

Ellora's Cave Publishing offers three levels of Romantica™ reading entertainment: S (S-ensuous), E (E-rotic), and X (X-treme).

The following material contains graphic sexual content meant for mature readers. This story has been rated E–rotic.

S-*ensuous* love scenes are explicit and leave nothing to the imagination.

E-*rotic* love scenes are explicit, leave nothing to the imagination, and are high in volume per the overall word count. E-rated titles might contain material that some readers find objectionable — in other words, almost anything goes, sexually. E-rated titles are the most graphic titles we carry in terms of both sexual language and descriptiveness in these works of literature.

X-*treme* titles differ from E-rated titles only in plot premise and storyline execution. Stories designated with the letter X tend to contain difficult or controversial subject matter not for the faint of heart.

About the Author

❧

Cat Marsters lives in a fairytale cottage with a Prince Charming husband who helpfully brings her delicious treats while she writes, and is more than happy to inspire a steamy love scene at a moment's notice. In fact, he walks around half-naked for this very purpose.

And then she wakes up. In actual fact, Cat lives in a village in southeast England which, while not quite a fairytale setting, is nonetheless very pretty and was mentioned in the Domesday Book of 1087. She shares a house with only slightly batty parents who hardly ever tell her to get a real job, and a musician brother who knows there's no chance she'll ever get one if he doesn't. Life is kept from being boring by the often hilarious antics of a pair of kinetically charged fluffballs who will apparently grow into normal cats.

Cat has been writing all her life, but in order to keep herself rich in shoes and chocolate, she's also worked as an airline check-in agent, video rental clerk, stationery shop assistant, and laboratory technician. She's still aiming for the fairytale cottage and asks all potential Prince Charmings to apply in writing with pictures of themselves and their Aston Martins.

Cat welcomes comments from readers. You can find her website and email address on her author bio page at www.ellorascave.com.

Tell Us What You Think

We appreciate hearing reader opinions about our books. You can email us at Comments@EllorasCave.com.

ALMOST HUMAN

శ

Glossary

൪

The Wall—Separates the Realms. A shining violet curtain that can't be penetrated except by Faeries, or by humans under heavy enchantment—and even then only at weak places known as Bridges.

Realm of Euskara

Galatea—Romantic, aristocratic country where the Association is based.

Paseilles—Capital of Galatea.

Severeges—Galatean coastal town.

Iberia—Hot, sensual country to the west of Galatea.

Colacochea—Iberian town at the foot of the mountains.

Basque—Kelfish tribe living in the Iberian-Galatean mountains.

Dacia—Northern country.

Dacstein—Dacian town near the Third Bridge.

First Bridge—leads to Asiatica.

Third Bridge—leads to Peneggan.

Realm of Peneggan

Port Jaret—Southern port, city closest to Koskwim.

Koskwim—Island by the Wall on the south coast, secret home of the Order. Believed by most Realms to be inhabited only by dangerous dragons. Site of the Second Bridge.

Peneggan City—Capital of Peneggan.

Elvyrn—Second city, famously genteel.

Srheged—Northern city.

Second Bridge—leads to Asiatica.

Third Bridge — leads to Euskara.
Fourth Bridge — leads to Angeland.
Sixth Bridge — leads to Zemlya.

Realm of Zemlya

Vaznafjörður — River port closest to the Sixth Bridge.
Tir na nÓg — Castle fortress, home of the Empress.
Saoirsefjörd — Capital city, near the Fifth Bridge.
Fifth Bridge — leads to Angeland.
Sixth Bridge — leads to Peneggan.

Realm of Angeland

Lorekdell — City on the River Lorek.
Fifth Bridge — leads to Zemlya.
Fourth Bridge — leads to Peneggan.

Organizations

The Order — Based on the island of Koskwim, Peneggan, the secretive Order takes in orphans and young volunteers and trains them as Knights — an elite military. Standard rank is the Dragon, advanced rank is the Phoenix.

The Association — A collective of highly desirable women, known as Associées, for hire as male companions. Trainees begin as Fillies and can rise to the rank of Lady. Based in Paseilles, Galatea, in the Realm of Euskara.

The Federacion — Mysterious rival of the Order. Based in Iberia, Euskara.

Prologue

ഔ

I knew it was going to be a lousy day when I woke to a woman screaming in my ear that I was a fucking pervert, but I think the real highlight came when I fell five hundred feet and smashed my skull into half a dozen pieces.

Still, as Lady Belleveuve was so fond of telling me, there's no such thing as lousy. The word is "difficult".

It was a difficult day.

There was a deliciously soft, warm bundle of smooth skin in my arms and a hot, sweet mouth suckling gently at my breast. The lady of the house. Not that I'm usually into girls, but they do pay well and they're so grateful. It's awful what these wives have to go through, a gilded cage of sexual neglect. Just dreadful. There ought to be laws against it.

Anyway, there we were, lying all tangled together under her silken sheets, her ladyship quite obviously up for doing the naughty again, when the maid came in and started screaming. I opened my eyes and glared sleepily at her.

"Do I tell you you're a fucking pervert for doing your job?"

"I cannot work under these conditions!" the girl cried, her words carrying a slight Iberian accent. "It is dreadful, a house of perversity! First the stable boys and now this—this *puta*!"

"Hey," I said severely, "I am not a whore, I am a registered Associée. Gimme some respe—"

What she'd said before that suddenly registered, and I turned to her ladyship, who was cowering beside me. Cowering in her own bed. Dear oh dear. "Stable boys?"

"I thought a younger man might help," she whispered.

I rolled my eyes. Her efforts were commendable, but if you like girls, you like girls, and no amount of strapping young men will help.

Now, me? I love strapping young men. Really love them. They're something of a hobby of mine.

The maid flounced out and her ladyship yanked on a robe and ran after her, pleading in Iberian. At first I thought it was pathetic—then I thought about how hard it really was to find someone who could do your hair properly, and relented.

I wandered downstairs, where the rest of the staff were suitably subservient, and snagged some breakfast from a hot young thing in the kitchen.

"You are my lady's guest?" he asked, bowing as he poured more tea from a silver pot.

"Guess so."

"It is an honor, madam."

See, that's why I like working in Galatea. They respect me here—the maid notwithstanding. They understand what an Associée really is. Not a geisha, not a whore. Something in between. You need a beautiful woman for any purpose, I'm yours—at a price, anyway.

I suppose I ought to introduce myself. Since you're paying, I'll do it the traditional way. Belle jour. I am Chance, Lady of the Association. Your desires are my pleasure.

A Lady is a senior member. High-ranking. One of the best. I started as a Filly when I was a day over the required age. It didn't take me long to rise to my current position. They say I have natural skill. Well, it's only to be expected.

By the time I wandered back upstairs the screaming had died down and her ladyship was sitting at her writing desk, dressed in a beautiful brocade robe. I stepped up behind her silently, pressing a kiss to the back of her neck.

She shivered delightfully. "I'm sorry about all the screaming."

"It's all right," I said. "I've had wives come after me with crossbows before."

"I didn't know your lifestyle was so dangerous."

"You have no idea."

I left her and went in search of my clothes. Mirabella, the shocked maid, had politely taken them away last night before she realized how sinful things were going to get. I found them in the dressing room, in shreds.

"Can I borrow a frock?" I called through.

Her ladyship laughed throatily. "*Ma cherie*, after last night, you can borrow anything."

Hmm.

Appropriately dressed — for an Associée is always appropriately dressed — I took my leave of her. She was glowing, beautiful. Yesterday when I'd arrived she'd been ever so shy, a little mouse. It's good to get some job satisfaction.

In several ways.

The most sophisticated form of transport available in the Realm of Euskara these days is the horse-drawn carriage. In Peneggan you can fly on dragonback. In Angeland they even have an iron railroad. But here in Euskara it's horses all the way. Quaint.

Lazily, I penned last night's details in my log as the carriage rattled away, occasionally staring out the window at the scenery. It's pretty here, hazy lavender fields stretching into the distance, scenting the air. Soothing me.

I had a hotel room in town, from where I could take messages from the Association headquarters in Paseilles. The coach was halfway there when my scryer buzzed.

I pulled the hemisphere of rock out of my bag and turned the polished black surface to my face. It shimmered red for a second or two, then cleared as the connection came through. The image was hazy and green, which meant my caller was off-Realm — and, seeing as how I was being contacted by

15

scryer, obviously it was someone from my *other* job. The less fun one.

"Phoenix 20572?"

I sighed. I just love dealing with the Order, they're so warm and personal.

"Tyra, my love. Eaten any men lately?"

She gave me a stern look. Tyra is a siren, but I only know that because I'm special. To the rest of the Realm she's a buttoned-down librarian in sensible shoes. "They give me indigestion. Where are you?"

"Euskara."

"Yes, I know that, but where exactly?"

"Galatea. On my way to Severeges. Why? Got a job for me?"

"I have an extremely important meeting for you. The Order is calling all Knights of Phoenix rank and above." Tyra looked troubled. "This has never happened before."

"Sure it has," I said lazily, "when that psycho chick tried to take over the island. Everyone was on red alert."

"This is different," Tyra said. "How soon can you get here?"

I frowned. "I guess I could get a ship to Dacia and then…I don't know—it's overland to the Bridge. A day and a half at the least. More like two, maybe three."

"Can't you manage any faster?"

I narrowed my eyes at her. Tyra might be scary as shit but I'm no slouch myself.

"I travel at the same speed as everyone else," I said levelly. "You know that."

She gave an impatient sigh. "Can't your father—"

"No," I said firmly. "No, he can't."

That was a direct lie. He could. Whatever the task, he could. But I didn't let him. I made a solemn vow a long time ago that I'd never let myself turn into my father. I'm halfway to becoming my mother—which is still a faintly scary prospect—but I refuse to give in to my father's heritage.

I told Tyra I'd be there as soon as humanly possible—stressing the "humanly"—and signed off. Dammit. I was enjoying my sojourn in Galatea. Euskara is my favorite Realm, courteous and beautiful and highly sensual. I loved the grace and pomp of the high court in Paseilles, the bronzed Iberian beach bodies of Puerta Nueva, the dark menace of the Carthageans, the all-out hedonism that swarms through southern Sisilia.

I didn't want to go back to Peneggan—backward, dusty Peneggan, with its antiquated government systems and its high monster population.

No doubt my parents would be there, adding to said monster population.

The coast road to Severeges winds steeply down the cliffs as it nears the town. Up ahead I could see the tall, murderous mountains rearing above me, the town sliding precariously down the lower slopes toward a sea that sparkled and shone like diamonds.

I sighed and started planning my trip. If I sent a runner to the docks as soon as I arrived at the hotel, by the time I got packed, ship passage could be sorted out. I'd need to send a copy of my log to the Association's HQ in Paseilles—the hotel Kelfs could do that for me. After which I'd need to—

There was a sudden jolt and the carriage wobbled alarmingly. I was thrown into the far corner—thank the gods the carriage was so soft and squishy on the inside or that would have hurt a lot more. As it was I felt bruised, and I hammered on the roof of the carriage, yelling to the driver Kelf.

"What the hell was that?"

"I'm sorry, my lady, the road is uneven."

"Well, find a more even bit! I don't want to go plunging into the sea."

"Yes, my lady."

I glanced out of the window. The road was separated from the sheer drop down to the sea by a wooden fence. Great barrier. I'm sure that will stop me plunging headlong to my death.

We started along again, slowly, unsurely. Things didn't feel right.

"Is something wrong?" I called up.

"I think one of the horses was injured when it stumbled," the Kelf said.

"Okay, stop the coach," I said. "Maybe there's something I can—"

Another heavy jolt had me losing my footing as I stood up, and I tumbled to the floor of the carriage.

"Can you steady it? I'm trying to get out," I said, but either the Kelf didn't hear me or—well, he must not have heard me. Kelfs don't disobey. Even outside of Euskara, where they're not starved and demeaned as part of the training process, it's part of a Kelf's intrinsic nature to be helpful to humans.

When I moved to the door I sent the carriage tilting to the right, which made me fall against the door. Which made the door open.

I swung out, heart hammering, clinging to the doorframe. The carriage tilted with me, and I felt it slowly start to waver.

Then air was rushing past me and we were falling, hard and fast, down through the clouds and the mist and the spray to the water below. The water—and the jagged rocks.

Chapter One

ɛɔ

Unconsciousness is not something I'm unfamiliar with. In fact, we've become quite good friends over the years. People who try to come between us usually get short shrift from me.

The guy who woke me in the fierce waves by forcing air into my lungs was, therefore, down for a hell of a kicking. As soon as I got my legs moving, anyway.

I knew I was in a bad way when he tied me on his back and started climbing back up the cliff. I couldn't move, couldn't speak, couldn't see—couldn't do anything at all except breathe pain. So I slipped back toward the arms of the familiar and hung out with unconsciousness again.

I woke once more possibly hours later, possibly days. Now I appeared to be in a bed. Not a particularly comfortable bed, but then I have become accustomed to sprung, feathered mattresses with the highest quality sheets. Silk if possible. Yeah, I'm expensive.

I cranked my eyes open, which hurt like death, and tried to focus on the room. I was at least able to move, which was a slight improvement on my earlier condition. Still, when I raised my hand, I felt the bones of my arm shift and slide against each other in broken shards. Something was pressing against my lungs. Maybe pressing through them. It was hard to tell with all the hurting.

"What are you?"

The voice came from the darkness. A lamp burned low by the bed, but it didn't illuminate all corners of the room. He was out there somewhere, in the blackness where my hazy vision couldn't penetrate.

A deep, dark voice, bringing with it a resonant shudder that jarred my shattered body.

"Hurt," I replied. My voice was a whisper.

"Why aren't you dead?"

Ah. Interesting question. "I'm...different."

Movement in the corner. From the shadows a figure emerged.

I couldn't see him well. I think my skull was cracked or something — vision was blurry, moving, swaying. Like being in one of those fairground haunted houses where the walls move.

He came toward me and I guess I should have been frightened. He was powerful, this much I could tell. Gleaming skin, dark hair — and that was all. My swaying vision was making me nauseous, so I closed my eyes.

"It's a full moon," he said.

That's nice.

"You're still human — human-shaped, anyway — so I don't think you're Were."

I tried to frown but gave up because it hurt.

"I saw you fall in the daytime, so I don't think you're vamp. Besides," he took something from around his neck and pressed it to my forehead, "this does nothing."

"Nice and cold," I said. "What is it?"

"Pentacle."

It took a moment to understand. It was a religious symbol — or it could be, if you believed in it. Plus, I figured it was silver. Good for Weres.

"And it's iron," he said, "so I don't think you're Fae."

So I was wrong. I've got a cracked skull, cut me a break.

He studied me a while. I felt the heat of his gaze through my eyelids.

"Are you Kelfish?"

"Do I look Kelfish?"

"You look like a corpse."

"Sure, hit me when I'm down." I tried to lift my hand to check for the vial I usually wear on my person—last seen on a chain around my neck—but I couldn't move it far, because it just hurt too much.

I licked my lips. "Do me a favor?"

"What?"

"Is there a chain 'round my neck? A necklace?"

"There was," he said. "It fell."

Panic set in. "Did you catch it?"

"Yeah, I have it."

I opened my eyes to see him dangling the chain from one hand. The vial swung in front of me. Actually, four vials. My vision was really in trouble.

"I need to drink it," I said.

"What is it?"

I went for the honest answer. "Magic."

"You're a sorceress?"

I swallowed. "Not really. But I need that."

"What will it do?"

"Just give me the damn drink!"

After a moment's hesitation he obeyed, unscrewing the lid of the vial and tipping it to my lips.

The warm liquid slid down my throat, burned for a second, then I was shaking hands with my old friend Blackout again.

Next time I opened my eyes I could see.

What I could see was that I was in a dull, empty room. There was a bed and a wooden chest, a lamp and a rug. That was about it.

There was also a warm, naked body right behind me.

Hmm. Is it Mr. Tall, Dark and Suspicious? Why yes, I think it is. He had one leg slung over mine and both his arms wrapped around me. I felt him breathe, deep and even, his skin hot against my back. His body was hard—hard muscle and bone and hard—

Well. Hello.

It's not that I'm not used to it. One of the first things an Associée is trained to do is subtly ignore a stiffie until the appropriate moment. Well, hey—we're the most desirable women in the Realm, and that's quantifiable. We'd be offended if men didn't get raging hard-ons at the sight—and feel—of us. Lying here naked with my certifiably perfect ass tucked up against his happy bits, I was perfectly pleased that said happy bits were standing up and cheering for me.

I shifted against him, reveling in the heat and strength of his erection. I didn't need to see it to know how big it was. Trust me when I say I'm an expert on this.

When I moved I realized I was healed. Not totally—my body still ached in places and I could feel the sting of a few cuts and bruises here and there, but my major organs were all in the right places and my bones weren't sticking in them anymore. It felt good, unbelievably good, to no longer be in horrific pain.

I stretched, luxuriating in my own body. I felt great. I'd kicked death in the teeth and now I had a sexy man wrapped around me.

And how did I know he was sexy? Come on. I'd heard his voice—his rough, dark voice, the memory of which still sent shivers through me. And I felt his body. Oh boy, did I feel it.

I let my arm slip back over his ribs and beyond to feel it some more. Mmm. Hard, sculpted back. Rocky biceps. Nice dusting of hair on the forearms. I'm not a fan of hairy men—if I wanted fuzz I'd go shag a gorilla—but on the other hand those completely hairless men remind me of either bulked-up male escorts or little boys. And I'm not into those, either. A little hair goes a long way in my book.

My hand roamed a little lower, surveying the territory. And what marvelous territory it was, too! I arched my back, enjoying my pain-free muscles, and reached down to encounter one of the most perfectly formed buttocks I'd ever felt in my life. I was just stretching a little more to see if its twin was as sweetly made when an iron vise clamped around my wrist.

Actually I think it was his hand, but you know—it felt more like a vise to me.

"You're feeling better."

His voice rumbled through me. Gods, it was sexy. I stretched again, demonstrating my newfound wellness, and his hand loosened its grip.

"I'm feeling good," I purred. Really, really good. That hot hard body and big hard cock of his were making me feel much better than I should have. Hey, I've found the cure for all the Realms' ills—a sexy man to rub his hot naked body against yours. Never be unwell again!

"What are you?" he asked again.

If I'd been facing him, I'd have given him my most smoldering look. As it was, I let my fingers do the talking, trailing my hand over the hot skin of his naked hip, wriggling my bottom against him before slipping my hand between us and wrapping my fingers around his long, swollen length.

I wanted him inside me. Quite suddenly, I wanted it so fiercely that for a moment I couldn't breathe.

I felt his body tense. A low rumble started in his chest. It sent vibrations through my body, making my skin hot and my muscles ripple with need. Moisture flooded my pussy, hot and wild. Beneath the arm he had wrapped around my chest, my nipples hardened, and I knew he felt them.

"I'm hot," I breathed.

Cat Marsters

He didn't say anything. He didn't have to. His hand found my breast, his fingers squeezing my flesh, thumb rubbing my aching nipple. I felt his mouth on the back of my neck, a hard kiss against my skin, and my whole body shuddered. He was unshaven, the rough hair on his jaw creating a glorious friction.

I moved my hand down his cock, stroking the base, and he thrust his hips against me, trapping my hand between us. No matter. I wriggled a little bit and found his balls, and began cupping and stroking and fondling.

His teeth dug into my shoulder and I arched, whimpering at the dark eroticism. My legs parted and I rolled my hips back, rubbing myself against him, letting him feel how wet I was, how much I wanted him. That huge hot cock of his slid against my desperate, slippery folds, and I almost came there and then.

But before I had the chance he shoved me on my belly, pulled me onto my knees and drove deep inside me.

I cried out. I couldn't help it. It felt so animal, so primitive, to be fucked this hard and this deep by someone whose name I didn't know, whose face I hadn't seen. He thrust deeper into me and my whole body surged forward on the bed. But next time I was ready for him, bracing my hands against the mattress and arching my back, plunging my hips back to meet his as he rammed into me.

Gods, he went so deep I swear I felt him in my throat.

His hands were on my hips, grabbing me to him as he thrust over and over, harder and deeper each time, a deep slide of intense heat, the pleasure so strong it was almost pain. I threw my head back and begged with incoherent words for him to fuck me harder, faster, showing him with my body when words failed me.

One hand left my hip and dragged up to my breast, squeezing hard, the pinch of his fingers on my nipple almost

24

enough to send me over the edge. My fingers tore holes in the sheet and I moaned, a low, desperate sound.

But it wasn't until he stretched over me and sank his teeth into my shoulder again—like a wild beast claiming his mate—that I flew into orgasm, screaming so loud the walls shook as pain spiked pleasure. My body rocked and writhed as agonizing spasms of glorious heat shocked through me. I yelped and shrieked and possibly even prayed as I came so hard I thought I might have blacked out.

The only reason I'm sure I didn't was that I felt him as he came right behind me, literally, letting out the most fearsome roar as he throbbed and pumped into me until I had spunk dripping down my legs.

I don't remember falling backward to the bed atop him. I don't remember him wrapping his arms around me again, tighter than before, holding me to him while his soft cock rested inside me, impressive even in repose. I was drifting on a cloud of happy pink ecstasy, my body occasionally shivering with remembered pleasure. The feel of his body once more wrapped around mine only made it harder to connect with reality.

I came back to myself when he whispered tightly, fiercely in my ear, "I'm sorry."

I blinked. "What?"

"I'm sorry. That was—it was brutal, and I...I'm not myself, I didn't mean to hurt you—"

"You didn't hurt me," I said. "I really am feeling much better." I stretched again, felt his cock twitch inside me.

"I couldn't control myself."

"Mmm. Then don't try to."

"You enjoyed that?"

He sounded disbelieving. Well, I suppose some women wouldn't. That was, I guess, exactly the sort of sex that her ladyship had been having for years, and hated. It's not the soft, mutually giving sort of sex the Association is fond of.

But, you know, there's a time and place for soft, sweet, tender sex. And there's a time and place for hard, wild, brutal, animalistic sex. And that, my friend, was it.

"Honey," I wriggled against him again, just to feel that hot body so close to mine, "if I'd enjoyed it any more, chunks would have been falling out of the ceiling. I think the whole Realm heard me come."

Was that another stir of interest in my pussy? Why, yes, I believe so. He was getting harder inside me, and the power I felt at that was almost enough to give me another orgasm.

I still had no idea where I was. How long I'd been here. What had happened to my clothes, my possessions. Who the hell this man—with his cock stiffening inside me—actually was.

I didn't know anything, in fact, except that I wanted to feel him moving in me again.

Still lying on my back on top of him, I moved my legs apart, raising my knees as I did so that my feet rested on either side of his legs. Then I ran one hand over my body, over my breasts which were swollen and aching for attention, stroked along his arm, down over my wet, full pussy, shivering slightly as my own fingers brushed against the needy folds buried around his cock.

If he'd been getting hard before, it was nothing compared to what happened when I started stroking him, inside and out. I tensed the muscles inside myself, squeezing him with an undulating motion. Took a long time to learn that, but it's never failed me yet.

He let out a hiss of breath. I smiled and ran my fingers over the base of his cock.

He swore.

I stroked his balls.

"Again," he moaned.

Well, I can be a good girl sometimes. I did as I was told. I stroked his balls, cupped them, loving the weight in my hand.

I wanted to taste them, but that'd have to wait. Right now he was hard inside me, and more than anything else I just wanted to feel him fucking me again. Wanted him to lose control and drive that hot, throbbing cock so deep inside me that I screamed. I wanted to lose control, too.

His cock twitched inside me. I let out a little sigh and started moving, gently, feeling the slide of his hot, hard flesh inside me. He shifted behind me, his hand moving to my breast to roll my aching nipple between his fingers. I closed my eyes, breathing faster, and bucked my hips harder against him, feeling his belly tense against my backside, feeling his cock jump inside me.

His other hand trailed down my body, making me gasp as the mere brush of his fingertips against my stomach sent a heated thrill right through me. My pussy clenched involuntarily and he grunted as I squeezed his cock inside me.

His fingers brushed my folds and I moaned. When he touched my clit I cried out, "Again!"

He removed his hand and my eyes flew open. I wanted more, dammit! But then his hand closed over mine, over his balls, and I realized I'd stopped stroking him. His hand started a rhythm, moving my fingers over his delicate sac, stroking, gently squeezing, then sliding my fingers around his staff — fucking him with my hand while he fucked me with his cock.

His breath was hot against my neck. He licked me and I moaned, so he kissed me and I gasped—then he bit me and I writhed against his mouth, pleasure mounting higher and higher inside me.

I started moving again, my eyes closed, lost in the rhythm of his hand over mine and his cock as he thrust gently into me. Then his hand left mine and returned to my pussy, stroking my folds, pinching my clit, stroking so perfectly, so relentlessly, that my back arched and I came, hard. Gasping and crying, thrusting my hips down to feel his cock all the way inside me, I bucked against his hand and his mouth as he bit down on me again, the pain pushing the pleasure higher.

I didn't want it to end. I jerked away from his mouth, thrusting my breasts forward and rising with arched back to sit on him, my legs splayed and my hand still buried between us. He angled his hips, raising his knees to brace himself against the bed as I rose up then down, riding him like a jockey with the gold cup in sight.

And what a finish! He thrust beneath me, my stallion, galloping ahead so fast and furious it was all I could do to keep up. His cock pistoned into me, harder and harder. My hand lost its grip on his cock and his balls, and I leaned forward, hands on his knees, riding him for all I was worth.

"Harder," I managed to gasp. "Harder, do it harder!"

He suddenly sat up, pushing his cock forward inside me until it pressed against the front of my pussy, and he grabbed my hips and pulled me down on him so hard I thought his dick might go right through me and out my pussy through my belly.

It didn't. But it did shove me into another bucking, screaming orgasm, words spilling from me, begging him to fuck me harder, longer, don't stop, oh gods, please don't ever stop.

"I'm not going to," he breathed in my ear, and another ripple of pleasure shot through me. "I'm going to fuck you so hard you pass out."

"Yes," I moaned.

"You want that? You want my cock inside you?"

"Don't ever take it out," I begged.

"No?" Suddenly he did just that, shoving me off him, flipping me over so that I lay sprawled on the bed with him poised above me, the head of his cock rubbing my clit, the light hair on his chest chafing my nipples, his eyes boring into mine.

I finally saw his face, and the sight tipped me back into the outer suburbs of orgasm-ville.

He was incredible. His eyes were amber, dark and stormy, his face an intense, hard chiseled masterpiece. His hair was midnight black and disheveled, and what I'd taken for unshaven cheeks actually turned out to be whiskers, dark and coarse against his jawline. The whole of it was like a mane around his glorious head. Like being fucked by a lion.

Hail lionesses!

"Fuck me," I managed, and he did, impaling me with his cock as his mouth took mine, his lips firm, his teeth sharp, his tongue unbelievably talented. He fucked me with his mouth as he fucked me with his cock, a total possession of my body, and I loved it so much I came twice more before he erupted inside me, his orgasm so fierce it made my body shake.

For a long time I couldn't move, and the realization hit me that this man had just made me come three times before I even saw his face. His cock was still buried inside me, his weight pressing me down. He was breathing hard against my neck, his whiskers stroking my skin.

All the strength I could muster was just enough to move my hand a little and twine a few strands of his sweat-dampened hair around my fingers. I didn't know what I'd expected him to look like, but when I thought about the man who'd fucked me like an animal, I wasn't surprised he looked so — so feral.

I remembered his eyes, the dark storm in them as he came, and my pussy clenched around his cock.

He lifted his head and his expression was inscrutable. He looked like a man who was seldom at peace, a man who had a lot to think about — a man who rarely had cause to smile. He looked full of blackness inside.

"What?" he asked, his voice a low rumble.

"Dark," I said, because he was. Dark hair, dark expression, darkness behind those brilliant amber eyes.

He stiffened—and I mean his body, not his cock. Although that wasn't quite relaxed, either. A deep furrow appeared between his eyes.

"How do you—" He cut himself off.

"What?"

He hesitated then said, "My brother called me that."

I frowned. "He called you Dark?"

He nodded and a sudden smile escaped me. "It suits you!"

He said nothing.

"What's your real name?" I asked, and he suddenly pulled out of me, rolling fluidly to his feet.

"It doesn't matter."

I frowned. Well, it was odd, but never mind. "I'll call you Dark, then?"

He shrugged, his back to me, and bent to mess with the fire that was burning low in the grate. I looked around the room again, a proper look this time, and didn't see much new. It looked like a rented room, stark and bare with tatty fixtures, crumbling walls, an old quilt on the bed and a dirty fireplace. And a really hot naked man who wouldn't tell me his name.

Never mind. I knew the important things about him. He was hot as all hell, had a gigantic cock and knew how to use it. What else was I going to be interested in?

"This is a tavern?" I guessed out loud.

"Yeah."

"Where?"

"Just outside Severeges."

"What happened to my coach? The Kelf?"

"The Kelf is downstairs. Your coach is in small pieces, floating out to sea." He paused in stoking the fire. "The horses too. I'm sorry."

"Oh." Horrible way to die. I should know. I went through it too. "You saw it happen?"

"One of the horses stumbled. I saw you fall out, knocking the coach off balance. The whole thing fell into the sea. I went down to help the Kelf as he was pulling you to the surface. Neither of us could believe you were still alive."

"Well, I'm a tough cookie," I said vaguely. I didn't really want to get into the peculiarities of my rubber-boned body.

Dark stood, and I took a minute to admire the back view of him before he turned and regarded me. I shivered. Those eyes of his were amazing. It was like being watched by a big cat, all coiled strength, ready to pounce and devour you.

My own cat revved up in appreciation. Those who knew me prior to my initiation into the Association said that it was the career I was born for. It's not that I'm a nymphomaniac, it's just that… Okay, maybe I am. I love sex. Who the hell doesn't? Faced with the prospect of a hard-bodied man with dark eyes and a thick cock, my pussy gets all hot and slippery and I can't breathe for thinking about how he might feel sliding inside me, filling that aching space. Sucking on my breasts. Digging his fingertips into every inch of me. Driving that cock wherever he wants—I'm more than happy to take it.

I looked at Dark's cock, which was getting hard again, and marveled at his stamina. Usually the only time I get this much cock there is more than one man in bed with me.

He saw me licking my lips. I wanted that cock in my mouth. Dear gods, I wanted it. Wanted to taste it, suck it, feel it fill my throat. I wanted to feel his balls against my chin but I doubted he'd fit in that far. My mouth just wasn't that big.

"So, you want to fuck me again?" I asked.

He was on me in seconds.

Chapter Two

♋

I woke to a rustle of clothing. It's a sound I'm quite attuned to. Dark was dressing, and I opened my eyes in time to see him fasten the last button on a pair of dark denims. That in itself warranted further thought—while workmen in Peneggan wear rough jeans and everyone in Angeland wears them as fashion, they haven't caught on in Euskara. This Realm is very elegant and old-fashioned in its attire. But while buckskins can do marvelous things for a man's lower half, I started thinking there was nothing like a good, worn pair of denims to make a guy look really, really hot. Especially when you know what he looks like under them.

Dark must be an off-Realmer. His Galatean was flawless, but so is my own and I was born in the Realm of Peneggan.

This was interesting.

"Where are you going?" I asked, admiring his beautiful chest and perfect stomach. Sunlight was streaming in through the half-open shutters, gleaming off his skin.

"I have to leave."

I frowned. I was still half asleep, to be honest. We'd fucked each other into oblivion last night, and now the sun was high and I was exhausted. My body, which had felt so marvelous when Dark was touching it, was now reminding me it had been through a lot of trauma in the last sun cycle.

"The Kelf is waiting for you," Dark continued, pulling on a loose shirt. "I bought him from the hotel in Severeges, he's indentured to you."

"Oh," I said, unsure what to say to that.

"His name is Varnus," Dark said.

"Right."

I wanted to ask where he was going but I had a feeling he wasn't going to tell me. He didn't seem the sort to volunteer information. Hell, we hadn't even exchanged names.

"Are you going home?" I asked.

His face darkened even more. "No."

"Then —"

He cut me off with a kiss. Gods, but that man had a glorious mouth. I wondered if there was an Association for men I hadn't heard about. He could make a hell of a living if there was.

"Are you hungry?"

I curved my arm around his neck. "Oh, yeah."

He didn't smile, but his eyes sort of gleamed. I guessed that was Dark's idea of a big grin. It was sexy, anyway.

"I meant for food."

"Oh." I thought about it, realized I was ravenous. "Starving," I admitted.

"I'll get you something."

He stepped away, picked up a kitbag from the floor and paused. I knew he wasn't going to wait around for my food and bring it up to me. Once he left the room, he'd be gone.

I wanted to say goodbye but at the same time, I didn't. Part of me thought that if I did, it'd be too final, and I really rather wanted to bump into him again.

He went to the door, reached for the handle and a voice cried, "Dark!"

I realized it was mine.

Dark stopped, utterly still. He didn't turn. There was silence for a long moment while I tried to think of something to say that wasn't going to sound like goodbye.

"Thank you," I said eventually, and his head moved in a very slight nod. Then the door opened, closed, and he was gone.

I was alone.

Varnus the Kelf was coweringly apologetic about very nearly getting me killed. He pledged his life to my service, which was nice, but since Kelfs couldn't cross the Wall and I needed to get out of the Realm, I figured it wasn't an arrangement that would last for long.

Varnus explained that we were at a coaching inn about sixty miles from Severeges. I vaguely recalled passing one before the coach went haywire. To get into town would take too long—I'd already lost a day and Tyra had been awfully insistent about the urgency of the meeting. I needed clothes and a new scryer, and a Bridge pass too, since mine had been destroyed along with everything else in the crash. All I had was the small purse of money that had been tucked into the bodice of my dress. The dress itself was ruined, having been cut off me by Dark.

That thought sent a rush of heat through me, and a spike of longing too. Ludicrous to miss someone I barely knew—it wasn't as if that was the first time I'd had amazing sex with a stranger. I didn't know what exactly it was about him that made me wish he was still with me. But it was unlikely I'd ever see him again and it wouldn't do to dwell on the past.

"Varnus," I said to my devoted slave of the last ten minutes, "I need you to get me some things."

"Anything, my lady."

"First, clothes. I know everything in the carriage was destroyed, but I had some things at the hotel in Severeges. Can you call them and get them to pack everything up and book me passage on a ship to Dacia, please? Dacstein, if possible."

"Call them?" The Kelf tried to look innocent, and I sighed. Kelfs just can't act. Plus, most of them think that humans have no idea what a scryer is. Well, they'd be right for the most part. Those of us in the know keep it quiet.

"Yes. On your scryer. Don't look so shocked, I know what they are and how they work. And I need one of them too. Mine was lost along with everything else. Are there any Kelfs near here?"

He nodded reluctantly. "Some Basques out fishing. They made camp not far from here."

"Right. See if you can get any clothes from them."

"But my lady, Kelfish clothes…"

I knew what he meant. Kelfs hardly feel the climate, and when left to their own devices don't wear much. Also, being that your average Kelf is about four feet tall, any clothes Varnus could find for me would be barely decent.

"All right, fine. Just…see if you can get any human clothes for me. And I really need that scryer."

I ate the bouillabaisse sent up for me, took a bath in lukewarm water, looked out the window at the rolling sea and waited.

Varnus returned not long after I'd sent him out—Kelfs can be damn quick when they want—with a few scraps of Kelf clothing and a new scryer. The clothes were, of course, far too small to even get into. Even if I'd managed to wriggle the minuscule skirt past my hips, my girlie parts would have been on display for anyone who wanted to see them. And while some people may not believe it, I don't show my pussy to just anyone.

I sighed and looked around the room for inspiration. No curtains, but there were sheets on the bed. I tugged on one experimentally. Well, I'd worn worse.

I fashioned for myself a sort of kilt and ripped up the rest of the cloth to wrap crosswise over my breasts. I made sure my Associée mark was well visible, the three short parallel lines on my right breast that denoted my high rank within the Association. Most people respect an Associée's social rank and training—and if they don't, then the well-known fact that all Associées are schooled in self-defense usually does the trick.

I got a few whistles and catcalls as I made my way through the tavern, but no one really bothered me. Varnus had secured a couple of horses and we set off for the docks. The Kelf had indeed bought passage on a ship to Dacstein, and after we docked he found us overland passage to the Third Bridge. I napped on the stagecoach and woke to see Striker's face a few inches from my own.

I yelped. I'm a fairly tough cookie, but Striker is a damn scary-looking guy. Well, not just scary-looking. He's bloody terrifying—inside as well as out. But his cold, hard eyes, chiseled cheekbones, ice-blond hair and usual ferocious expression generally do the trick of conveying to you what a truly frightening person he is.

"Gods alive, Striker, you nearly gave me a heart attack," I said, straightening in my seat and rearranging my clothing.

"I'm sure your heart's perfectly strong, pet," he said, stepping back out of the coach. "Not sure if it's any good at the warm and fuzzies, but it ain't gonna pack up on you anytime soon."

I scowled and scrambled out of the cramped carriage into the dusk. Striker was fetching my luggage off the roof rack— probably each piece weighed as much as I did, but he hefted them as if they were full of cotton candy.

"Showoff," I said.

A figure came out of the darkness—tall, slender, impossibly stylish in her chic gown and picture hat. She had long, straight dark hair, a generous mouth and beautiful eyes, and she didn't look a day over thirty. This was interesting, since I knew she'd been thirty-five when I was born.

"Chance," she cried, and enveloped me in a hug.

"Hi, Mum."

"Your father said you'd been having some problems," she said. "Lost your Bridge pass?"

"Er, yeah." I turned to Varnus, who was standing quietly by the coach. "Thank you," I said. "I'm leaving the Realm now. You're free to go."

He stared at me for a moment. "Free?"

"Yep. You belong to yourself. Go back to your tribe, go get a paying job." I gave him a couple hundred *ors*. "Go nuts."

Varnus looked at the money, grinned widely and vanished into the darkness.

"That was sweet of you," my mother said. Striker made a disparaging sound.

"I can be capable of sweetness," I said, and he made the noise again, louder. "Did you bring my Bridge pass?"

"Couldn't get one in time," my mother apologized. "Talis is ever so busy."

Talis is the king of Peneggan. Like, the whole freaking Realm. He is sovereign to millions and millions of people, and also something in the way of a family friend. Which is to say he sort of likes my mother and tries to keep on Striker's good side. King Talis isn't stupid. He knows that there's no such thing as being Striker's friend.

"So what do we do?" I asked.

"I'll make us a Bridge," Striker said, as if he was talking about making a cake or something. "I ain't gonna pay those Bridge fees," he added with a curl of his lip.

"Like you couldn't afford it," I scoffed. "You know Bridge fees pay the wages of the free Kelfs who work here," I added. "They get a pittance as it is and they work twenty-hour days—"

"Spare me the lecture, love, or I'll leave you here wrapped in your bedsheet," Striker said.

I scowled at him, and my mother laughed.

"What?"

"You looked just like your father then," she said, and both of us scowled at her for that.

Yeah. Striker is my father. It's not a well-known fact that the Realms' most evil man has a daughter, mostly because, I suspect, he doesn't want anyone to think he's become a softie. Which he hasn't. Whereas most fathers protect and cherish their little girls, buy them ponies and tell them fairy stories, mine gave me a sword, taught me some swear words and regaled me with tales of how many people he'd slaughtered horribly that day.

Sometimes I wonder how Chalia puts up with him. She's not really all that normal in the traditional sense of the word, but she doesn't know any magic and she needs to sleep at night. She's human through and through. Striker hasn't been human for many years.

No one quite knows where in between the two I actually fall.

I have my mother's wide mouth, expressive eyes and slender build, but most people—those who know, anyway—comment that I resemble my father more closely. I was pretty pleased to get his cheekbones, I have to admit, although I could have done without eyes that look like holes in the ice and hair that's several shades paler than my skin. Still, blondes are rare in southern Euskara. I can fetch a fairly high price just by uncovering my head.

We moved away from the Bridge compound. The way it works is, the Wall surrounds and separates the Realms, pulsing and flowing gently like an iridescent violet curtain. It's quite beautiful, and I've known people to stand for hours staring at it. But like many beautiful things, the Wall is also deadly. People call it female, like a siren, because it can entrance you so much you don't realize how much closer it's crept until it's on you, burning you, consuming you. The Wall is hungry, and damn sneaky to boot.

The only creatures who can pass through totally unharmed are Faeries. Humans need to be enchanted against the Wall's harm—it's a tricky process and can easily go wrong. At the six Bridge sites, the Wall has been breached so many times it's weaker, and so safer to pass through. Children can't be enchanted, and neither can animals, Kelfs or inanimate objects much bigger than a rucksack.

Unless they happen to be with Striker.

If you asked anyone whether it was possible to cross the Wall without paying the fees and being enchanted by one of the wizards at the Bridge ports, they'd say it wasn't. Unless you happened to be asking Striker, that is. He creates his own Bridge. Always has. And it doesn't have to be near an established Bridge, either. He can do it anywhere along the Wall.

He sent my luggage through first then made the incantation over my mother. It was creepy, watching her stand so utterly still, like a statue, before she shimmered out of sight to the other side of the Wall.

Then Striker came to me, and I closed my eyes and made myself as still as possible. Until I felt his fingers touch my face, lifting my chin, and I opened my eyes as he said, "What's been happening to you, kid?"

His fingertips probed a sensitive spot on my cheekbone and I winced. While the tonic had done its job in mending my body, it hadn't done much with the superficial cuts and scrapes all over me. I hadn't seen myself in a mirror yet, but I could see the damage on my arms and legs. I was amazed neither of my parents had said anything yet.

"Just a little accident," I said. "I'm okay now."

His eyes scanned me. "Need more of that tonic?"

I hesitated. Then I nodded.

Striker nodded too, and didn't say anything else. The only way I knew he was concerned at all was because he'd asked me about it in the first place.

I closed my eyes and he murmured the words of enchantment over me. It's a strange feeling, and not really a pleasant one. After the total stillness required for the incantation to take, you're frozen in place, and then you start to disintegrate, like turning into sand. Sand that flows apart and flies wide in the wind. Going through the Wall is like being pulled apart, piece by tiny piece, and then mushed back together on the other side. Well, it's not *like* that. It *is* that. I don't particularly enjoy it, but I have the best reaction to it of anyone I've ever met. Apart from Striker, obviously.

Five minutes later I was flowing to the ground in sunny green Peneggan, laughing at my mother who was curled a few feet away, looking wretched.

"I bloody hate Bridge travel," she moaned, wiping her mouth.

"You didn't have to come over with Striker," I said.

"I know. I wanted to see you."

I gave her some water and we waited for Striker to appear. He had a dragon tethered nearby, the small cabin strapped to its back lined with cushions. I climbed up, settled down and drifted off to sleep for a few hours while Striker flew us to the small island of Koskwim, several hundred miles away to the east.

My dreams were dirty. You might think this is an occupational hazard, but in truth I spend so much time planning sex, thinking about the psychology of it, practicing what are not always personally fulfilling sexual acts, that my brain is too full of it and I don't think about it when I'm asleep. It'd be like a miner dreaming about coal.

Maybe it was because the sex I'd had with Dark was just so inhumanly good. My brain kept replaying it over and over. I wanted Dark again, wanted his hands and his mouth on me, wanted to feel his cock driving deep inside me, hear his deep voice whispering filthy things in my ear. I dreamt I arrived at Koskwim and he was waiting for me, there in my bed, naked but for a white sheet that made such a perfect contrast against the dark of his skin that it took my breath away. He pulled me into his arms, the rough hair on his chest abrading my sensitive nipples, and kissed me long and hard as his fingers shaped my buttocks, delved between them, stroking me.

His cock grew between us and excitement pounded through me at the thought — the amazing, incredible thought — that soon that delicious rod of hard flesh would be pounding into me. I pushed his head down toward my breasts, but he wouldn't lick me there, wouldn't suck, wouldn't bite down on my aching nipples the way I wanted him to.

It was only just occurring to me that this was because he never had, in real life, put his mouth to my tits, when a tilt and jolt brought me awake with tearing memories of the coach crash.

But it was just the dragon coming in to land. The island of Koskwim, to the south of the huge landmass that is Peneggan, is barely enclosed by the Wall. In fact, the Second Bridge, from the Realm of Asiatica to Peneggan, comes in on the island, spewing forth tourists every single day. But none of them know that the Order is here — that anything's here. The story put around is that the island is home to a colony of vicious, hungry, deadly dragons, and consequently the Bridge traffic coming through gets off the island pretty damn quick.

It's not a lie about the dragons. Not totally. There are big, scaly, fire-breathing creatures inhabiting the island, but they're not remotely dangerous. Not once they've been properly trained, anyway.

The really deadly Dragons walk on two legs.

I've known about the Order all my life, in complete contrast with your average normal person, who has no idea it exists. Only heads of state and very important ministers know about it. I came here as a child, before I'd ever heard of the Association, eager to join the Order's academy.

And what do they teach here? It's a little like the Association's academy, only it's also overwhelmingly — *not*. The Association teaches you to become the ultimate desirable female. Here on the beautiful volcanic island of Koskwim, the Order teaches you to become the ultimate killer.

There are other things a Knight learns—language skills, diplomacy, healing—but basically, if you come to the Order, you join a group of killers. Highly paid, utterly discreet and very, very elite, but killers nonetheless—in the same way that a charming Associée is, at the end of the day, a very high-class whore.

We're mercenaries, and that's that.

I think I hold some sort of record for youngest-ever Dragon Knight. I was thirteen when I graduated. Dragon's the standard level, but I went one better—mostly to spite Striker—and got the Phoenix. The Phoenix test is deadly, by which I mean they kill you if you don't pass. I did, and got my standard Dragon tattoo—crossed swords and my graduation number—upgraded to incorporate a Phoenix design. I wasn't frightened of failing the test. I'd figured out by then that I was pretty much invincible.

Pretty much.

Chapter Three

ဆ

Striker didn't bother to take the dragon to her paddock. He jumped down the ladder, left me to bring my own luggage and strolled on ahead with his arm around Chalia. I swore at him, grabbed my heavy trunks and lugged them after me like a dead dog.

People called out greetings to Chalia as she and Striker made their way through the beautiful courtyard at the center of the island. She's one of those people who find it easy to make friends—mostly because she does a lot of things that people laugh at, and she laughs with them. People like someone who can take the piss out of themselves.

My mother, unlike Striker, never attended the Koskwim academy, but due to a rather long and drawn-out set of circumstances, she's one of very few outsiders allowed on the island. She even has her own room here in the huge white tower where all the Knights and students sleep.

No one called out to me. I'd only been here a few months when I asked Striker to do something for me—to cast a glamour on the inhabitants of the island so that they wouldn't remember I was Striker's daughter. It caused too many problems. I don't want to be like my father. I never did. He frightens me.

If I want to kill and maim, I shall do it the human way, thank you so very much.

Consequently, I never really made any friends. I was just another student, albeit a very good one. The senior Knights know, though. They know everything. But the students and the Dragons and most of the Phoenixes have no idea of my lineage. Suits me.

Koskwim Knights have loose morals and high sex drives—hell, you're on an island with a couple hundred physically perfect specimens, and there's a very high chance you could die tomorrow. Sex is big over here. I was never cast out as promiscuous.

I caught the eye of a few former lovers, and they gave me vague smiles. One of them openly checked me out as if he'd never seen me before. Sometimes Striker's spell works too well. It's supposed to make people forget the connection between us, not forget me altogether. But that's Striker for you. He probably did it on purpose.

As soon as we entered the soaring white tower, with its peaceful fountains and abundant greenery, Tyra raced over to us. As usual, she was dressed demurely in a boring suit, flat shoes and spectacles—which I knew she didn't need—but sexuality still oozed from her every pore.

"Come on," she said, taking my arm. "We've been waiting days for you. You're the last to arrive, you know."

"I had a few problems," I said, signaling to a student to take my luggage to my room.

"Well, now you're here. Striker, what are you doing here? We didn't call you."

He shrugged. "Ain't a party without me, love," he said.

"It's a 'party' for Phoenixes," Tyra said. "You're a Dragon."

I grinned. I never get tired of reminding Striker I outrank him.

"You don't want me there?"

"No," she sighed. "No, you might have some input. Come along. Chalia, I'm afraid we really can't let you in."

"No prob," my mother said. "I'll amuse myself."

Tyra hustled Striker and me back out into the courtyard and across to the low, hulking red buildings that house the Order's offices and Tyra's huge library. It was the library we were taken to, where maybe fifty people were seated around a huge table. I recognized some, but most were strangers to me. A lot of them were about my parents' ages—a Phoenix never retires, but a lot of them go off active duty when they're forty or fifty. It's not old, but when you live such a hard, fast life, forty is more like sixty.

Unless you're Striker, who stopped aging at thirty-three.

"Now that everyone is finally here," Tyra said, shoving me toward a seat while Striker leaned rebelliously against the wall, "we can begin."

"Striker's not a Phoenix," said a dark-haired girl on the far side of the table. I knew her—actually she's my cousin on Chalia's side. I thought she was a Dragon, but maybe she'd passed the Phoenix when I wasn't looking. Her mother had been a famous shapeshifter, and so while Kett inherited my uncle's silvery eyes and bad temper, she also inherited her mother's ability to bend her form into whatever she wanted.

She told me it made sex pretty mind-blowing.

No one paid any attention to Kett, apart from Striker, who smirked. Everyone there knew Striker had more power in a single eyelash than all the Phoenixes in the room combined. But Kett's a bit of a shit-stirrer. It's why I like her.

I slid low in my seat and looked around as one of the senior members of the Order started speaking. I didn't pay a lot of attention to start with—she was droning on about some Euskaran faction and I guess she was looking for a large number of Knights to deal with it.

"…intel has shown that the Federacion, as they have taken to calling themselves, are based in…"

There was Jalen, who is possibly as close to a friend as I have on the island. Mostly we're friends because no one else likes us. Her father is King Talis, she's dating an inter-Realm star and she can kill with a look. Beautiful as anything, with long blonde hair and big blue eyes, she's one of the hardest, smartest sharp-tongued women I've ever met.

"...reports have shown that work is flooding in for the Federacion, and we have noticed a distinct decline in interest from the western reaches of..."

A little farther down was a very tall, very handsome man with long, shaggy dark hair and eyes that could cut through hard metal. Another cousin, as it happens. For some reason my mother's family closet is just bursting with skeletons, and Mac is one of them. He's also sleeping with Rosie, who is a relation of mine in a very distant sort of way. Rosie is training for the Dragon, although she's older than me and therefore, in Koskwim terms, past it. All her classmates are teenagers.

"...missions in Asiatica, although none have so far encroached into Peneggan..."

Mac sat next to his prospective father-in-law, Rosie's father Tanner. One of the big Koskwim heroes. The Order doesn't just send Knights out to assassinate and spy—there's a lot of diplomacy involved. Before taking up his current position, running the Elvyrn Royal Guard, Tanner had negotiated the peace in a very tricky settlement in Qarat, Asiatica. The fighting had gone on there for years, and Tanner's presence had been instrumental in ending it.

I admire him in a professional sense, but we rarely speak to each other. Old problems get in the way. Family issues. Scars that run deep.

"...been living in Euskara for the past three years, as I understand. Have you had any dealings with them?"

I became slowly aware that the room was silent.

"Chance?"

The senior Knight—I think her name is Elwyn—was glaring at me. Behind me, Striker sniggered.

"What?" I said.

"I would be interested," Elwyn said in a frosty tone, "to know what, if anything, you have heard of the Federacion. But if you're demonstrating to me your usual level of attention, then I would surmise that you've heard nothing."

I glowered at her and sunk lower in my seat. "I haven't been paying much attention to politics," I muttered. "I've been too busy."

"Ah, yes. Your famous Association. I understand that the Association carries out background checks on many prospective clients?"

I could feel disapproval rolling off Tanner and Mac in waves. *Oh, piss off*, I thought. I knew for a fact that Tanner used to be a thief who killed a man when he was eleven, and that Mac spent a good few weeks spying on his precious Rosie before he ever got her into bed.

"Yes," I said, knowing what was coming.

"And are those clients of the illustrious Association not wealthy citizens, often prominent businessmen and politicians?"

"Okay, yes," I snapped, glaring at her with all the force of my father's eyes. It worked—I saw her flinch. "But cut me a break, okay? This time yesterday I had two ribs breaking through my skin and my skull was in half a dozen pieces. I'm not really feeling my best at the moment, and I can't bring myself to pay attention to this mind-numbing drivel you're spouting."

There was a short silence. I wondered if Striker might say anything.

"Half a dozen?" Kett said disdainfully. "Honey, until you've actually been on a slab in the morgue, it doesn't really count."

I glared at her. Just because she'd died once she seemed to think she was part of some exclusive little club. Well, I belong to an even more exclusive club—the Descendants of Striker Party, where it seems that not even a broken spine and smashed skull means death.

"Do you have any contacts within Euskara you could use for information?" Elwyn asked.

I sighed. "I don't know. Yes—but then, how am I supposed to contact them?"

"By Faerie," Elwyn said, as if I was a child.

"Uh, hello," Striker spoke up from behind me. "Remember who you're talking to, here? Faeries don't exactly like playing with—"

"Me," I broke in quickly. Elwyn knows why, and Kett and Tanner and some of them, but for the rest it'd just be too complicated to explain. "Faeries hate me. You know how weird they are..."

It was true. While most Knights had one or two Faeries in their service that could carry messages almost instantly, neither Striker nor I did. Because he'd killed a Faerie many years before I was even born, they now refused to come anywhere near him, or Chalia or me. It was why I used a scryer to communicate. In Euskara, I had used it to call a Kelf who could contact a Faerie for me when needed. But right now, I didn't feel like being so helpful.

Elwyn frowned, nodding. No one else seemed to be interested. Bloody Striker. Sometimes I think he's out to get me.

"How about if one of us contacts the Association for information?" asked a low-voiced Asiatic girl I didn't know. "Professionally. Surely some of the senior members must be aware of our existence?"

"They are," I said, "but they won't help. An Associée never tells."

"Not even when it's life or death?" Tanner asked, his tone carefully neutral.

"Not even when," Striker rumbled behind me. "She ain't lying, Captain."

Striker and Tanner hate each other. It's all about my mother—she was once engaged to Tanner but she left him for Striker, and neither of them has forgotten it. Tanner is a decent man, but Striker can never resist trying to get one up on him. It's one of those male pissing contests, and it drives me mad.

"Maybe we should take another route," Tanner suggested, his eyes never even flickering in Striker's direction. I'll give him credit—he has a lot more grace than my father ever possessed.

The meeting flowed back into order, and I half listened. It seemed the Order was concerned about a rival group that was operating out of Iberia, on the west coast of Euskara. The Federacion had been recruiting for some time now, and while the Order had initially sent one or two spies in to keep any eye on things, as they were wont to do, those spies had been rooted out and ruthlessly dispatched. Elwyn got quite graphic on the subject of what had been done to them.

"I knew those tattoos were a dumb idea," Striker opined.

Everyone turned to look at him.

"What? S'like a beacon, yelling out to the whole bloody Realm who you are and what you do. If we know about them then they'll know about us—and about these little indicators. You can't infiltrate them when you've got a bloody great tattoo plastered across your arse."

There was a pause, then Elwyn spoke.

"What he says is true. It appears the Federacion inspects every new recruit. If the Koskwim tattoo is found, it's cut off and sent to us. The recruit is, of course, killed."

"What about scarring it?" Jalen asked. She's a gal who knows a thing or two about scars. "You could cut the tat off or burn it so it's indistinct."

"Not too painful," Mac scoffed.

"Fuck off," she said succinctly.

"It's a possibility," Elwyn said. "We did have another plan."

"How jolly exciting," Striker muttered, and I heard him light up a cigarette. No one told him to put it out—it'd have been completely pointless anyway.

"Kett," Elwyn said, and Kett looked up. "You can change your appearance. Can you make your tattoo vanish?"

She shrugged. "I guess, but not for long."

"I've seen you hold a tiger shape for three days," a male Phoenix said to her. "You can make something as small as a tattoo vanish."

"Excuse me. Am I the shapeshifter or you? Can you change your hand into a fucking talon? No. Then shut the fuck up," Kett said. "A whole shape is easier to hold. It's mimicry. Still takes a long time to perfect it though, a lot of practice before I can hold the shape for any length of time. Changing something small… Well, don't you wonder why I don't change my hair more often?"

"But it can be done?" Elwyn pressed.

"I guess." Kett smiled. "Wondered why I was the only Dragon *invited*." She flicked her eyes smugly at Striker, who ignored her totally. He doesn't care in the slightest whether he's invited to anything or not.

Elwyn turned to Striker. "What about you?"

"I ain't a shapeshifter."

"But you can heal yourself, bone, muscle and skin."

"Yeah. Still no difference."

"We found something you can't do?" Jalen asked with obvious glee.

"Shut the fuck up," I said, not out of any great familial loyalty to Striker, but in the interests of preserving Jalen's life.

"I could incinerate whoever was looking for the tats, if it'd make you happy?" Striker offered sarcastically.

"We may take you up on that offer," Elwyn said.

The meeting dragged on and on, and I started to wish I'd learned a bit more from Striker, like how to make myself invisible so I could get the hell out of there. I didn't even seem to be needed in this great Fight the Federacion plot they were cooking up. If I'd been willing to betray my Associée discretion, then I might have been useful. But I do have some integrity, and a promise is a promise.

When the meeting eventually ended I stumbled up the stairs to my room—which was on the seventh floor and the counterweight elevator was broken. Every room in the tower is the same—pristine white marble walls, floor and ceiling that look like they were all carved out of the huge block of the tower. The windows are arched, like those of a church, and beautiful marble angels support the mirror over the mantelpiece and the canopy over the bed. Everything is white—furniture, sheets, everything. It might look stark, but the glow from the hundreds of tiny gaslights around the room adds warmth and somehow, it's quite restive. Angels to guard me while I sleep. A Knight doesn't get to see many angels.

I tried to get some sleep, after all it was getting dark, but my hearing seemed to be on overdrive and all I could concentrate on was the couple in the next room fucking vigorously. There were creaks and groans as they tested each piece of furniture, screams as they came, loud begging for more cock, harder, deeper, oh baby oh baby.

Whatever.

I dragged myself into the shower, put on some clean clothes and took a small dragon over to the mainland, where a town called Port Jaret serves the Bridge traffic from Asiatica, and also holds the postal addresses and meeting rooms used by the Order for external communications.

I wandered down to the docks and spent some time educating the whores there on how to deep-throat without choking yourself. I like to give a little back to the community.

One of the girls, a pretty, sweet little thing who hadn't been there long, seemed in need of extra tuition. Okay, I felt sorry for her and she wasn't too dirty. So when a sailor client came along, I booked us a room in one of the hourly taverns and gave her a personal lesson in oral sex—after I'd given them both a bath. I'm quite particular about what I bury my face in.

We fell asleep together, her sweet body nestled close to mine, his arms wrapped around us both, and my last thought was how sad it was that I, one of the Realm's most desirable women, had to pay a cheap whore to sleep in my arms. Right now it wasn't the sex I wanted. It was the human comfort.

Chapter Four

ಬ

"Wake up, whore, and tell me the truth before you die."

I swear that's what woke me. That and the cold blade pressed to my throat. I opened my eyes, slowly, trying to adjust to the gloom.

And then I nearly had a heart attack as my brain got the delayed signals from my ears and my eyes all at the same time, and I realized that the man holding his sword to my throat was Dark.

He looked as shocked as I felt, but he didn't move the sword.

"Chance?"

"Uh-huh?" I squeaked.

"Phoenix 20572?"

I nodded and swallowed, painfully. The blade nicked my skin.

Dark looked like an animal. In the dim light that filtered through the dirty window from the gas lamp outside, he was like a big cat, and I was the gazelle he'd earmarked for lunch. His eyes glowed, somehow more feline than before, and I'd swear his teeth were like fangs.

"You killed my brother," Dark said, and I stared at him.

"I don't even know —"

"Tell me where my sister is."

"Who the fuck is your sister?"

"Tell me and I'll kill you quickly," Dark said.

Okay, he was a psycho.

"Look," I said. "I think you have me confused with someone else—"

With his free hand he whipped away the sheet covering us. The whore stirred, making a small sound in her sleep as the cool air hit her skin.

Dark grabbed my ankle and glared at the tattoo on the sole of my foot. "Phoenix 20572," he said. "No confusion."

Okay, so he hadn't seen the tat before. Why would he have? There are much more interesting areas of my body than the sole of my foot. That's why I had the tattoo placed there— every Knight has one, and it's supposed to be in a place where it won't be seen easily. On my body, that doesn't leave a lot of choices.

"Or maybe I'm confused," I said, wrenching my foot back. "You *are* the guy who fucked me six ways to Sunday the night before last, aren't you? You don't have a twin?"

Those fabulous eyes darkened. "I do," he said, "and he has claws."

The truth hit me then, of what he was, why he was so feral, who his brother was. But I didn't get to say anything because right then the door slammed open and a crossbow bolt shot straight at Dark.

I don't know how I got there in time. One of those things I didn't know I could do. One moment I was lying in the bed between two naked bodies, the next I was flying through the air, my hand flung out to catch the bolt as it shot toward Dark's head.

It went through my hand instead, the tip scraping Dark's cheek. I cried out, losing momentum and crumpling to a heap on the floor.

Striker stared at me. Who else would it have been? Dark stared too. The whore and the sailor woke suddenly, took in the scene and wisely decided to get the hell out of there as fast as their naked legs would take them.

Which left me lying on the floor, once again bleeding and naked with Dark's eyes on me. Striker's, too.

"What the fuck are you doing?" Striker snarled.

"Right back at you!" I cradled my hand to my chest. Fuck, it hurt. Striker had probably tipped the bolt, too. Fan-fucking-tastic. "You can't just come in here and shoot at people like that!"

"It may have escaped your notice, pet, but he had a bloody great sword to your throat and was telling you he was going to kill you."

I transferred my glare to Dark, who returned it full force. "Yeah, and what's that about?"

"You killed my brother," he said. "Now I'm going to kill you."

"You see?" Striker said, a trifle smugly.

"Bite me, Striker. Dark. Look. I can explain this—"

"I'm sure you can," Dark said. "I'm still going to kill you."

There was a whoosh as a fireball appeared in Striker's palm. Oh marvelous, another pissing contest.

"Stop it," I said, in a voice I learned from Tyra. "Both of you. Dark, put that sword away. Striker, no fireballs. This whole place will go up if that gets any bigger."

They both stared at me.

"I *said*," I began, and they hurriedly did as they were told. Hah. I couldn't speak for Dark, but I knew that in the dim and distant past Striker had once had to answer to Nanny, the most frightening woman in the world for a nursery child. I guess it's universal. That voice has never failed me yet.

"Striker," I asked, turning to him as if I wasn't sprawled there naked and bloody with a fucking crossbow bolt stuck through my hand, "this poisoned?"

He gave a bare nod.

"You want to give me the antidote?"

He looked annoyed, but knelt in front of me, took my palm in his and touched the bolt. I hissed in a sharp breath. I could see my own flesh torn and distorted by the barbed metal, the tip of which was sticking out through the back of my hand.

Striker reached into a pocket of the black leather duster he always wears, and brought out a packet of some powder or other. I don't understand the things he does with these herbs and stuff—I think they're more props than anything.

Dark just stood there, sword loose by his side, watching me.

While Striker worked, he asked, "Why'd you do that?"

"Do what?"

"Stop me killing him."

I looked up at Dark, whose face was inscrutable. Truth was, I didn't really know. I went for the obvious answer.

"Because he's a bloody good fuck."

Striker shrugged as if this figured. You may have realized by now that we don't exactly have a very normal relationship.

Dark glared down at me. "I'm still going to kill you."

"Then how will you ever find out where your sister is?"

His nostrils flared. *That's done you*, I thought, then winced as Striker pulled the bolt out of my hand.

"You want me to make it all better," he asked, "or just stop it killing you?"

"A bolt through her hand won't kill her right away," Dark said impatiently.

"One of his will," I said, and Striker looked smug. "Just—leave it. I need to talk to Dark."

Striker stood and looked Dark over. He didn't seem to be impressed. "You'll be all right?" he asked me.

I nodded. I have my pride.

Striker handed me a little vial full of the tonic I'd used up before. Then he paused before handing me another. Very funny.

"You know where I'll be," he said cryptically, and walked out.

I started to get up, and Dark pushed me onto the bed. Grumbling beneath my breath, I reached for my clothes and started to pull them on. I'd dressed for the docks—long skirt, blouse, corset. Right now the corset seemed like too much trouble. I pulled on the blouse then broke off in dressing to tear some strips off the bedsheet and wrap them around my hand, which was still bleeding.

The tip of Dark's sword touched my breast, traced the Associée marks there. "How ironic your status is called 'lady'," he said.

I held my tongue and carried on wrapping.

"You will help me find my sister," he said.

"I thought you were going to kill me?"

"When you've found her."

"That's not much of an incentive."

"If you don't, I'll kill you anyway."

"Whatever happened to just fucking me?"

"I found out who you really are."

"What, you were following me?" Impossible. Quite apart from the fact that I've been on dragonback since entering the Realm, no one follows Striker and gets away with it.

My scryer buzzed, and I reached for it before Dark could stop me. He glared as my hand touched the scryer and the connection opened up.

"Chance." It was Tyra, and I knew something was urgent by the way she used my name, not my rank and number. "Where are you?"

"Port Jaret."

"Alone?"

I glanced at Dark. "You can talk."

"You need to come back here immediately. Something has — occurred — and we need to talk to you."

"We?"

"The senior Knights and myself."

I've never been sure just what Tyra's rank was. Probably she runs the place.

"What is it?" I asked. I wasn't terribly alarmed. My first thought was that something had happened to one of my parents, but if it had been my mother then Striker would have taken care of it and if it had been Striker — well, it just wouldn't have been Striker.

"There's been an information leak," she said. "One of the students lost control of her Faerie and someone used it to get information from me."

I frowned. Faeries are usually extremely pissy about working for anyone who doesn't hold their amulet, and therefore directly control them. "Who —" I began, and then I realized. The answer was staring me in the face.

Well, actually, it was glaring me in the face and aiming a sword at my tit.

"A Nasc," I said. "He got the Faerie, didn't he?"

"Yes," Tyra said. "He asked me who killed his brother."

"And that someone was me."

Dark growled low in his throat.

"Is there someone there with you?" Tyra asked.

"No. It's all right. Tyra, did you tell him anything else?"

"No. I realized something was wrong. But Chance, he could find you. The Nasc are very protective of their families. He's after revenge, of that I am quite certain."

Boy, she was smart.

"I can take care of myself," I said.

Dark snorted.

"There *is* someone with you," Tyra said.

"It's no one. Just someone I hooked up with," I said. "It's fine. Look, Tyra—go easy on the kid, okay? We all know the Nasc are pretty powerful."

Tyra made a tsking noise. "I'm powerful," she said pityingly. "Your father is powerful. The Nasc are just humans with integrated pets."

With a roar, Dark swiped the scryer out of my hand, and it flew across the room to shatter in a hundred pieces on the far wall.

It was my turn to glare at him. I go through so many scryers these days. "What'd you do that for? I only just got it."

"Pets?" he snarled. "My twin is not a pet!"

"No," I said soothingly, "of course not."

He glowered at me, grabbed me by the wrist and hauled me to my feet. His chest was heaving, his eyes were glowing—he was furious as hell and so sexy my knees went weak. My nipples punched through my thin blouse. My pussy throbbed with sudden heat. I was so turned on that I actually felt faint.

Now that I knew what Dark was, at least I knew why I wanted him so much. It was just pheromones, just chemistry. Everyone knows the Nasc are powerfully sexual beings. It's their animal magnetism. Literally. Every Nasc has an animal twin—the stronger the human, the stronger his twin. I wondered if Dark's twin was a panther or a bull or something.

"What are you?" I whispered, and I'm ashamed to say I was trembling.

Dark didn't answer. Hauled as close to him as I was, I could feel the rapidly hardening ridge of his cock against me. He was incredibly angry, fury pouring off him in waves, and what with one thing and another I wasn't really in any mood to get nearly killed again. Or, you know, actually killed. That would suck a lot.

I needed to distract him. And fortunately, my body already had a plan in motion.

If he was surprised when I kissed him, he didn't show it. I fastened my mouth to his, thrust my tongue inside and felt the sharpness of his teeth. At my guess, Dark and his twin had been separated too long—that would account for his increasingly feral nature, the simplicity of his actions. Kill and fuck—wasn't that what big, scary animals did best?

And I knew, as he sucked my tongue into his mouth and shoved me hard against the wall, that big and scary he most certainly was. I wasn't dealing with a fluffy bunny or a puppy dog here. Dark was a tiger, a bear, a wolf, a fucking *dragon*.

My head crashed into the wall, the rough plaster scraping my back through my blouse. I wasn't wearing anything else, and as I lifted my legs to wrap them around Dark's waist, I felt the press of his big, hard cock against my hot pussy, separated only by the rough jeans he wore. That barrier ought to have been a frustration, but the way he ground against me, the coarse fabric rubbing my incredibly sensitive flesh—gods, I nearly came there and then.

I tore my mouth away from his to suck in a gasp of air, and he dropped his head and bit my neck. Gods, yes—that felt so fucking good. I'd had plenty of clients who got off on the pleasure-pain thing, but I'd never truly understood it until now.

I wedged my hand between us and prized his jeans open. His cock sprang into my hand, happy to see me again, eager to get reacquainted. I gave it a welcoming stroke.

Dark growled, not a human growl but the low, undulating rumble of a really big, really dangerous cat, and ripped my blouse open. His teeth closed over my nipple and I cried out, spots dancing in front of my eyes. If he'd touched my clit then I'd have come in one big, loud explosion.

But he didn't. He bit and sucked at my tender flesh as I stroked him, rubbed my thumb over the pearl of moisture that seeped out of his cock, switched hands and brought my damp fingers up to my lips as he watched.

I sucked my fingers, one by one, and I'd only got to the third finger when Dark shoved my hand away and rammed that huge, hard cock of his all the way up inside me.

Well, I came then. I came so hard I nearly blacked out, and it was only the insistent, driving rhythm of his cock pounding me into the wall that kept me from slithering to the floor. It felt so good, so big, so deep, that even when I could see again the waves of ecstasy washing over me rose to a flood almost immediately, and I kept coming, over and over again, harder and harder, until Dark was fucking a writhing, screaming bundle of thrashing limbs. I bucked and cried and shoved myself harder against him, clamping my pussy muscles down around his thick pumping cock, and chunks of plaster started falling out of the walls, the ceiling, and raining down on us.

I don't think I'd have even noticed his orgasm if he hadn't come so hard, so much, spurting thick jets of cum into me and roaring a deep guttural sound that made the walls shake and the windows shatter.

He fucked me so fiercely I felt the wall splinter behind me as his semen gushed into me, and as the final force of my endless orgasm gripped me, the wall gave way and we crashed through, out onto the landing that overlooked the tavern. I screamed so loud as the force of the fall shoved Dark's cock ever deeper into me that all the windows in the place shattered at once.

I think I actually did black out there for a second or two, and only came to when the sound of applause roused me. Dark yanked me to my feet—still looking mighty angry—and dragged me through the hole in the wall, back to the squalid little bedroom where he'd found me.

He shoved me at the bed and tucked his limp, shiny cock back into his jeans, not looking at me at all.

"Get dressed," he said, and I glanced down dreamily to see my bitten, swollen red nipples thrusting brazenly toward him through what was left of my blouse.

"Sure you don't want another round?" I pouted.

"No. Put some clothes on."

The whore had left behind her shirt, but I didn't fancy putting that on. I laced myself back into my corset, letting my bare breasts rub against the hard whalebone and loving the friction. I'd just fastened my skirt into place when Dark grabbed my wrist again, and I winced. I'd forgotten about the huge hole in my hand. That's how good a fuck it was.

Chapter Five

❧

A word about the Nasc. They're not Werefolk, who are forced by the moon to change into a second shape. They're not Shapeshifters, like Kett, who can choose which form to be in.

A Nasc has one soul and two bodies. They can merge into one form or separate into two. They're born human, and shortly after birth they separate into an animal form. There's not a huge amount known about them—they're very private people—but my understanding is that every now and then the two forms must merge, or each starts to weaken. The animal becomes more human, the human more animal.

Dark had obviously been apart from his animal form for some time.

He hauled me, stumbling and barefoot, down the stairs into the wrecked tavern. The landlord started shouting at us, but Dark snarled at him so viciously the man just shrank back behind his bar and let us walk out.

"How do you get there?" Dark asked as he dragged me along in the sunlight.

"Where?"

"Koskwim."

"You don't."

He turned that ferocious glare on me.

"I'm sorry Dark, but you don't. Rules are rules. They don't allow outsiders on the island."

"I am the ruler of my people."

"I'm sure you are," I said, "but you're still not allowed on the island. They wouldn't let you on."

"We'll see about that," he said.

He kept a death grip on my wrist, the wrist with my injured hand attached, and I didn't have the strength to pull away. He led me to the ngardaí, the watchhouse, and simply stalked into the back room, past the astonished garda at the desk.

"Hey, you can't—"

Dark swiped at him like he was a mosquito, and the garda fell away.

"That wasn't very nice," I said.

"You're the killer," he replied tonelessly.

"Yes, but that was different, I—"

"Shut the fuck up," Dark snarled. "I don't want to hear your excuses."

Personally, I'd call them "explanations", but each to his own.

Dark selected a set of heavy-duty handcuffs from a rack in the back room and snapped one bracelet around my wrist.

"So you *are* up for another round," I purred.

He snapped the other cuff around his own wrist and walked out, giving me no choice but to be tugged after him.

"This is getting tiresome," I said. "Where are we going? If you want to have sex in the street then that's fine, but I'll warn you the gardaí are probably already pretty pissed off with you."

He ignored me, and pulled me halfway across town toward a building I recognized—it was one where the Order held an office or two. They used it for meetings with prospective clients.

Dark stalked inside.

"Look," I said, "I don't know what you think you're going to achieve by getting all growly with them, but the Order is not going to let you on the island. They have never allowed outsiders and they never will."

That wasn't strictly true, but he was really pissing me off now.

"They will," Dark said confidently, striding into an office without knocking. The Knight at the desk, a young pretty girl, started in surprise and reached for her weapons.

"You have a scryer?" Dark said to her, and she gave him a wary look.

"Who are you?"

"Just give him the scryer," I said.

"I can't." She looked at me reproachfully, and I sighed and showed her the bare, dirty sole of my foot, where my Phoenix tattoo was visible.

"It'll mess my scryer up if I do that."

"Call Elwyn," Dark said. "Tell her to send a dragon over to pick us up."

"Show me your tattoo," she said.

"He doesn't have one," I told her. "Not a Knight."

"Then I can't do that," the girl said firmly. "You don't go near the Order unless—"

"Yes?" Dark said softly, and I knew from that tone and the look on his face—like he was about to pounce—that his Nasc twin was undoubtedly a cat of some kind.

"Unless you're a Knight," the girl finished.

"Wrong," Dark said, and ripped a hole in my neck with his teeth.

All hell broke loose. I cried out—at least, to begin with I did. Then the sound died out to a nasty sort of bubbling noise, and I couldn't seem to draw breath to scream again. My lungs felt fizzy.

Oh fuck, not again.

The young Knight had her sword at Dark's throat, and my scream had drawn the attention of several other people from different parts of the building. They all flooded into the room, maybe half a dozen of them, and stared at me in horror. Probably most of them were still students and the horrifying gore of the battlefield was still light-years ahead of them.

The girl Knight raised her sword to cut off Dark's head, but I shoved at her and she lost her balance, glaring at me quizzically.

"Don't—" I began, but the sound just bubbled out and died. Dammit, I was sick of getting injured defending this man! *Life would be so much simpler*, I thought as my vision began to fade, *if I just stopped stopping other people from killing him.*

I was vaguely aware of Striker erupting into the room like a tornado, scattering everyone else, whirling me up into his arms. There was a flash and the crackle of fire, and I smelled burnt flesh.

Someone snarled, and I think it was Dark. My arm hung limply where it was still cuffed to his.

Then I lost interest in the Realm, and faded back inside myself, back into the arms of my old friend Oblivion.

I woke in my own room in the white tower. I was alone, no one watching over me while I slept. My hand throbbed under a fat bandage and my neck stung where Dark's teeth had ripped into it, but I didn't feel like I was dying anymore. In fact, I had a suspicion that if I removed the bandages, I'd already be half healed.

I heard a toilet flush, then the door from the bathroom opened and Chalia came out, her eyes going straight to mine.

"Sweetheart," she said, "how are you feeling?"

I shrugged experimentally. "I'm alive," I said, and was pleased to find my voice coming out normally, no bubbles of blood or anything.

She smiled and sat down in a chair by the bed, but her smile didn't look very natural.

"Where's Striker?" I asked.

"Beating the crap out of some students in the tourney ring," she answered, in the sort of tone a normal person might use to describe a tennis match. "Don't worry—I made him promise not to kill anyone."

"What about seriously maim?" I asked, knowing Striker's tendency to find loopholes in most of my mother's explicit commands to not hurt people.

She sighed, and hauled out her scryer.

"I haven't killed anyone," he said without preamble.

I had to smile at that.

"Cut off any limbs?"

"No. Can I?"

"No! And no maiming, either. Make sure they all walk off alive, Striker, and with all the faculties they brought onto the pitch."

"You're no bloody fun. How'm I supposed to blow off steam if you won't let me kill the wanker who bit Chance and you won't let me maim any students? That's what they're here for, anyway."

My mother rolled her eyes, but I was intrigued. He'd tried to kill Dark? Wow. That was almost like parental concern. Bit of a novelty.

She signed off and tucked her scryer back into its pouch on her belt. Chalia is always beautifully dressed, even if her fashions aren't always entirely appropriate for the weather, or indeed, the Realm. Today she was sporting a little beaded sari bodice and full embroidered skirt, like women wear on the stage in Pradesh. Her long dark hair was bound in a plait that hung down her back. She looked not much older than me.

Exposed by her cropped bodice was the vicious, deep scar that ran across her stomach. Someone had killed Chalia once, but Striker wouldn't let her go.

I was beginning to empathize with my mother more than usual.

"What happened to Dark?" I asked.

"Dark?"

"The guy who bit me. The Nasc with the mane and the cat's eyes."

She smiled a little at my description. "What is he to you?"

"I'll tell you after you tell me how many pieces Striker broke him into."

"None. But only just. He was ready to tear him limb from limb for what he did to you." Chalia looked proud, as well she might, because she's been trying to teach Striker some paternal values ever since I was born. Usually the only things he does for me, he does to please Chalia.

I sat up against my pillows and looked at her expectantly.

"Since he was still handcuffed to you at the time and I wouldn't let him cut—what did you call him?"

"Dark."

My mother considered this. "Good name. I wouldn't let him cut Dark's hand off, so we brought him along too."

I very nearly asked how Striker had even known I was in trouble again, but that was pointless. He knows where Chalia is, every moment of every day, and how she's feeling, and probably what she's wearing too. He has a similar, if less powerful, link to me and a couple of other people. I'm not very close to Striker emotionally—no one is, except for Chalia—but we do have a blood bond, after all.

"The Order gave him a room and locked him in it—probably for his protection as much as yours—while they decide what to do with him," Chalia finished.

"Is he okay?" I asked, not sure why I cared.

My mother made a face. "Striker burned him a bit," she said. "Well, okay, a lot. He was pretty mad. If I hadn't made him stop, he…"

She didn't need to finish that. Striker had destroyed cities before. Incinerating one man and a building or two wouldn't be much work for him.

I ran my hand through my hair. "What room is he in?"

Chalia narrowed her eyes at me. "What are you going to do?"

"I just want to see him."

"See the man who tried to kill you twice in the space of an hour?"

"He wasn't trying to kill me the second time," I said doubtfully, feeling at the wound on my neck through the bandage.

"Looks like it to me."

I scowled. "Well, I'm still alive, aren't I?"

"Thanks to your father," Chalia said tartly, and I glared hard at her. "Don't you give me that look, young lady, I invented it. You know if it weren't for him you'd have died half a dozen times before now." Her face didn't change, but I saw her fingers tighten in the folds of her skirt. "One way or another, you owe your life to him."

Yes, and I'm never going to be able to forget it. Every time I look in the mirror I'm reminded of who I am, what I am.

"Thanks for the pep talk," I said, and swung out of bed. I felt a little bit dizzy, but otherwise I was okay. "What's his room number?"

My mother sighed, well used to stubborn people. "947."

"Thank you."

I took myself into the bathroom, contemplated a shower, then looked at my mittened hand and decided to wash at the sink instead. When I came out, looking a little better thanks to some makeup and a hairbrush, Chalia was still sitting there, looking pensive.

"What is he to you?" she asked again as I started looking for clothes.

"Who?"

"The Nasc."

I shrugged. "We met in Euskara."

My mother hesitated. "One of your clients?"

"No. We just met."

"Did he have anything to do with you using up your potion?"

My eyes slid sideways to her. "Yes, but not that way."

She cocked an eyebrow.

"It was an accident. My carriage tipped over the cliffs outside Severeges. Dark brought me back up, out of the sea. If it wasn't for him I'd probably have been eaten by some sharks."

"Do they have sharks in Euskara?"

"They have sharks everywhere."

I stepped into a loose cotton skirt and a cropped top. Koskwim is the only place in all the Realms where you can wear what the hell you like and not get arrested for it. The girls' summer uniform, which is really only worn by students, consists of a cropped top and hot pants. You've gotta love that.

Chalia came with me as far as the stairs, where she went down to see some friends in the courtyard. I started up toward the ninth floor, but then paused and thought about it. Dark was likely to be pretty pissed off, and I'd seen how violent he got when he *wasn't* in a bad mood. If I just walked in there he'd probably rip me to shreds, and I was feeling fragile enough as it was.

Besides, there was some research I had to do.

I made my way down to the lobby and crossed the courtyard with all its tinkling, shining fountains. In the sunshine the white tower gleamed like ivory. Probably it is ivory. The tusk of a Realm-sized mammoth from prehistory. No one can really tell for sure what it is made of. There just aren't any records to prove it.

Speaking of records, I ducked into the shady cavern of the library, seeking out Tyra in her cool, ordered office. She was looking cool and ordered too, in a neat little suit, her hair in a chignon. She wore her usual spectacles, though why I'm not sure because her eyesight is as supernaturally brilliant as my own.

"It's on the table," she said without looking up from her desk.

I hesitated. "What is?"

"The file on the Nasc royal family."

Okay, how did she know? How? "I don't—"

"I do recognize people from their file pictures," Tyra said, still not looking up.

She'd seen Dark. But, given that he'd never been here before, that was a hell of a memory leap. "Do you know him?"

"Never met him before. Very angry young man."

"Tell that to my neck," I said, touching the bandage.

She glanced at me. "How is it?"

"Healing."

"Thought so. If you need anything else, I'll be here."

I backed out, a little freaked. But then I'm always a little freaked by Tyra. It amazes me that hardly anyone else on the island can tell what she is—she even has the golden wings that sprout from her temples when she's angry! But then, pretty much everyone else on the island is human.

I mean, not that I'm not. Human, I mean. I am. I'm just...a little different.

Oh, shut up.

I found the file on the huge, endless table that runs down the middle of the library. Sitting not far from it was my sort-of cousin Rosie and her best friend, Brack. He ran a hand through his brilliant auburn hair when he saw me and cried, "Chance! Babe, who was that divine man who came in handcuffed to you, and does that mean he's taken?"

Oh yeah. Brack's gay.

"I don't know, and I don't know," I told him, sitting down opposite. "But I do know he likes girls."

"You know this personally?" Rosie asked, as Brack pouted. His hair was fluffed up into spikes now and he looked like a puppy.

"Yep. Sorry."

She shrugged, and I guess it made no never mind to her. She's got her own chunk of tall, dark and psychotic to go home to. Brack looked tortured though. I guessed it must be tough, being the only outed gay on the island. Especially when there are so many highly sexed, perfect male specimens running around to frustrate you.

I pulled the Nasc file toward me.

"Did he really try to rip your throat out?" Rosie asked me.

I nodded.

"So is that like a Nasc mating ritual or what?"

I shuddered, mostly at the word "mating" which has all sorts of fun, primitive meanings in terms of sex—but which takes on a very frightening tint when used in conjunction with the word "ritual". Marriage is a mating ritual.

Shudder.

"No," I said, "but it's a reasonably effective way of killing someone."

A short silence. "His animal form isn't a praying mantis, is it?" Brack asked.

I laughed at the thought of Dark being a little insect. "No. Says here he's a mountain lion. A big one."

"Figures," Brack said dreamily.

"Besides, it's the females who kill the males after mating," Rosie told him. "Don't you know anything?"

I tuned out of their bickering as I read through the file. I ought to have read it years ago, of course, only I—well, I couldn't be bothered. I got the important bits and went off to do my job.

My job had been to assassinate Jonal. Dark's brother.

Dark isn't his real name, obviously. It's Talvéan—or more accurately, it's Tal, and Véan is his animal form. The mountain lion. According to the file, Véan is fully eight feet from nose to tail, and as tall as a horse at the withers. Well, that figures— Dark's a pretty big guy in, ahem, all respects.

Véan also has a dark mane, which is unusual in mountain lions, as it affords almost no camouflage. But then, he isn't a true lion, any more than Tal is a true human.

That thought gave me pause. But he isn't the first supernatural being I've been with. The Association is quite popular with vampires, although they have to sign a contract promising to leave the Associée they choose with enough blood to be healthy. And I'd been with a Were or two in my time. I once got a rather tempting offer from a mage who told me I'd make an excellent succubus, but in the end I decided I'd rather keep sex for recreation and food for sustaining my life force. I like food.

I carried on reading. There was some background information on the Nasc in general and Dark's family in particular. It seems that he, his sister Venara and late brother Jonal were the children of the Nasc monarch, or at least they had been until—

Oh no.

Oh *fuck*.

They had been the children of the monarch of the Nasc, a great stag named Kovel, and his mate, a unicorn by the name of Calmira. But Kovel and Calmira, along with a dozen of their most trusted ministers, advisors and friends, had been slaughtered five years ago. By Striker.

This is going to be really difficult.

To make matters worse, my esteemed pater had gone on to truly degenerate Nasc/Striker relations by killing every one of them he came across since. I wasn't a hundred percent surprised by this news—Striker has been known to kill people just because they were standing in his way—but I was grimly fascinated that he'd killed so many of the Nasc, a people whose ruler had my name on an arrow.

Well, this is just peachy.

I read on. Tyra had added a note to check the Vance family files for reference, and I realized she'd gotten them out as well. I was intrigued—Vance is my mother's surname (and, incidentally, the reason I never took a surname. Striker doesn't have one and Chance Vance is just bloody ridiculous).

The file detailed all the usual facts of Chalia's family—her grandfather had established an expensive boarding school, had a town named after him, the family had lots of money and rarely saw Chalia nowadays since, (a) she hadn't aged since the day she pledged herself to Striker, and (b) she's the soul mate of a vicious killer, which is a bit of a downer at family parties.

I'd met my maternal grandmother once, when I was about seven, and she seemed all right to me. The rest of the family treated me with extreme caution, as if I might accidentally blow something up. Which was mean. I'd gotten the hang of not exploding things by my sixth birthday.

There was an interesting sidebar about my great-grandfather, who had been in the army before he retired to teach—which I guess is why the school is so successful, ha ha. Apparently his battalion had toured Asiatica, where the Anglish still had a small colony or two, and had done some tiger hunting in Pradesh. Which turned out to be a mistake, as the tiger he shot turned out to be the monarch of the Nasc.

I was beginning to see a pattern here and I didn't like it one bit. No wonder Dark hated me so much.

"Rosie," I said, closing the Vance file, "have you seen Striker today?"

She nodded. "I passed him in the lobby. He looked like he was off to kill something."

"Did he say anything to you about Dark?"

"Who?"

Apparently this isn't a nickname he's shared with many people. "Talvéan. Tal."

"Uh…" Her forehead wrinkled. "He said Chalia wouldn't let him rip Tal to shreds. Said that was your job. He seemed to be looking quite hopeful as he said it."

No doubt. Striker always seems to be a little disappointed that I don't make more use of my finely honed killing skills.

"Did you see Dar—Tal?"

She looked regretful. "No. But Jalen did and she said he's in a hell of a state. Looks like Striker did one of his fireball specials."

I winced at the thought of all that gorgeous skin burned and charred. "I really ought to go see him," I said reluctantly, standing up and gathering the files.

"You want to borrow my sword?" Brack offered gallantly.

"Why?"

"Well, I figure you're going to need some defense."

I smiled at him. "That's very sweet of you honey, but the day I need a sword to defend myself is the day I throw myself on it."

Rosie rolled her eyes. "Phoenixes."

"Don't let your boyfriend hear you say that."

I passed Captain Tanner on the way out. His eyes flickered over me then he gave a nod.

"How are you?"

I was a little surprised he asked. "I'm okay."

"Your father patched you up."

"I guess." See what a brilliant conversationalist I am?

Tanner paused. "The Nasc—I don't know his name—"

"Tal."

"Right. He's the king of his people, isn't he?"

"Apparently."

Tanner paused again. "He—his family has been through a lot..."

"Most of it caused by my family," I said grimly.

He cracked a smile. "If your family was normal they wouldn't let you on the island," he said, and I knew that his own family history—past and present—was extremely complicated and not a little bit notorious.

"Striker did him some pretty serious damage," Tanner said.

"So Rosie told me."

"Which I suppose puts paid to my doubts about his paternal instincts."

"Oh, no," I assured him cheerfully, "you were right. He only did it because he knew Chalia would get mad if he didn't."

Tanner cocked his head and he seemed to be reading me. Most Phoenixes are extremely good at headology, and Tanner is no exception. Hell, he's a garda and a father, not to mention the countless peacekeeping efforts he'd been renowned for before he left the Order's active duty list.

He didn't say anything about my comment though, just said, "Doc's been trying to replicate that green paste Striker uses for healing. She's got a reasonable facsimile if you want to take some to Tal."

I blinked at him, surprised. I was about to suggest that I take the doc with me instead, but something told me that Dark wouldn't like that. I was walking on broken glass going up there myself.

"Good idea," I said. "Thanks."

Tanner nodded and moved past me to the library. Then he paused again. "Oh, and you know where the body armor is, right?"

I rolled my eyes at him, and he laughed and walked on.

Chapter Six

જી

I collected the green gunk and made my way up the nine flights in a leisurely fashion. Because my Phoenix training is fairly ingrained, I was packing a reasonable amount of heat but my light summer clothes made it hard to conceal much. Not that I figured concealment was the issue, but I like to be subtle.

I thought over my conversation with Tanner as I climbed. It seemed strange that he'd stopped to talk to me at all, but then maybe he was just offering advice in a fatherly capacity. I mean, I guess that's what fathers generally do. Rosie says he's always butting in her affairs. Mac had a lot of work to do before Tanner accepted him.

Striker, on the other hand, seems to view any man in my life as a form of entertainment. Our connection has never been emotional on any level, but it is solid and biological—no one in their right mind would doubt that Striker is my father, even without our strong physical resemblance.

I stopped off in my room to unwind the bandage around my hand. There was an angry red weal in the center of my palm, and to be honest the whole thing hurt like hell, but considering it had been stuck through with a crossbow bolt not too long ago, it was looking bloody good.

The rip on my neck wasn't healed so well. It would probably leave a scar—just in case I felt inclined to forget about Dark.

I followed the running channel of water around the ninth-floor open landing that overlooked the lobby far below, and turned off down the corridor toward Dark's room. I hesitated just a moment outside the door then knocked.

"Fuck off," came the reply.

Yep, this was his room.

The door was locked, but that's no problem for a Phoenix. I learned to pick a lock practically before I could walk. I let myself in, one hand cautiously on the throwing dagger at my waist.

It was dark in the room, appropriately. Outside it was late afternoon and the sun was still bright, but Dark—or someone—had drawn the curtains at the high arched windows. Only the gleaming whiteness of the marble illuminated the bed, and the sprawled figure upon it.

I sucked in a breath as I looked at Dark. Striker really *had* done a number on him. He was lying on his back, totally naked, eyes closed, and his chest and arms were horribly burned. Obviously the fireball had hit him dead center.

I sneaked a glance lower and was incredibly relieved to see the damage hadn't spread below his waist. If that magic cock of his had been damaged I might have cried.

"I said fuck off," Dark said.

"I've come to help."

"The hell you have."

"Open your eyes," I said.

He didn't.

"Open you eyes and see what I've brought you."

That did it. Apparently even half-animal kings can't resist a present. I held out the medical bag I'd brought up, and he frowned at it a moment before bringing those feral eyes up to mine.

"Don't tease me."

"Honey, if I was teasing you, you'd be enjoying it. I told you, I've come to help. Striker could've killed you—"

"Why didn't he?"

I shrugged. "Chalia made him stop."

"You mother is insane," Dark said, his lip curling.

Pretty much, I thought, but I said, "For stopping Striker from killing you?"

"For being with him in the first place. For spawning you."

"That's not a very nice way to talk to someone bearing bandages."

I looked closer at him. His shoulder was swollen and discolored, and the way his arm lay didn't look right at all. I winced as I realized that had probably been part of Striker's efforts to get us un-cuffed. Unnecessary, but fun in Strikerland.

I reached out and touched his arm. He flinched away. "Get your hands off me."

"I'm not going to hurt you."

"You already have." Dark glared at me. "Do you have any idea what your father did to my family? To my people?"

It was my turn to flinch. "Um...yes. I'm sorry."

"And you're following in his footsteps. You make me s—"

I shut him up with a well-placed blow to the neck. A useful trick I learned from Madame Belleveuve at the Association's academy. He fell silent—eyes closing, body going limp—and I climbed on the bed and set to work with what I'd borrowed from the infirmary, cleaning his burns and covering them with the green paste. Then I wrapped bandages around the worst of the wounds, sat back and thought about his shoulder. It was clearly dislocated, and I knew how to pop it back in, but I had a feeling that might wake Dark from his slumber.

I leaned forward and felt at the joint with my fingers, and his eyelids fluttered.

Damn.

I sat on my heels again and looked him over. Thank the gods Chalia had intervened when she had. I'd bandaged Dark's wrist where the handcuff had nearly rubbed his skin off, but I couldn't do much more without waking him. I needed a distraction.

Heat flooded me as I recalled the way I'd distracted him this morning in the tavern. That had worked out reasonably well for all concerned.

I looked down at his cock. Even in repose it was a damn impressive sight. Hell, it looked big enough to please as it was—I had no idea how it had ever fit into me when it was all hard and fat and erect and hard and…

My fingers strayed toward it. Dare I?

Don't be silly, Chance. Of course you dare.

I pulled off my shoulder harness for better maneuverability, leaned forward and ran my fingers over Dark's penis. Gave it a few experimental strokes. I hadn't really gotten to know it properly yet, hadn't studied it. I let my fingers do the walking and set out to discover this magnificent cock that had already afforded me some pretty astounding orgasms. It seemed impolite that we'd been on such intimate terms and yet not properly introduced.

I scooted over between Dark's lean thighs and took a proper look at it. It was rising slightly now, stiffening as I played with it. I slid my other hand into play, exploring his balls, getting to know the weight of them in my hand.

Dark didn't stir, but I noticed his nipples pushing through the bandage on his chest. One had been burned a little, which had to have bloody hurt. I decided I ought to kiss it better when the green stuff had been washed off.

Speaking of kissing better—a little drop of moisture had seeped out of Dark's rapidly hardening cock, and it looked mighty tasty to me. I know a lot of women don't like giving head, but personally I love it. I love the taste of it, the meaty, thick feeling of a cock in my mouth. I don't even really mind the taste of cum sliding down my throat.

I ran my tongue over the ridge around the head of his cock. It twitched.

I licked up the main vein. It jumped.

I slid my mouth over it as far as it would go, which was quite a long way, but somehow not even halfway down this magnificent hard-on, and Dark's eyes came open.

I winked at him and pushed my head down a little farther, taking him into the back of my throat.

"Fuck," he gasped, eloquently.

Later, I thought, and did it again.

Dark's whole body bucked and I smoothed my hands over his hips, pulling him to me. He thrust into my mouth, and I slipped one hand around to caress his balls as I sucked and licked.

Dark gasped, swore and panted. I smiled around his cock, withdrew my mouth and licked his balls.

"Fucking hell," he hissed.

"No, fucking heaven," I murmured, cupping his balls with my tongue. Dark's fingers splayed in my hair, holding me to him. As if I was going anywhere.

That thought reminded me that there was something I needed to do. I was seducing him for a reason. But my pussy was getting pretty slippery by now and demanding some attention. I squeezed my thighs together, rubbed my nipples lightly against the soft hair on his thighs.

It wasn't enough. With my mouth once more wrapped firmly around Dark's thick, straining cock, I slipped one hand down my body and between my legs. For some reason when I'd gotten dressed I hadn't bothered with knickers. Maybe I'd subconsciously known what I'd end up doing here with Dark. My pussy was wetter than I'd realized, slick and hot with wanting for Dark's cock. Gods, how I wanted that cock. I wanted to feel it pushing deep into me, filling me, thrusting hard against my dripping, needy flesh.

I thrust two fingers inside myself, trying to angle them forward but failing. Wrong angle. My thumb rubbed my clit as my other hand fondled Dark's balls.

I felt them clench. He was going to come soon.

And I wanted to come too, but somehow I felt that I'd never manage it unless I had his cock inside me. I let it slip out of my mouth, slid up his body and rubbed my wet cunt against him. Dark shifted restlessly, his eyes flashing fire at me, his hands moving to my hips to position me over him.

I flexed my muscles, thrust out my tits and slid down onto him.

"Oh yes," Dark groaned. "*Gods, yes.*"

I felt the same way. With his cock inside me once again, his balls pressed against my hot flesh, his fingers digging in my hips, it was easy to forget exactly why I was doing this.

Maybe I ought to just get in a good fuck or two before doing what I had to.

No. It needed to be fixed now or all the fucking would just make it worse.

I rose up on his cock, and when I came back down again Dark thrust to meet me. See, this is what amazed me our first night together. There was no need to tell him what I wanted, or even show him. He just knew and did it, and it felt so incredibly good.

His hands started moving upward, toward my breasts, but only one made it under my top. The other fell back, hampered by his dislocated shoulder, and a look of frustration crossed Dark's face.

I squeezed my pussy muscles to distract him a little, cupped his good hand over my tit and slid the other to my pussy, which was within easy reach and had a swollen, needy clit just begging for his attention.

Dark obliged by stroking me, looking up at me with those dark amber eyes, thrusting heat and passion into me, and on impulse I leaned down and kissed him.

Our tongues met and danced, and I felt the sharpness of his lion teeth on my lip as his cock pushed deeper into me at this different angle.

He was going to come soon. I could feel it—I'm pretty good at sensing this. I kept on kissing him, roaming my hands over his poor burnt chest and arms, careful not to press down too much, getting a good grip on his injured arm.

"Come in me," I breathed against his mouth. "I want to feel you come."

"You too," Dark gasped as I squeezed my pussy around him again.

"I'll come whenever you want, honey," I told him, and rubbed my thumb over his nipple through the bandage.

Dark's breath hitched and he thrust into me a little more violently. "Come on," I whispered. "Come inside me. All the way deep inside me. Gods, Dark, no one's ever been this deep," I moaned, as his fingers pinched my clit and he throbbed inside me.

"Next time," Dark said, around stolen breaths and half-kisses, "you come first." And he erupted, a long, hard flow of hot semen pumping into me.

I gripped his arm and twisted it back into place.

Dark's roar of pleasure turned into a howl of pain, his eyes flying open, his hand clutching my breast so hard I thought it might burst open.

"What the *fuck*—"

He really did look in pain. Probably I ought to make it up to him. I leaned down to kiss him, but he shoved me away.

"Get off me, you bloody menace," he spat.

"But—" I knew I'd meant to say something about his shoulder, but all that came to mind was that he'd just come inside me—and how!—and I still hadn't gotten my happies yet. And I wanted those happies. I'd been so focused on getting him to come so I could pop his shoulder back in place that I hadn't let myself orgasm. Now I wanted it, desperately, especially since I still felt his cock inside me.

Dark gave me a shove with both hands and I toppled off him to land in a sticky, cum-drenched tangle on the hard, cold floor.

That knocked some sense into me and I glared up at him. "How did that feel?"

"You mean the fucking or the deliberate molestation of my dislocated shoulder?"

"Your *relocated* shoulder." I shakily pushed myself to my knees and then my feet, reluctantly impressed at his coherent use of long words. Dark was leaning back on his elbows, and now a look of confusion crossed his face as he realized he could move his shoulder more easily.

"What did you do?" he asked warily.

"I popped it back in. Sorry it hurt, but I tried to—"

"What's this?" He'd noticed the bandages, the mess of gunk smeared all over him.

"It's some healing paste for your burns—"

"I don't need it," Dark said coldly.

"Well, I beg to differ. It'll accelerate the healing process tenfold, you'll feel much better in a day and if you're lucky it might not permanently scar—"

"Is it magic?"

I shrugged. "I guess. Sort of."

His eyes went dark. "Striker's magic?"

"No. It was made by the doc here."

Dark didn't look impressed. He sat up, moving much more easily than you'd think a man with such extensive tissue damage could, then stood up. Barefoot, he towered over me, and I'm not exactly little.

My heart rate picked up. My nipples tightened.

Dark shoved past me and slammed into the bathroom, and before I could really process it, he'd switched on the shower.

I stood for a long moment, stunned. Then it hit me.

Little ingrate! I spend all this time trying my bloody best to heal him and look what he does! Gods, he made me mad. It's one thing when someone tries to kill you or playfully rips out your throat for attention, but to be so bloody ungrateful? *Oooh!*

I waited for one minute, two, five. The shower water still ran.

My patience ended.

I stormed into the bathroom and ripped back the shower curtain.

"How dare you—" I began, and then stopped. Dark stood there all naked and soapy, having managed to get most of the green stuff off already. Water cascaded down his chest—his magnificent, scarred chest—past his stomach, down to his groin, where his hand rested on his own cock. He was hard.

I stared, all the anger whacked out of me by the sight of him. It's a failing—one day my utter inability to function when faced with a hot naked man is really going to get me in serious trouble, but right now I didn't care.

"I locked the door," Dark said. Steam rose around him and I figured it was probably his body heat making the water boil.

"I didn't notice."

He removed his fingers from his cock, but my own hand shot out and stopped him.

"You're a witch," he breathed. "You've possessed me."

My pussy clenched at the thought. "You were—you were doing that for me?"

His eyes bored into mine, and my hand moved up and down on his cock. Dark let out a sharp breath and then in a second he'd yanked me in to the shower with him, the water beating down on my clothes, soaking me to the skin.

I didn't care. I hardly noticed. My body was plastered against Dark's and my mouth was glued to his. I couldn't stop kissing him. In the back of my mind I knew he hated me, knew he despised me, knew that one day he was going to stand over my dead body and smile. But right now all that mattered was the heat and the darkness and strength of him, his hot skin against mine, his cock in my hand, his fingers thrusting into my pussy. He yanked my skirt off and I think it tore but I wasn't really interested.

I came quickly, hard, convulsing around his hand, and then he was shoving me against the wall, ripping open my sodden T-shirt, pulling my legs apart and driving that cock of his deep inside me.

It was hard and fast and glorious. The water hammered down on us, steam rose around us and still Dark drove himself relentlessly, deep and hard inside me. I lifted my legs, wrapping them around his waist as he slammed me against the cold wall with every thrust. His head rolled back, a rumble arising in his chest, the deep purr of a big, satisfied cat. His wet, rough skin chafed my bare, aching nipples, the water cascading between us adding slide to the friction, and the glory of it made me moan, an honest-to-gods *moan*.

I nipped at his throat with my teeth and he rewarded me by fucking me just a little bit harder. That glorious chest of his was right there in front of me and I fastened my mouth on one nipple—the unburnt one—feasting on it, loving the taste and the hardness of it scraping against my lips.

Dark growled and dug his fingers into my hips. I spread kisses all over his chest, licking him, the salt of his skin, the wet of the shower, the bitterness of the herbs. The heat and power in his body so fierce it made me tremble before I came, fingers digging into the hard muscle of his back, clenching around him, crying out as wave after wave of sweet, hot pleasure crashed through me, wringing me dry, the big orgasm I'd been wanting ever since I saw him sprawled on that bed.

I think Dark came too. To be honest, I wasn't really paying attention. I was squished between a rock and hard place—or Dark and the wall—and my body felt fucking wonderful, and I didn't really care about anything.

I'm sure sex used to be good before this. I'm sure it used to be fantastic. Time was, I could spend all night merrily boinking my little brains out—and yet, right then, it was hard to imagine ever having good sex with anyone else.

Dark's head dropped to my shoulder, his face buried in my neck.

"What have you done to me?" he murmured.

I lifted a hand to stroke his wet hair. "I didn't do anything, honey—that was all you."

Dark was breathing hard, his body heavy where it pinned mine to the wall. I felt like a butterfly, trapped and spread open.

"I can't stop wanting you," he breathed.

"Well, it's nice to see I haven't lost my touch."

Then he lifted his head and his expression wasn't nice. "That's right," he said. "How could I have forgotten you're a whore?"

He slid out of me then, turning away to wash himself before stepping out of the shower. Bastard. Just when I think he's thawing toward me, he goes and says something like that.

"For your information," I said, following him out of the bathroom, "I am no such thing."

"You fuck people for money. That's what whores do."

"And you rip out people's throats for attention. That's what Striker does."

I regretted the words as soon as I'd said them. Dark gave me a ferocious glare and strode to the door, which, I realized with a sudden stab of panic, I'd forgotten to lock again. Oh fuck, the Order was going to *kill* me.

"No!" I yelped, rushing over to bar the exit with my body. As I ran I lost my grip on the towel I'd wrapped around me, so I was naked but for a soaking garter holster when I threw myself against the door. Dark—who hadn't bothered with a towel—grabbed my shoulders and attempted to move me.

Right then I wished I had a smidgen of Striker's powers, so I could stop him. But all I had was my own physical strength, and I planted my damp feet square on the marble floor and stood my ground. Dark growled, an animal sound, and shoved at me. I growled back at him and stayed where I was—or nearly where I was, anyway.

Glaring hard at him, I said, "I'm not letting you out of this room."

"The hell you aren't."

"No," I said, "I'm really not. You're not allowed to leave, that's why they locked you in."

"Slave to your orders?"

"Sensible orders," I cried. "You did try to kill me twice this morning."

"Only once," Dark growled. "Call the second a love bite."

A hot shiver ran through me at that, and Dark, the ratfink, used the opportunity to shove me to the floor. But I'm not a Phoenix Knight for nothing, so I tackled him as I toppled over and pulled him down with me in a tangle of hot, wet, naked limbs.

Okay. I wasn't interested in fighting so much anymore. Hot, wet, naked Dark was always going to be fun, and I was just starting to give up the fight and reach down to see if he wanted to play when the door burst open, slamming into my thigh, and I looked up to see my parents looking down at me.

Chapter Seven

ॐ

So there I was, wrestling naked and dripping on the floor with an equally naked and dripping man who, let's face it, my body had plans for other than grievous harm—and in the doorway stood Chalia and Striker. She clapped her hands over her eyes. He started to laugh.

"This isn't what it looks like," I began.

"Oh yes it is," piped up a voice from behind my mother, and I peered around her skirts to see a young Dragon looking down at me, a blush staining her cheeks. "I, uh, have the room next door," she explained.

Ah, fuck.

I kicked at Dark and he had the good sense to get off me, moving away to grab the towel I'd discarded.

Bastard wrapped it around his own waist instead of handing it to me, like a gentleman would.

I pulled myself to my feet and raised my chin. It's not like this is the first time I've been seen stark naked in public. Hell, this morning I was *fucking* in public. And anyway, I was armed. That's not totally naked.

But to my absolute horror, it wasn't just Striker, Chalia and the little Dragon girl who'd come to call. Elwyn was there too. And Tanner. And Tyra, her usual clipboard in hand.

Oh, fuck. Fuckety fuck.

I took a deep breath and tried to look normal. A hand brushed mine, and I saw Dark holding out the sheet from the bed.

In that moment, I loved him.

Instead of throwing myself at his feet and kissing his toes, however, I just accepted the sheet with a tight smile, and wrapped it around me. Still no one had said anything, although Striker's shoulders were shaking with laughter.

"Did you want something?" I asked regally.

"Can I open my eyes now?" Chalia asked, peeking between her fingers.

"Yes," I said.

"They're not doing the nasty anymore," Striker informed her solemnly.

"We were not—we weren't—he was trying to escape," I said with dignity, "and I was trying to stop him."

"Naked?" Tanner said. He looked kinda amused, too.

"We just got out of the shower," I said, and then winced. Striker's shoulders were heaving. "I mean—oh, fuck."

"Later," Dark said, and I think I blushed, for maybe the third time in my entire life. "And I was not trying to escape. I merely wished to find a senior member of the Order to talk to."

"Naked?" I enquired.

He glared at me.

"So what did you want?" I asked the crowd at the door, hitching my sheet a little higher.

"You healed him," Striker said, his laughter finally fading, a frown creeping in. He looked a little older when he frowned, but still not old enough to be my father.

"I used that green paste stuff Doc made," I said.

"Doesn't heal that quickly," Tanner said. He was frowning too.

I looked at Dark's chest. Now that the water had dried off, I could see clearly what had happened to the horrible burns that had covered his chest.

They were gone.

Well, nearly gone. Here and there the skin still looked sore, uneven, but for the most part he looked as if he'd been healing for weeks, months.

He looked like Striker had healed him.

He looked really mad.

"What did you do?" Dark asked in a low voice.

"I didn't do anything! I just put that stuff on you."

"It doesn't work like that," said the young Dragon, and we all looked at her. Senior staff, Phoenixes and legends—she looked bloody terrified. "I mean, last year Derry Jopville got burned mucking out the dragon paddock and Doc put that stuff on him, and it eased it a bit but it still took a long time before it stopped hurting and he still has the scars even now."

Striker raised an eyebrow at me.

"Oh, honey," Chalia said.

"Don't you 'oh honey' me," I said crossly, folding my arms. "I didn't do anything."

"Well, you must have," Tyra said practicably. "Look at him."

We all looked. The Dragon girl licked her lips and I glared at her.

She shrank back.

"I. Didn't. Do. Anything," I said.

"You used your—" Striker began, and I shot my glare at him.

"Don't say it. Don't you *dare* say it."

But Striker is Striker, so he said it.

"You used your magic," he said.

"I don't have any frigging magic!"

They all stared at me. Striker looked smug. Chalia looked disappointed, like I'd been caught lying. Elwyn, Tanner and Tyra all exchanged knowing glances.

"Don't you do that look thingy," I said. "I know what that look thingy means. It means you think I have magic and I've just been hiding it all along. Well, I haven't and I haven't, and even if I did I would have."

"Uh." Chalia looked confused.

"Never mind," I snapped.

"Then explain this," Dark said.

I looked at that lovely smooth skin, skin I'd been kissing and licking only a few minutes before…

Oh fuck.

"I can't," I said finally.

Striker snorted.

"Did you all want something?" I asked again.

"Yes." Elwyn marched into the room, Tyra following like an obedient secretary. Tanner strolled after them, and finally Striker and Chalia came in, too. The young Dragon crept away. There wasn't really anywhere to sit but the bed and one single chair, which Striker took, pulling Chalia down onto his lap.

Tanner glared out the window. Dark glared at me.

"Is there a title you would prefer?" Elwyn asked Dark.

"Tal will be fine."

She nodded. "Tal, then. You know you're not supposed to be on this island? The very fact that you know where it *is,* is a gross breach of protocol."

He inclined his head gracefully. "I know, and you have my most sincere apologies. I regret my use of that young Knight. Please do not punish her. The fault was all mine."

Elwyn fixed him with a steely glare. "The fault was entirely hers. For a fully qualified Dragon Knight to allow such a lapse in judgment is wholly unacceptable. Her punishment has been severe."

I don't know why I happened to glance over at Striker at that point, but he met my eyes and looked very pleased with himself. Oh gods. I do not want to know what he did to that poor child.

"Nevertheless, we do realize why you took such extreme measures."

I transferred my attention back to Dark, who was looking far more regal than should be possible in just a towel.

"Honor is very important to my people," he said fiercely. "I must avenge the death of my brother."

Elwyn nodded, but she said, "You realize we cannot disclose to you who commissioned us?"

"If Tyra hadn't been such an avid graphologist he probably would have found out," Tanner said.

Striker sneered over "graphologist". I've no doubt he knew what it meant, but he didn't use long words. They were too poncy for him.

"It doesn't matter," Dark said, looking at me, and I knew what that look meant. It meant that he was going to make me tell him. Well, he could go fuck himself for that, because nothing that walked the Realms could pull that out of me.

Nothing.

"Ordinarily," Elwyn went on, "such violations of our rules would probably earn you death."

A flash of—I don't know, was it pain?—went through me then. Striker smirked, and for that alone I hated him.

"But the Nasc have seen enough tragedy in recent years that to put another member to death would nudge you closer to extinction," Elwyn went on.

"Added to which, if you killed me, my people would declare war," Dark said, almost pleasantly. "Nearing extinction we may be, but we are a fierce people."

"I'll put that in your file," Tyra murmured.

"Therefore the Order has come to a decision," Tanner said. "Due to the wrongs done to your family by one of our number," here he heroically managed not to look at Striker, "we have decided not to prosecute you."

"Prosecute now, is it?" Striker said, and I rolled my eyes. He just can't resist. "Spent too long as a copper, you have."

Tanner manfully ignored him, and not for the first time I wished he was my dad.

"If," Elwyn said, her tone steely, "you agree not to pursue the matter."

There was a long pause. I could feel the air burning between Striker and Dark.

"He slaughtered my people," Dark said in a low voice.

"One of 'em looked at me funny," Striker said glibly.

"That's not funny," I snapped. "What would you do if someone slaughtered all the people you care about? If they took a personal dislike and just killed everyone you loved for no reason at all? Oh no, I forget," I added, glaring at him like a teenager, "that would be impossible. I don't believe you've ever cared for anyone in your life. I don't think you're even capable of loving anyone, except *her*." I jerked my head at my mother, incensed at her for just allowing it. "And that's only because she's a bloody good fuck."

The air got a little thinner as everyone sucked in a breath. Striker had leapt to his feet when I brought Chalia into this, and she stood with her hand on his arm.

"Striker, don't."

He snarled at her and swatted her away, and then the full force of his glare was turned on me. I stood my ground. I'd meant what I said, and if push came to shove I knew I had a trick or two up my sleeve to slow him down.

Stopping him was another matter. I don't think anyone could do that.

"Don't you dare say that about her," Striker breathed, low and menacing.

"I can say what I bloody like, she's my mother. And it's true. Name one person you've ever cared for, *ever*, except for her."

Silence. You could have heard a corpse breathe in that room.

Tears pricked my eyes as I realized what sort of hole I was digging myself into. Striker didn't love me, I'd always known that. He barely tolerated me. I knew this, and yet it still hurt that he said nothing.

Besides which, so far I was having a *really* bad day.

"You know, this would be a really good place for you to jump in and say, 'You, Chance, I love you'," I prompted sharply. "'You're my flesh and blood, the impossible child who should never have been, and even though I rarely show it I do find you precious.' But you can't even pretend for me, because you don't like me any more than you like...*Tanner*. In fact, you probably like me less, since Tanner's hardly caused you any trouble compared to all I've managed to disrupt. My gods, think of all the sex you could have been having that I got in the way of!"

I didn't see it coming because he moved so damn fast. But I felt the sharp, bone-cracking sting of Striker's palm hitting my face, felt my cheekbone shudder and snap and in that instant, all hell broke loose. Chalia started yelling, screaming at Striker, and Tanner did too. Elwyn grabbed my arm and pulled me back, away from Striker. And Dark—

Dark launched himself at the man who'd hit me, suddenly less of a man himself than a snarling, enraged beast, all teeth and hair and wild, ferocious eyes. I would swear blind that his fingers evolved into claws, and he attacked Striker like a wild animal. Like the mountain lion he was inside.

Everything else stopped for a second as we all stared in astonishment, first at the insanity of attacking Striker, and then at the ferocity with which Dark was doing so. Striker was on the ground, fighting back, but Dark seemed to be all teeth and claws and for once, it looked like Striker didn't know what to do with himself.

"Stay the fuck away," a snarl arose from the whirling mass of fury that Dark had become, "from my woman."

And that made every single one of us freeze, until Tyra managed to recover her senses a little. She took the clasp from her hair, shook out the golden wings that seemed to disappear most of the time and opened her mouth on one beautiful, clear blue note.

And I mean blue. I could see it. I could actually see the music pouring from her beautiful mouth, and I was utterly entranced by it. Maybe it was because I'm occasionally into the girl thing, I don't know. I thought that most of the time I was pretty straight. But while Chalia and Elwyn were unaffected enough to start pulling Striker and Dark apart, I was terribly distracted by the noise.

Tanner, Striker and Dark were all completely enchanted by it. Unable to do anything but what they were bidden, which, let me tell you, is no small feat for even Tanner and Dark. I'd never seen Striker so completely helpless in all my life.

I started to fall a little bit in love with Tyra.

Elwyn hustled me out of the room, pulling Dark with her too, and marched us down the hall. As the siren's song faded, I came back to my senses and clutched my sheet closer around me.

Dark, I noticed, had lost his towel and was completely naked again. He didn't seem to have realized.

"What was that?" he mumbled.

"Nothing," Elwyn said smoothly.

"But I—I felt—"

"Tal, look at me," Elwyn said, and he did, confused. "I promise I will not tell anyone that your Nascene animal senses temporarily overwhelmed you. I have heard that it can occasionally cause delusion and temporary memory loss when Nasc twins have been apart for some time."

I was impressed. Dark, in his befuddled state, just nodded blearily.

"I would suggest you try to get some sleep. In the morning you are free to go. Chance, you are responsible for him from now on."

She shoved us toward the stairs then marched back to the room to clean up the mess.

I didn't know where else to take Dark, so I led him back to my room. He seemed highly confused, and indeed I didn't feel quite myself. I'd never heard a siren's song before, but it was fucking powerful stuff. I could quite see how men might be lured to their deaths by it.

Dark didn't seem to realize he was naked, although every female—and a few males too, I must tell Brack—stopped and absolutely gaped.

I let us into my room and propelled Dark toward the bed. "Stay here," I told him, "I'll get you some clothes."

He did as he was told. Man, what I wouldn't give for some of Tyra's mojo.

The room opposite mine had formerly been held by a rather tasty young hunk of Dragon who had a passion for playing Treegan and for dirty sex in the gryphon stables. I knocked on his door, hoping he was still around, and was relieved when he answered.

"Hi," I said. "I need to borrow some clothes."

"Chance?" He stared at me, then propped himself against the doorframe, grinning sexily. "I heard you were back on the island. Long time no see! What's all this stuff going on with you and Striker? Anyone ever tell you, you look a bit like him? You could be family or something!" He laughed at the absurdity of the idea.

I gave him my most charming smile, the one I always bring out when I want to dazzle people into not making the connection between me and the most evil man history has ever known.

"Nothing interesting," I said. "Could you just lend me some trousers and a shirt? Shoes if you have them."

He certainly did, and whenever he asked questions I just dazzled him a little bit more. See, who needs magic when you have a big smile and a lot of bare skin?

Back in my room, I was relieved to find Dark hadn't gone anywhere, but slightly disturbed to find him just sitting there, frowning into space.

"I brought you some clothes," I said.

He nodded vaguely. At least he'd heard me.

"It's late though," I said, glancing at the clock by the bed. "Probably you ought to get some sleep. What with the whole, er, Nasc senses thing—"

"She was a siren," Dark corrected me, still staring at nothing.

Oh crap.

"There's no such thing as a—"

"Yes there is, and she was it." He rubbed his face with his hands and finally looked up at me. "Never seen one before."

"I've never seen another one," I said, giving in. "Only Tyra. Striker said—" I began, then winced. I shook myself, then went to my clothes chest and pulled out a shirt to sleep in. I don't usually bother with pajamas unless it's cold, and even then I prefer to warm myself up another way.

But right now, I didn't quite feel like getting hot and sweaty with Dark. He looked greatly disturbed and I didn't feel much better. I pulled on the shirt and went into the bathroom to get my first-aid kit. Every room has one—it stops us from bothering Doc with minor injuries. Well, I say minor— there's stuff in there for local anesthetics and stitches.

He flinched back when I reached out with a damp cloth to wipe away the blood on his face.

"If you leave it, it could get infected," I said, and he relented and let me clean the scratches on his cheek, his shoulder — the deep gashes on his rib cage where Striker had apparently developed some sort of claws. I wondered what sort of state *he* was in. Dark had been pretty vicious.

"Why did you attack him?" I asked after long hesitation, as I was taping a dressing over his side.

Dark didn't answer for a while. He'd been silent and compliant as I tended to him, and eventually he said, "I was angry."

"Well, duh."

"He killed so many of them," Dark said, sounding distant. "Needlessly. We did nothing to him."

Brief hope. Why do I bother?

"That's not how Striker works," I said.

"'One of 'em looked at me funny'," Dark quoted bitterly.

"I think it's his idea of a joke."

"Joke? *He slaughtered dozens of people!*"

I felt the anger vibrating through him and I could have wept for him, I really could.

"Striker has an unfortunate sense of humor," I muttered. Before Dark could respond I took his face in my hands and said, "I'm sorry."

He looked at me with troubled amber eyes and asked, "For what?"

"For what he did. For not being able to stop him. For everything he is. I'm sorry."

Dark looked at me for a long moment. Then he turned away, lay down on the bed and was silent for the rest of the night.

Chapter Eight

ഔ

It would be nice to say how sweet it was to wake in Dark's arms, but the truth is he woke me by prodding at my cheek, which was incredibly sore where Striker had hit me.

"Bloody ow," I said, without opening my eyes.

"I think it's broken."

"Yeah. Me too. Stop poking it."

He did, but the throbbing still remained. I peeled open one eye to see first the clock, which said it was barely morning, and then Dark, propped on one elbow next to me, the cuts on his face and body making him look even more sinful than usual. Like a warrior fresh from battle.

Mmm.

"There's a doctor on the island?"

"Yeah," I said, running my eyes over his beautiful chest.

"You should see her."

My eyes stopped their descent into paradise and zoomed back up to his face. "Excuse me?"

"Your cheekbone may need to be reset. There's a lot of swelling. Maybe she could give you something for that."

I stared at him. "Aren't you the guy who wants me dead? Wait—when you said you had a twin did you mean like a human one? Did someone swap you?"

He made a sarcastic face. "Until you find my sister you get to live."

"Yes, but what good is resetting my cheekbone going to do until then? You're only going to kill me eventually anyway."

I don't know why I was reminding him. Dark didn't seem like the type to back down on a vow like that.

He turned away from me, lay on his back with one arm behind his head, looking like sin itself. I ran my eyes down the curve of muscle that flowed beautifully from biceps to hip and then I got distracted.

"Remember the first time we woke up together?" I asked a little breathlessly, and even if Dark didn't remember, his cock did.

"Don't," Dark said. "I feel like hell this morning."

"Me too," I said. "We could feel like hell together."

"No."

Well, hell. I wasn't used to this sort of rejection. I leaned over and licked at the cut on his chest. Dark's skin jumped in appreciation.

"What are you doing?"

"Seemed to help last night."

Silence. Mmm, he tasted good, even with the metallic taste of blood tainting his skin.

"You said you had no magic."

I lied.

"I don't."

See, I lied again.

"But obviously you—do." He sucked in a breath as he spoke, which may or may not have had anything to do with my tongue flicking over his nipple. Well, okay, that wasn't hurt, but there was a little cut close by.

"Well, of a certain kind," I said, sliding my hand over his hip, loving the ridge of bone, the indentation, the hard muscle, the—

His hand stopped mine.

"I'm magic in bed," I breathed.

"You have a magic tongue."

"Glad you noticed," I purred.

"You know that's not what I meant."

"Okay, I'm like a dog. My saliva heals."

"Charming imagery. But then maybe you're right. You can be a bitch."

He was remarkably eloquent for a man with someone licking his chest.

"You'd better believe it," I told him, well aware that the angel of mercy persona I'd been affecting last night wasn't entirely accurate. I didn't want to give him the wrong impression.

I moved on to the cut on his hip.

"Chance, what are you—" He sounded slightly strangled.

"Trying to heal you."

"Why?"

"Shame to see that lovely body ruined."

Besides, I had plans for said lovely body.

"Chance, *please* stop."

I looked up. "You don't like it?"

His rapidly rising erection said otherwise. Wow, I'd never known anyone to get a hard-on as fast as this guy. Surely that had to hurt?

"This isn't a good idea," Dark said, but he didn't sound very convinced.

I left the cut on his hip, thought about going for his cock but then decided to pay his face some attention. He'd find me harder to ignore that way.

I ran my lips over the cut on his cheek in the barest of kisses. Then I slid my tongue over the wound.

Dark was breathing fast now. Losing interest in healing as his hands slid up my back, I dragged my mouth to his, tasting those soft, full lips of his before nipping with my teeth and finally nudging inside, thrusting into his mouth the way he thrust into my pussy, taking him, sprawling across him and consuming him.

Dark didn't resist anymore. His arms came around me, he rolled me to my back and he kissed me—hard, sweet, perfect. He settled between my legs, hips cradled against mine, so comfortable, so hot. I felt his cock nudging against me, the roughness of his chest against my nipples, and I wrapped my arms around him, needing to feel his big, solid body cradled by my own. The muscles in his arms and back moved under my hands, rippling beneath his skin, and I ran my fingers restlessly over his back, down to that sweet ass of his, so tight and perfect. I wanted to bite it. But I never wanted to stop kissing him.

I can't remember ever being so addicted to a kiss.

I was in so deep I hardly heard my scryer buzzing until Dark raised his head from mine, looking dazed, and said, "What's that?"

"Wha?" I felt drugged.

"That buzzing…"

Probably my ears, I thought, but then with a sinking feeling I realized someone was trying to call me. Damn Chalia for getting me a new scryer.

"Bollocks." I wriggled out from under Dark and reached for the little rock on the nightstand. "Don't go anywhere."

Dark looked at me like I was insane, through eyes with pupils the size of sovereign pieces.

I grabbed my scryer and immediately wished I hadn't.

"Look, she can't be that upset, she's shagging him right now," Striker said to someone offstage left.

"You," I said, all my warm fuzzies just draining away. "I don't want to speak to you."

Striker glared at me. "I'm sorry," he said, and didn't look it at all.

Suddenly I was really angry.

"No, you're not."

"Hey! Don't you tell me what I am and am not, kid. I've said I'm sorry and —"

"Did Mum put you up to this?"

He looked really sulky.

"She did, didn't she? And she's sitting there listening. What'd she threaten you with?"

"Shut the fuck up," Striker said.

"She wouldn't sleep with you, would she? Until you'd apologized to me. Well, tough. I don't accept it."

"What do you mean, you don't accept it?" Striker looked outraged.

"I mean, I don't accept it," I said in slow, speaking-to-idiot tones. "You don't mean it, do you?"

Striker narrowed his eyes, drew down his brows and sucked in his cheeks. I knew that look. I was pretty good at it myself.

"Don't go giving me that cheekbone look," I said. "Either say you're sorry and mean it or fuck off."

He glared at me.

"Fuck off then," I said, and dropped the scryer.

Dark was lying back on the bed, not looking quite so liquidly tempting anymore.

"Excuse me one moment," I said, and got up off the bed. I looked around for a second, until my eyes fell on the angels holding up the mirror over the mantel. I saw myself reflected, and I looked mad as hell. My hair was mussed, my lips were swollen, my cheeks were flushed and I might have looked quite sexy if it wasn't for the utter Strikerness of my eyes. And the swollen bruise on my cheek.

Even my reflection couldn't escape him.

I grabbed the mirror, hauled it over my head and aimed it through the window. Dark started when it struck the pane, but the marble-framed mirror sailed through unharmed in a shower of shattering glass, noisy as hell, but not destructive enough.

I grabbed a crossbow from the weapons chest by the bed and aimed it after the mirror. My aim was good, and the bolt struck dead center.

The mirror exploded in a fountain of light, rainbow shards glittering in the sunlight as they fell to earth.

I felt a little better.

Dark, however, raced to the window, looked down and yelled, "Take cover!"

Oh yeah. How thoughtful of him.

"That was fucking stupid," he said, turning back to me.

"Yeah. Well. Get used to it." I was still mad as hell. Random destruction had only taken the edge off. I looked at Dark and thought about just attacking him and fucking him into the ground, but the way he was looking at me wasn't inviting and besides, right now I just wasn't in the mood for sex.

There must be something wrong with me.

"I'm hungry," I announced. "You want to eat?"

Dark looked at me like I was mad.

"Either come with me or stay here," I said. "It's up to you. I can't let you roam around the island on your own."

His eyes narrowed, but then he nodded. I threw at him the clothes I'd gotten last night and shoved myself into some random garments of my own. Not bothering with a hairbrush or makeup, I grabbed Dark's arm as soon as he'd tugged his shirt on and yanked him outside.

He didn't say anything as I hauled him down the stairs and toward the cafeteria. My mood wasn't much improved by the scent of slowly roasted dodo meat, but my appetite definitely appreciated it. Dark got himself an extra-large helping—macho git—and I stomped back outside again, towing him after me.

Tanner, Rosie and Mac were sitting at one of the stone tables outside. Tanner was picking at his food, looking disgusted as his daughter and her boyfriend fed each other bits of dodo meat.

I slapped my tray down on the table. "Morning."

They looked up and from the expressions of horror on their faces, I knew the bruise on my face had gotten a little worse.

"What the fuck happened to you?" Rosie stared at me.

"You haven't heard?" I stabbed a carrot with my fork.

"Striker," Tanner said grimly.

Mac and Rosie looked appalled. "He hit you?" Rosie gasped.

I shrugged and hacked at a venroot. I hate venroots. They don't taste of anything. Why do people serve them?

"Have you seen him this morning?" Tanner asked after a short pause.

"He called me."

"And?"

"Chalia tried to make him apologize."

"And?"

"And, he didn't." I mutilated an asparagus tip.

"Not strictly true," Dark murmured. I sent him a death glare. A lesser man might have keeled over.

"One of those fake 'she made me say it' apologies?" Rosie guessed, and I nodded. "I hate that."

"You do it all the time." Tanner rolled his eyes.

"I do not!"

"Yes, you do. 'I'm sorry I was late, I'm sorry I failed the test, I'm sorry I forgot to take the dog out—'"

"Da-ad—"

"Children," Mac said.

"Don't you 'children' me," Tanner said, but he said it mildly, and I felt a burst of jealousy. The only sparring I ever did with Striker usually resulted in bruises for both of us. We never just bickered. It was cozy. I liked it.

I ripped some dodo meat to shreds. Hey, dodos are stupid. They deserve to be eaten.

"How are you feeling this morning?" Tanner asked Dark, carefully.

"Fine." The word was clipped.

"Elwyn explained about your Nasc senses—"

"Did she explain about the siren?"

I winced. Everyone else froze.

"Uh, ixnay on the irensay," I muttered.

"What?"

"It's not common knowledge," Tanner translated.

"Siren?" Rosie said.

"Uh," I said. Yeah. Smooth. You can see how I passed the Phoenix so easily, huh?

"It doesn't matter," Tanner said, and shot her a warning look.

"No," Dark frowned, seeing it. "It doesn't."

Silence. I forked up some meat.

"Rosie, how's your training going?" I asked, just to break the silence, and Rosie sighed dramatically and launched into an impassioned retelling of her latest catastrophe, with sympathetic and occasionally caustic asides from her father and boyfriend.

Striker never paid the slightest bit of attention to my achievements. When I passed the Dragon he'd asked what took me so long. When I got the Phoenix he'd said it was a pointless test and he could do it from inside a lead coffin.

I offered to take him up on that. He thought I was joking.

Dark's eyes were closed. He looked like he was thinking, hard. I frowned, touching his arm. "Dark?"

He shrugged me off irritably and his expression grew more intense. Finally his eyes opened, he looked at me and said, "We need to go to Zemlya."

I blinked. "We?"

"If you'd prefer not to help me find Venara, I could kill you right now."

"The hell you could," Tanner said mildly, and I gazed at him adoringly.

"Will you be my dad?"

He laughed at that, but I was serious.

"Take him," Rosie said. "I have too many anyway."

"No you don't." Mac rolled his eyes.

"Come on—I have him and a stepdad, and I swear Tyrnan seems to think he should be in there too, and Striker—"

"Striker you can keep," I told her.

"No," Tanner stood up, pushing his chair back abruptly, "she can't. He's all yours."

He stomped away. And this time it was Rosie who broke the silence.

"Tal," she addressed Dark, "maybe you could look in the library and see if Tyra has any information on your sister."

"She doesn't," I said. "I looked."

"I'd like to look myself," Dark said.

"Trust me, you don't want to tangle with Tyra right now," I said, and I meant it. She always got out of sorts when the whole siren thing came up. She was likely to bite the head off anyone who pissed her off—and I don't mean that as a figure of speech.

Dark looked at me then gave an almost imperceptible nod.

"We must go to Zemlya," he repeated. "Soon. Now."

I thought about it. By dragon it would only take a few hours to get to the Sixth Bridge, between Peneggan and Zemlya—if the Order let us take a dragon on unofficial business, which they probably wouldn't. Although, once we got there we'd probably have to cross the Leac—that huge frozen expanse of nothingness where only Kelfs were able to live—or take a long boat trip around it.

We could go over the Fourth Bridge, into Angeland, and take the railroad to the Fifth Bridge. It would be slower, but not as unpleasant. The Fifth opened onto the civilized part of southern Zemlya, close to the capital. All of Zemlya was cold, all year round, but at least it was possible to actually live in the southern part.

"Where exactly in Zemlya?" I asked Dark.

He closed his eyes. "I'll know when we get there."

"That's not very helpful."

"Somewhere cold."

"Duh. Icy, frozen wasteland."

His eyes opened and glared at me. "I don't know where exactly," he said. "I'll know when we get there."

Fine. Very helpful.

"If you want to go north, we're flying back to Elvyrn today," Rosie said. "That's half the way."

"Thanks. We might go via Angeland. I'll have to think about it."

"Flying?" Dark said. He looked confused.

"By dragon. They can be tamed, harnessed—you put a sort of cab on their back and steer them like a horse. They fly incredibly fast—a couple hundred miles in an hour."

He didn't look convinced. "With good horses we could make the Fourth Bridge in—"

"In about ten times as long," I interrupted. "And it's exhausting. Going north is probably our best bet."

"With a very long journey at the other end," Dark pointed out. "It takes hours to get to Vaznafjörður from the Sixth Bridge."

I was impressed at how he'd managed to pronounce the tricky Zemlyan name correctly. Zemlyan is a language half derived from Kelfish — it's not easy to wrap your tongue around unless you're used to it. Of course, I started learning when I was pretty young. As Dark must have done...

"It'll take us hours to get to the Fourth," I said, "and after that we've still got the railroad to negotiate. And you know how unreliable the Anglish can be..."

"You know," Mac said to Rosie, "they bicker just like we do."

"We don't bicker," she said.

"Uh, yes honey, we do."

"We discuss things in a calm and rational manner."

"No, we bicker."

"We don't!"

"Look, what are we doing now?"

I shook my head at them and got up to move away. Dark followed me as I took my plate back to the cafeteria, snatched up some chocolate cake and walked away eating it.

"We really would be better going west," he said.

"Nope. North."

He caught me around the waist as I took the first step up toward my room, pushing me back against the banister.

My breath caught in my throat as he pressed his long, hard body against mine.

"West."

"North," I breathed.

"The boat is hideous."

"The railroad is unreliable."

His breath was hot against my ear. "So is the boat. Those ice floes…"

"Anglish inefficiency…"

"The Anglish are light-years ahead of everyone else in terms of technology, engineering…"

Dark's tongue snaked around my earlobe. I was finding it hard to think. "The ship is powered by Kelfs. They know ice."

"Kelfs don't like Nasc."

"Are you afraid?"

"No. They are."

His fingers were creeping up under my shirt, fluttering against my belly. My breath caught again.

"How about we settle this somewhere else?" I squeaked.

Listen to me! I'm an Associée. I'm a goddamn Phoenix. I don't *squeak*.

"Like where?"

"Like my bed."

Dark drew back just enough to meet my eyes. His gaze was hot, deep, steamy.

I leaned forward and whispered in his ear. "How about a race?"

"A race?"

"First one to come…loses."

For a second or two he was utterly still. Then he said, "How far is your room again?"

"Seven flights."

"We'll never make it."

And to my utter astonishment, his fingers crept up farther toward my breasts.

"Dark, we're in the lobby."

"Mmm." His mouth was hot on my neck.

So he wanted to do this here? He really did?

Well, ha. I'm trained for this, buddy. I know every single trick there is and even some there aren't. I've made grown men come in their pants so often it's not even special anymore.

I slid my hands up under his shirt, enjoying the heat of his skin and the play of his muscles under my fingers, and let him kiss my neck as I detached.

Or at least tried to.

Usually I don't bother. I like getting my pleasure, thank you so very much, and since, unlike a man, I'm good to go again and again even after I've gotten my jollies, I don't usually put a limit on myself. I don't bother to detach from the pleasure.

I tried it now, and it didn't work.

Dark's hand was warm against my stomach, caressing me, sweeping in gentle circles ever higher, higher, but never quite brushing my breast.

Well, you ain't gonna get me off that way, I thought, and forced his mouth to mine. I kissed him, slowly, tongue delving in and tracing all the delicious contours of his mouth, and let my hands roam over his back, his buttocks, pulling him closer to me. I could feel the rapidly hardening ridge of his cock against my stomach, and I willed myself not to move and rub my cunt against it. I wasn't going to lose this race. It had nothing to do with routes and flying and trains now—it had to do with pride. In myself and in my profession.

I was the best, dammit. I could make him come without even touching his cock.

"You want to fuck me right here?" I murmured in his ear, my hand slipping 'round under his shirt, caressing his nipple.

"I will if I have to."

"Not have to, Dark, want to. Do you *want* to fuck me here, in public?"

He replied by finally touching my breast, his knuckles rubbing the nipple.

"You do," I told him, licking his ear between words. "You want to slide that big, throbbing cock of yours right inside me. You want me to unfasten your fly, reach inside and stroke it. Don't you?"

Dark bit my neck.

"And stroke your balls," I whispered. "You love it when I do that. Stroke them, cup them, run my finger up and down the vein in your cock. Around the head. Mmm. That delicious little ridge."

He was breathing hard now, his fingers really working my nipple. He tried to force a thigh between my legs, but I crossed them, aware of how wet my pussy was getting. I was trying not to get turned on here, but the thought of actually doing what I was describing was clouding my detachment.

Or lack of it.

"I love the taste of that ridge," I murmured, and Dark wedged his body closer to mine. "I love the feel of it in my mouth. Mmm. Mmmmm. I could suck you for hours. Lick you and taste you. Slide under and let your balls fall on my tongue. Do you like it when I do that? Lick them and suck on them? Take your balls into my mouth? Mmm, they taste so good."

His cock was so hard it felt as if it was denting me. Dark's hand was almost painful on my breast. Almost.

"But you know what I bet would taste even better? Your cum, Dark. I never felt you come in my mouth. All those times you came inside me, pumped all that thick creamy cum into my pussy, and I never got a taste of it. I want to taste it. I want to feel your cock, your gorgeous, thick, meaty cock, pumping in my mouth, pushing to the back of my throat. It's so big I can't get it all in but I'll try. I want it all in my mouth. I want you to come down my throat, fill my mouth up with your—"

He cut me off by gluing his mouth to mine. About time. I was getting seriously excited here.

Part of me was slightly aware that we were standing at the bottom of the stairs, leaning against the marble balustrade, and he had his hand up my shirt. It would have been fairly obvious to anyone walking by that we were making out pretty seriously.

I focused on the doorway, hoping it might ground me. *I'm in a public place*, I reminded myself, *someone could walk by. Tyra, Tanner, Striker for the gods' sakes. Imagine Elwyn striding in here right now. Imagine Lady Belleveuve watching you, scoring you, knocking off points for distraction by means of personal arousal. Arousal is all very well and good, so long as you don't let it distract you.*

Dear gods, I was so distracted.

I ripped my mouth away from Dark's as his fingers slid around my buttocks and wormed their way between my legs from behind.

"That's cheating," I moaned, glad I wasn't wearing a skirt so he couldn't get direct access to my pussy.

"And talking dirty isn't?"

"It's not dirty talk," I informed him, "it's just an honest rundown of stuff I want to do to you. With you. For you. *Around* you."

Dark shuddered against me. I could feel the throbbing heat of his cock pushing insistently against my belly, and I knew he was close.

"Around you," I repeated. "Lips, tongue, cunt. Which do you prefer, Dark? You want to be in my mouth or in my cunt? Mmm, you can feel how hot it is for you. How wet. Don't you want to just slip inside? All that heat, that throbbing. I could ease that for you. Just think how good it would feel to slide inside my tight, wet pussy, warm and welcoming for you. Close around your cock and stroke it better. You want that?"

His tongue flickered around my earlobe. Dammit, he must have picked up before how much I like that. His hand had made its way between my legs deep enough that his fingers were stroking my labia through my clothes. Sweet fuck, it felt good.

"Or would you prefer my mouth?" I asked desperately.

Dark left my ear alone for a moment and bit down on my lower lip. "I'd prefer you to keep it shut," he murmured.

"Shut around your cock?"

His tongue slid inside my mouth then, and I almost gave in to the temptation to up the stakes a bit by wedging my hand between us and stroking his cock. Even with his trousers still on, all it'd take was a few strokes and he'd be done. I could feel it—he was that close.

But I knew I could do this my way. I needed to prove it to myself.

I wrenched my mouth away, placed my hot, wet lips against his ear and whispered, "Or maybe you'd prefer to come in the back way?"

Dark's fingers squeezed my nipple so hard I thought he might pinch it off. I'd be annoyed if he did. I rather like my nipples where they are.

"Is that it?" I breathed. He sucked hard on my neck. "You want to come in my ass? Oh, Dark. It's been so long since anyone's done that. I'll be so tight. You've made me so hot…"

Dark's teeth broke the skin of my throat.

"I want you inside me," I whispered.

And he came.

Of course, the other good thing about being a girl is that if you come in your clothes it doesn't make such a big mess. Luckily for Dark, his trousers were black and they didn't show much of the wetness, but he still looked mightily pissed off with me.

I didn't care. I've still got it, babe.

I leaned forward, tugged his earlobe into my mouth with my teeth and murmured, "North."

Ha!

Chapter Nine

৵

Dark was in the shower when Rosie called me. She had her hair slung back in a plait and was moving things around with the hand not holding her scryer. Packing.

"Dad said you wanted a lift to Elvyrn," she said.

I smiled smugly. "Yes. We're going north."

"Don't tell Elwyn, though—you know how hot she is on not using dragons for personal business."

"Sure," I said. "No problem. Thanks Rosie."

"We're leaving in half an hour," she said, "can you be ready by then?"

"Absolutely. See you at the dragon pad."

As I cut the connection, Dark came out of the shower, a towel around his hips, looking like sex. I lost my breath for a moment then he said abruptly, "My sister is friends with the king's daughter. They might know where she is."

I got my focus back.

"King Talis' daughter? You mean Jalen? She's right here—"

"No," he frowned, "his younger daughter. Varia."

I called Jalen, who said her sister was at home in Peneggan City, then Rosie, who said she could drop us off on her way north.

"Looks like north is the way to go," I said, a tad smugly. "We might be able to catch up with the dragon at Elvyrn and take it up to the Sixth."

"It would be just as easy to go west from Peneggan City," Dark said.

"Yeah, but this way I get to tease you some more about being scared of flying," I said.

"I am not scared of flying. Venara and I—" He broke off, turning away.

"Yes? Venara and you what?"

"She liked to fly. When we were children. Before our forms settled, we were birds quite a lot. Only she wasn't good at it, so I flew with her."

His words came out stilted, reluctantly. This was the first personal thing he'd ever told me and disgustingly sentimental though it might be, I cherished it.

Then he turned back, his habitual scowl in place. "I need some clean clothes."

"Sure," I said, and gestured to the things I'd liberated from the room across the hall. Trousers, shirts, a sweater, thick socks and a fur-lined parka. Even in summer, Zemlya was less than balmy—and on the Leac, the temperature rarely rose above freezing.

"I didn't find any gloves or anything," I said. "But I think there's a place selling them when we get to the Bridge."

I put some of my own clothes into a bag—practical things, plus a few pretties, should I need them—and turned to go. "Ready?"

"Nearly," Dark said. He'd been messing around my clothes and weapons chests while I packed, picking out sharp shiny things and slicing them through the air. Consequently packing took a little longer than it should have, because I kept getting distracted by Dark's astonishing grace of movement as he swung a broadsword through the air or whipped a bow into stillness.

Having armed himself with a couple of subtle forms of death, he reached out and took my wrist. He stroked the sensitive skin there and I caught my breath, my eyes falling closed for a second.

They snapped open pretty sharply when Dark clipped a handcuff around my wrist.

"Oh, leave it out, will you?" I said, looking down in dismay as he clicked the other bracelet around his own arm. "I'm not going anywhere."

"I intend to hold you to that," Dark said. "Now come on."

He tugged me down the stairs and I followed grumpily. Getting up the ladder to the dragon cabin was going to be fun.

Usually, my favorite way to spend a long, hard journey is with a long, hard cock inside me. However, in the crowded dragon cabin with Tanner, Rosie, Mac and Jalen, privacy was a little hard to come by. No pun intended.

Dark decided to make it worse by torturing me with suggestive murmurs and stroking various innocuous parts of my body—my palm, my elbow, the back of my knee—with his magic fingers. It was as if he'd shoved his hand up my skirt and was stroking my clit. It felt so fucking good.

And the thing was, no one seemed to notice. Rosie curled up against Mac, dozing, while he talked quietly to Tanner about some case the captain was working on. Jalen concentrated on flying the dragon, occasionally offering her caustic opinion to the conversation.

No one noticed that Dark was, very effectively, doing to me just what I'd done to him a few hours ago. Their eyes flickered over the handcuffs, but no one said anything. I guess that tells you something about the people I know, huh?

The moment the dragon touched down in a clearing outside Peneggan City, I threw our luggage out and yanked Dark down the ladder after me.

"Have a nice trip…" Rosie's voice echoed around the clearing as the dragon lifted off, and I grabbed Dark to me, plastering his mouth against mine. Sweet heaven, the man could kiss. It was amazing. I'd never set so much store by kissing before, but right now if I wasn't so desperate for a fuck I'd have snogged him all day.

"That was dirty," I said when I could bear to let him go.

"Just a little payback," Dark murmured against my lips, backing me against a tree. His body pressed against mine and I could feel how hard he was. My entire body throbbed for him, my nipples almost poking holes in my shirt, my pussy weeping for him.

"Inside," I breathed, using my cuffed hand to hitch up my skirt, really glad I'd changed. Dark's hand inevitably followed, tracing up my thigh to my buttocks. His breath hitched when he realized I wasn't wearing any underwear.

"Inside where?"

"Right here," I said, blind with lust, my free hand ripping at his fly, desperate to feel that big hard cock in my hand.

"Where inside you?" Dark asked, and I nearly came there and then. A huge shudder ripped through me and my breath came in uneven pants. "You want me in your mouth, in your ass, in your dripping wet cunt?"

His fingers had discovered said cunt and were dipping inside, drawing out the slippery wetness and spreading it over my pussy lips, my clit, making me writhe and shudder with need. I scrabbled at his fly, wondering when it had become so fucking complicated to unfasten.

"Wherever you want," I begged, and it didn't occur to me until later that it was the first time in my life that I'd ever begged for something. I finally got my hand inside and wrapped my fingers around his steaming hard cock, tugging him none too gently toward me and rubbing my clit against the head.

Dark growled that fabulous, low sexy growl of his, and plunged into my dripping wet pussy, ramming me back against the tree with such force that I came straight away.

But he wasn't finished yet, not by half. He fucked me hard and vigorous, pounding me into the tree until the bark started to scrape my skin through my clothes. I didn't care. It felt good. Dark bit into my neck and thrust so deep his balls slammed into me, and I very nearly sobbed with the perfection of it. It was wild, raw, brutal and fabulous.

He roared when he came, spurting a hot, endless jet of spunk into me, and I came too, his cock bucking inside me, his teeth breaking the skin of my neck.

I wondered vaguely about this biting fetish he seemed to have. Not that I minded—in fact I liked it. That pleasure-pain thing again. It was such a primal thing to do. I guessed it was the lion in him. The longer he spent away from his twin the more feral he became, focused on eating, surviving, fucking. Branding me as he climaxed, marking his mate—

Oh fuck.

His mate.

We rode into Peneggan City on a hired mount. It didn't like Dark much, kept prancing, nostrils flaring, eyes rolling. It wasn't until I thought about the whole lion thing that I realized the poor creature was probably terrified of Dark.

It was summer in Peneggan, and hot as hell. We stopped only once, so I could get a new Bridge pass, and by the time we rode up to the castle I felt like a bit of old meat left out in the sun—dry, dusty, dead. I started having fantasies about cold water and wonderful showers. And then I thought about the man riding behind me, his hard body against mine, his arm wrapped around me as we were cuffed together, and I inserted him into the fantasy.

Mmmm.

The castle in PC is freaking ancient. I mean, it could give Koskwim a run for its money. A lot of Peneggan cities were devastated in a big war a couple of hundred years ago, and the ones that were rebuilt are all shiny and new and well-planned. The capital escaped such a fate, and is still full of dead-end alleys, perilously leaning buildings, dirty narrow streets and ancient hodgepodge architecture. I don't know if anyone actually designed the castle, or if it just sort of came together in a big rumble of dark, ancient stone. It's been modified and extended so many times over the years it's impossible to tell which bit belongs to which era.

We rode under the deep, long arch that's the only entrance through the five- or six- yard thick wall, and I basked in the coolness of the ancient stone before we were stopped by the uniformed guard. He was a big, hulking guy with a shaved head and a sword as big as me. Dark stiffened behind me.

"Hey, Charlie," I said. "King about?"

"Sure," he said. "Go on in."

There are advantages to having grown up the way I did.

Dark didn't stay anything as we rode in, and I dismounted first, twisting on the saddle to leap to the ground.

The steward on duty bowed and said, "My lady. I am afraid His Majesty is currently engaged in affairs of state, but Her Royal Highness Princess Nuala is in residence."

I smiled. Nuala was my aunt and I adored her. "Please tell her we're here."

"Certainly, my lady. If you would care to follow me, arrangements will be made for your refreshment."

"Thank you, Bryllan."

"Will you be staying with us?"

"I don't think so. But would it be possible to use a room so we could freshen up? It's so dusty out there."

"Certainly, my lady. If you'll follow me."

Dark and I dutifully followed the guy into the endless recesses of the castle. It's an odd place, built of stone and heavily fortified with massive iron gates and spikes in a lot of the inside walls, and yet most of it is carpeted, and there are tapestries and portraits and beautiful pieces of furniture dotted around between the battlements.

"My lady?" Dark enquired, sotto voce, as we followed the steward up one short set of stairs and down another. I'd lost count of which floor we might be on.

"He's just being polite. Peneggans don't know about the Association."

"I'm glad to hear it. I wondered if you'd picked up an ennoblement while I wasn't looking."

"Nope. Common as muck, me."

Dark gave me a flattering look of stark disbelief, and I preened.

Bryllan showed us to a suite of rooms and said he would enquire as to the availability of Nuala.

"Is Princess Varia here?" I asked.

"I believe she has gone shopping with Lady Eithne. I will enquire as to whether they have yet returned."

With a stately bow, the steward retreated, leaving us in the big stone chamber, little changed for several hundred years but for new gaslight fittings. I sighed. The king is a widower, his wife having died before I was born, but even when she was alive she hadn't much cared for fripperies. The king's winter palace in Elvyrn is a beautiful, comfortable place, mostly decorated by his little sister, Nuala—but her influence hasn't extended here to the draughty old castle.

"At least there's a shower stall," I said, peeking into the bathroom, "although I'm not sure if you'll fit in there."

It was an old-fashioned shower, more like a teepee than a proper cubicle, dark and cramped and really just for the purpose of getting clean quickly. There was a bathtub, but it was about eight feet long and would have taken hours to fill.

"I'll try," Dark said, shutting himself in the bathroom without inviting me in. Not that I'd have managed to fit in the shower, but anyway. It meant he'd unlocked the cuffs, which was a show of goodwill.

Bryllan came back while I was looking through my clothes and deciding what to wear to see Nuala, who always appreciated beautiful things, and told me that my aunt and uncle were taking lunch in the solar and that we were welcome to join them when we were ready.

"What name shall I announce?" the steward asked politely, glancing toward the bathroom where running water could be heard.

I hid a smile. "King Tal of the Nasc," I said, and watched Bryllan's eyebrows shoot up in surprise.

"Yes, my lady."

He left, and a few minutes later it occurred to me that I hadn't asked which solar — the old or new one. I stuck my head out and called, "Bryllan!"

He wasn't there, but an exquisite lady with long dark hair, beautiful eyes and the most gorgeous velvet and brocade gown came around the corner, looking at me inquisitively.

I blinked and stared, because while I knew her well it was so surprising to see her here, in this Realm, that it took me a moment to place her.

"Solana?"

Her perfect forehead wrinkled just a little, and then cleared as she saw past the creased traveling clothes and layers of dust and bruises to the Associée underneath. Solana and I had studied together at the Association's academy in Paseilles.

"*Bonne* Chance," she greeted me, smiling and coming forward. "It's been too long."

I embraced her, and she gallantly said nothing about the state of my appearance or what it was doing to her exquisite gown.

"What are you doing in Peneggan?" I asked, drawing her into the room.

"Working," Solana smiled, her voice a perfectly modulated, charmingly accented dream. "Accompanying the Iberian ambassador."

"I thought he was married," I said, recalling a portly middle-aged woman.

"He is," Solana dimpled prettily.

A thought occurred to me. "Solana, he's never mentioned anything to you about a Federacion, has he?"

She frowned beautifully. "Not that I recall. Why?"

"It's just...nothing. If he does, would you let me know?"

She looked puzzled, but nodded. She had a vague knowledge of my Order connections. Probably she thought I was in the Mob. "And you? What brings you here?"

"Oh, working too," I said. "Well, sort of."

I didn't get a chance to explain though, because right then the bathroom door opened and Dark strolled out, magnificently naked, droplets of water falling from his hair to the broad sweep of his shoulders.

I'm afraid I may have gaped at him. I was so transfixed it took me a second or two to notice the deep, deep curtsey Solana had fallen into the moment Dark appeared.

"Majesty," she murmured, her beautiful voice toned with awe.

"Stand up," Dark said. He didn't seem concerned that he was totally naked and I for one wasn't complaining. "Solana, yes?"

She nodded, barely daring to lift her eyes to him. I frowned. Maybe word had gotten around that Dark was king—but it was unlikely, and besides, Solana was behaving like a devoted subject.

Suddenly I recalled the perfectly elegant Xinjianese cat that had followed her everywhere at the academy. She'd called it Ana and the two were famed for their synchronicity.

"You're Nasc!" I gasped.

Solana nodded.

Dark rolled his eyes, grabbing some clothes. "You're smart."

I ignored him. "That cat of yours, it's—"

"My twin," Solana confirmed.

"Where is she now?"

"We are as one," Solana said.

"Okay," I said doubtfully, because while I knew how Nasc worked it was just odd to think of two creatures merging into one. Still, it explained her perfect, eerie feline beauty and grace.

"You know each other," Dark said.

"We graduated together," I said, and I saw his eyes go to the mark of the Lady on Solana's breast, proudly displayed by her carefully cut gown.

His face went immobile. "There is a Nasc within your ranks?"

"Majesty, I am one of three," Solana said, surprising me. "Tulsea and Jantara are Fillies."

"Literally?" I couldn't help asking.

She smiled her charming smile. "Tulsea is a falcon and Jantara a unicorn."

"Yet she is only a Filly?" Dark asked. "A unicorn will rise high."

"She is young," Solana said. "Everyone expects that she will outshine the whole Association."

Not if she's really a unicorn, I thought. Aren't they symbols of virginity? Any money the young Nasc would get snapped up by some handsome prince and treated to a life of innocent wealth for the rest of her life.

"Is there news on the Lady Venara, Majesty?" Solana asked.

"I hope to hear some from Princess Varia," Dark told her. I noticed that his speech became much more formal when he was talking to Solana. The speech of a king? Or that of a Nasc?

I left the two of them talking about other Nasc I'd never heard of and went to take a shower. When I came back Solana had gone, and one of my beautiful dresses was laid out on the bed. It was blue silk with gold inserts, brocade trim and trailing sleeves. The king's colors. It was an Associée's dress, tailored to show the mark on my breast.

"Solana says you should wear this," Dark nodded at it. He was dressed in dark trousers and a brocade-trimmed tunic, looking royal and forbidding and utterly edible.

"Solana has good taste," I said, dropping my towel and stretching. I was pleased to see Dark's eyes follow the movement. "Help me get dressed?"

I slipped on some silk underwear, which seemed to dismay Dark a little. Before I fastened the beautiful matching bra he pulled me to him, fingers caressing my breasts, and said, "How long do we have to spend here?"

"Long enough to talk to Varia and pay our compliments to the king and his sister."

He nuzzled the fresh bite mark on my neck, just below the tender scar where his teeth had ripped into my flesh the day before.

"I have to get dressed," I chided him.

He gave me a hot look, one that said as soon as we were done being polite and formal with royalty, he was going to fuck me silly.

My expensive silk knickers got damp at the thought.

I fastened my hair into a well-practiced, intricate style and put on a little makeup. I wasn't going to be outdone by Solana, feline that she was. Not that I feared I was going to lose Dark to her—for one thing, that was extremely unprofessional, and for another, it was me he was already having blistering, vigorous sex with.

That thought occupied me as we made our way through the warren of rooms to the new solar, where I figured Nuala was more likely to be. For someone whose eventual plan was to kill me, Dark seemed pretty eager to fuck me. Was he just killing time? Or was there something deeper than that going on? Or—could I hope—had he changed his mind about the killing?

A plan started to form in my mind. I'd made men addicted to me before without hardly trying. What if I so addicted Dark to sex with me that he couldn't bring himself to kill me? He'd said himself he couldn't stop touching me. What if I gave him the most amazing sex he'd ever had, gave it to him often, constantly, blinded him to anything but the ecstasy of my body, so much so that he couldn't live without it?

As we entered the solar, my mind wasn't on greeting my aunt or interviewing Varia. It was on surviving.

Chapter Ten

∞

"…but she's an infant!"

I rolled my eyes as I heard my uncle's voice echoing from the solar. Nuala's reasonable tones followed it.

"She's not an infant, Tyrnan, she is twenty-three. Which, might I remind you, is the same age I was when we got engaged."

"But this is different!"

"Why? Because she's your daughter?"

"Exactly."

Yet more parental concern. It wasn't bloody fair. When I told my parents I was going to become an Associée, my mother looked despairing and Striker thought it was hilarious. I couldn't possibly imagine Tyrnan ever letting one of his beloved daughters so much as kiss a man, let alone go to bed with one. He's Chalia's brother, older but definitely not wiser. Which is a feat, really.

Nuala, the king's sister and the closest thing my mother has to a good friend, always reminds me of an eager puppy. Small, round, blonde and as sweet as she is pretty, she leapt to her feet as soon as we entered the solar and threw her arms around me enthusiastically.

"Chance! Darling girl. Bryllan said you were here but I was doubting you'd ever come to see us!"

"Had to wash the heat off," I said. "It's good to see you, Aunt Nu."

"Yes, darling, you too! But whatever's happened to you?" she cried, taking my face in her hands. She had to stretch up quite a way to reach me.

"Oh, just the usual sparring, you know. Missed a few steps while I was training."

"It looks like something's been taking chunks out of you!"

I could feel Dark tensing beside me. "Yes, well, Phoenix training is rather brutal. Speaking of brutal, my parents send their regards."

She beamed at me and turned to Dark. "Your Majesty."

"Your Royal Highness," he responded with a courtly bow. "Please, call me Tal."

"And you must call me Nuala. I'm Chance's godmother, as well as her aunt," she explained proudly.

"Then she is lucky indeed."

Nuala grinned so widely I thought the top of her head would fall off. "And this is my husband Tyrnan, Earl of Nirya."

"I've just heard from Eithne," Nuala told me, while Tyrnan scowled in the background. "She's on her way back in with Varia."

"And is it Eithne who's gotten herself involved with some dastardly cradle-snatcher?" I asked mischievously.

"He's a garda," Tyrnan told me in tones of deep disgust. "She says she wants to marry him."

"He's not a garda." Nuala rolled her eyes. "He's the Captain of the Royal Guard here in PC, and he's utterly charming."

"He's a punk," Tyrnan snarled, "who only wants one thing."

"I think he's already had it, dear," Nuala murmured, just quiet enough for me to hear and not Tyrnan. I stifled a giggle.

Nuala insisted on serving us both gigantic portions of a delicious lunch and asking all about what I'd been up to in Euskara. I toned it down—Nuala's used to my parents' exploits, but I still didn't want to make her uncomfortable—and told her the more exciting, aunt-friendly bits. Gracious as ever, she refrained from asking Dark about his family. Nuala knows a lot more than she lets on.

We were eating dessert when Varia, the king's youngest daughter, and Eithne, the middle of Nuala and Tyrnan's triplets, wandered in, both looking beautiful and blonde. They were followed by several guards carrying hundreds of expensive carrier bags.

"Chance," Eithne said. "What brings you here?"

"Just popped in to say hello." I kissed both her and Varia on the cheek. "Your mother tells me you've found a young man."

She beamed, just like Nuala. "Oh, he's so wonderful. I know everyone says that when they fall in love, but he is!"

Tyrnan glowered but managed not to say anything.

"This is Da— This is King Tal of the Nasc," I introduced, and he made nice with both girls. Eithne was polite. Varia salivated, and I had to squash an interesting instinct to rip her head off. Instead I said, "Varia, I understand you know Tal's sister?"

Her pretty forehead wrinkled. She's a little like Nuala, a little like her deceased mother, and nothing at all like Talis, who is tall and dark. Varia is small, blonde, pretty and rather vague.

"Do remind me of her name," she said. "It seems everyone one knows is sister to some king or another."

"Her name is Venara," Dark said. "She is about five feet, nine inches tall, with long white hair and brown eyes. Quite slender."

Varia continued to look exquisitely puzzled. Dark rolled his eyes.

"Her twin is a pure white horse and she is mildly psychic," he clarified.

"Oh yes, *that* Venara," Varia tinkled. "I was trying to think of everyone I knew whose name started with 'princess'."

Gag me with a spoon.

"We don't often use human titles," Dark said.

"She's psychic?" I asked, intrigued, but Dark gave me, for want of a better expression, a dark look. I piped down and let him talk to Varia. I was impressed how he handled her — the young princess was pretty and sweet but her vacuous charm annoyed me after a while. Dark was patient and gracious.

"How is dear Ven?" Varia asked.

"I'm afraid I don't know. The last I heard she had been," he paused, and I could see him struggling for control, "she had been kidnapped."

Everyone expressed surprise. Eithne said that her dear darling captain might be of some assistance. Tyrnan offered his sword. Nuala, more practically, asked if the Order had been involved.

"No," Dark said, "neither in the capture nor the recovery. However, Chance has agreed to help me find her."

All eyes swiveled on me and I gave a little wave.

"We were hoping you might have some information on her," Dark went on, looking at Varia. "When was the last time you saw her?"

"Hmm." Varia looked off into the middle distance. "I know she was at Bunty Arvin's coming out, because it was a costume party and she came as that lady...hmm, who was she? The horse goddess...I can't remember. But anyway, in she trots on this unbelievably beautiful tall horse, completely starkers, only her hair covering her! It was quite the entrance, as you can imagine!"

"Completely naked?" Eithne gawped.

"Nudity is not an issue among my people," Dark said. "We dress in human environments but spend much of our time in an animal skin."

Not to mention that if his sister was half as beautiful as him, she'd have no problem showing off her body.

"When was this party?" Dark pressed.

"Oh. Hmm. Last season? I don't quite remember…"

"I think it was Amaril of last year," Nuala put in. "Bunty had the most beautiful white beaded dress."

"Oh yes," Varia said, "it was glorious. She was some snow queen or something, I think." Her eyes widened. "Was the horse Venara's twin?"

Boy, she was quick, huh?

"The horse would have been Ara," Dark agreed. "Ven is her human form."

"How absolutely fascinating," Varia said earnestly.

"Have you seen her since then? Amaril is…" he thought about it, "the fourth month of the Peneggan calendar."

She frowned again. "You know, it's just *so* difficult to keep up," she said. "One goes to party after party and sees the same old people *all* the time. Such a bore."

"Is Venara one of the people you see all the time?"

"Well, not recently. I suppose…" She thought hard about it. "I saw her in Angeland, I do recall that. But you know, I simply can't recall when that was. She did have the most exquisite blue chiffon frock, though. Aunt Nu, do you remember when I went to Angeland? I think it was some dull official thing. An anniversary."

"The Entente Cordiale?" I asked.

"Yes! I knew it was something Galatean. Odd, really."

"The anniversary of peace between Angeland and Galatea," I told her. "Representatives from all major governments attend."

"Oh, yes, now I remember," Nuala said. "Talis was ill and Jalen was off in Asiatica, so Varia and Emlyn went." Emlyn was the king's son, the middle child.

"That was in Bridelran," I said. "About six months ago."

"And you haven't seen her since?" Dark asked.

"I don't think so," Varia said slowly. "No…"

I glanced at Eithne, who shrugged apologetically. "I'm afraid I don't know her," she said.

"What about Emlyn?"

"He's in the east," Nuala said. "Athinisha or somewhere. Talis will know."

I looked at Dark, who shook his head, and we stood up.

"I don't think we really have time to wait for him," I said. "We have to get to Zemlya."

They all expressed disappointment that we weren't staying, but I could see that Dark was getting antsy about leaving. Coming to PC had been a dead end and it had cost us a lot of time—time that would have been better spent continuing to Elvyrn on the dragon, or possibly catching a lift with the Zemlyan Knights on their way home.

We collected our belongings and went down to the stables, where to my surprise a gryphon had been saddled and was waiting for us. Nuala stood with it.

"His name is Grandus," she said, stroking the beast's powerful back. "He was bred for Treegan but really he's just too big for competitive sports. He can carry the two of you easily to the Bridge, and then if you just let him go he'll come back here."

I looked at the huge beast, his lion's body and eagle's head massive and ferocious. I've been flying gryphons ever since I was old enough to grasp the reins, but I'd never seen one so huge before.

I glanced at Dark to gauge his reaction. He patted Grandus' head and the gryphon made a noise of agreement. Apparently he wasn't as frightened as our horse had been earlier.

"We ride," he said to me, and the words made me shiver.

Gryphons don't fly as high or fast as dragons, but they have more stamina than horses and of course aren't subject to the meanderings of roads. It took us five or six hours to get to the Bridge, by which time it was dark and we were all exhausted.

I was especially exhausted. Dark had cuffed us back together, which was actually slightly reassuring as we were up so high. The gryphon's saddle had a safety harness built in but it was only for one person, so I tied a rope around us both and fastened it to the saddle. Safety pays.

However, being tied so close was torture on my body. Dark was so hot, so hard behind me, each beat of the gryphon's wings setting us into a rhythm of falling against each other. I remembered my earlier plan, a ridiculous and desperate plan to save myself with sex. Well, hell. I'm a lover and a fighter, and part of my talent is knowing which to choose for which occasion.

I'd changed out of my dress and was back in a shirt and skirt again. Less practical for riding a horse or a gryphon, but bloody good for riding a man.

I wriggled my butt against Dark's crotch and felt an answering nudge from his cock.

"It's cold up here," I said.

"Not as cold as in Zemlya."

"Hmm. I'm glad I have you here to keep me warm," I said, wriggling again.

Dark's hand, fastened to mine, had been resting on my hip since my cuffed arm was wrapped around my body. He held the reins in one hand.

Now his fingers flexed through my thin skirt. "I could make you warmer," he murmured against my skin.

"Mmm. Tell me how," I said.

His fingers began walking the material of my skirt up, revealing inch after inch of bare thigh. "I'd rather show you."

He once more discovered that I wasn't wearing knickers—well, they seemed so pointless, and it wasn't as if I was going to freeze to death in the Peneggan summer—and lightly stroked the tops of my thighs, the sensitive skin around my pussy, while I gasped and pressed back against him.

"You like that?" Dark whispered.

"Oh, yes."

"How about this?"

His fingers brushed my labia, already slick with moisture. I moaned.

"Or this?"

His thumb flicked my clit.

"Gods, yes."

"Or this."

His own voice cracked as he slid two fingers inside me, and I could feel the rock-hard line of his penis against my back. I closed my eyes and fantasized about that penis as he thrust his fingers into me, imagining I was full of his cock. But no way were the fingers enough. Not only two of them.

"More," I groaned, and he obligingly inserted another finger as I spread my legs, hooking my ankles around his.

"We're flying over Srheged," Dark murmured in my ear, his voice a low, thrilling hum. "If someone looked up they could see me finger-fucking you."

"It's getting dark," I panted.

He added another finger, all four of them plunging inside me now as his thumb massaged my clit, and I cried out.

"Then they'll hear you," he said.

"You did that on purpose."

"Maybe I want them to hear you," he said. "I want them to know what I'm doing to you. Making you come up here, fifty miles an hour over the city, riding a gryphon with my fingers in your cunt."

I trembled around those fingers.

"I want you to cry out my name when you come," Dark whispered in my ear. "I want them all to know. *I'm* fucking you. *I'm* making you come."

"You're—not—fucking—me—yet," I panted.

"Yet," he purred, and I came, crying his name just as he'd ordered, convulsing around his fingers.

He bit my ear and I yelled, "Gods Dark, yes!"

"I'm going to fuck you now," Dark said, and he must have let go of the reins because he still had one hand inside me as he unfastened his pants. "I want you to keep yelling out my name."

"Yes," I whimpered.

"Tell everyone what I'm doing to you," he said as I felt his cock nudge me from behind. I wriggled against it, coating it with my juices, sliding my slippery wet pussy lips against it.

"I want you in me now," I moaned.

"Louder."

"In me," I cried.

"When?"

"Now! Fuck me now!"

Dark obliged, removing his hand and plunging his cock into me. I screamed with the pleasure of it. The gryphon started at the sound, bucking, and the movement shoved Dark's cock even deeper.

"Ohhhhh yes." My free arm moved up over my head, the movement thrusting my breasts out as I pressed Dark's head against my neck.

"Is this what you want?" Dark said in my ear.

"Yes!"

"Say it."

"I want—" I lost my breath for a moment as he withdrew and slid back into me. "I want your cock. Inside me."

"Like this?"

"Yes!"

"Is it good? Deep like this? Hard inside you?"

I moaned in reply.

"Say it," Dark ordered, "tell the Realm what I'm doing to you."

"You're fucking me," I whimpered as his hand guided my hips up and down, sliding on and off his cock, bouncing against his balls.

"Louder."

"You're fucking me, Dark," I yelled. "Fucking me from behind, deep and hard, and it's so good, it's so fucking good," I cried, nearly sobbing now.

"How good?"

"I'm going to come."

"Who's making you come?" Dark demanded.

"You! Your cock, Dark, it's making me—"

"My name?"

"Tal! Talvéan, King of Nasc, is fucking me with his big, hard cock and making me come my, my—" I couldn't finish. It was almost here.

"Yes?" Dark's voice was hot in my ear, his teeth scraping my flesh.

"Making me come my brains out!" I yelled, then suited action to words, and came so hard I blacked out.

Chapter Eleven

ഗ

We set down near the Bridge port and let Grandus, the poor thing, fly away. Dark pulled me into his arms and kissed me, hard, without explanation. What need was there for kissing? All it did was leave me wanting more.

Maybe that was his plan.

Considering I was supposed to be enslaving him, I was becoming pretty enslaved myself.

Having gotten my Bridge pass reissued, we crossed over into Zemlya without incident. I changed into my furs and threatened the staff of the small, closed convenience shop that if they didn't open up I'd set a mountain lion loose on them. Dark added some convincing sound effects, and a moment later was admitted to buy the furs, gloves and other cold-weather essentials he didn't have.

It was dusk on the Leac—the darkest it would get at this time of year—and several degrees below freezing. Still, it was better than in winter, when the wind alone could freeze you where you stood.

We stepped aboard the ship bound for Vaznafjörður, and a somewhat sulky Kelf showed us to our cabin. A small dingy room with a meager bunk. Not precisely the luxury accommodations the Association brochure promised its members.

"So why is it, exactly, that Kelfs don't like Nasc?" I asked as Dark prowled around, checking the lock on the door, pulling the porthole shutter tight.

"Animal senses," he said. "They find us unsettling."

Without any warning, he grabbed me to him and took my mouth in a hard, wild kiss that wiped away any vestiges of coldness remaining from outside.

"They're not the only ones," I said, trembling on jelly legs.

He kissed me again — no, not a kiss, a savage mating of his mouth with mine. He bit my tongue, sank his teeth into my lip, plunged his own tongue deep into my mouth in ferocious mimicry of the way his cock had slid so hard into me earlier.

We fell together onto the bunk, arms and legs tangling in the blankets. Dark didn't even bother taking off my furs as he wormed his fingers under my skirt, past the leggings I'd pulled on, and to the knickers I'd decided might be a good idea in this weather.

"The hell with these," he growled, ripping them off and throwing them across the room.

Then his fingers were inside me again. His teeth pulled at my shirt and he sucked my nipple into his mouth.

Accommodating as ever, I unfastened his fly and caressed his cock, but I hadn't gotten very far before Dark shoved me back on the bed, reared up between my legs and plunged straight into me.

The third time in one day I've had sex without taking my clothes off, I thought vaguely as he grasped my ankles and hooked them over his shoulders. I was totally open to him, although my face, left nipple and cunt were the only parts of me not covered by clothes. But hell, what else did I need?

He thrust into me, hard and fast, this new angle bringing alive every nerve ending I had. His left hand rested on my thigh, my right wrist chained only inches away. I slipped my hand between my legs and stroked my clit, looking up at Dark as he pumped into me, filling my cunt to stretching with his huge, thick cock, then pulling out, leaving me empty, unfulfilled, wanting.

"No," I whimpered, "again."

He thrust deep into me and I moaned at the sensation. I could let this man fuck me forever.

But he had to come some time, and he did — shortly after I screamed out my orgasm not just to please him but because I had no choice. He made me lose control.

He sank down onto me, breathing hard, trembling, and there was a clink as he uncuffed us. He stripped off his clothes then mine, then locked us back together and pulled me against him, our chained arms between us. I slid my leg over his, hooking him in and keeping him close as the hammering of my heart slowed down.

Somewhere in the back of my mind I remembered giggling over a book about animals when I was about twelve. The book had said that when a lioness was in heat she'd mate every twenty-five minutes for up to four days. At the time I'd thought that was insane. Now I was starting to understand it.

Dark was becoming more feral with every passing second. Marking his mate with bites. Fucking me at every opportunity.

He called me his woman.

I looked at him as he lay sleeping in my arms — well, okay, arm — his skin damp with sweat, his chest rising and falling. A low rumble sounded in his chest and while the rational part of me said it was just snoring, the rest of me said he was purring. I stroked his hair, and the handcuffs clinked quietly as I moved.

A chain between us, binding us. Damn him for reminding me what I was to him, what my whole family — my fucking dynasty — was to him. Damn him, damn Striker — and damn me for never breaking the chain.

I woke to a sudden silence and groggily realized that the ship's steam engines had stopped.

"Are we at Vaznafjörður?" I asked sleepily, turning my head to see Dark sitting beside me, half dressed and looking tense.

He gave a short nod, then unfastened the handcuffs and threw my clothes at me. "Get dressed," he said. "Quickly."

The man who'd fucked me into a stupor last night, the man who'd held my trembling body and fallen asleep with me—he was totally gone. Dark was silent, restless, edgy and scary as hell. I quickly pulled on my furs while he finished getting dressed, and then we were chained together again and leaving the cabin.

If anyone in Vaznafjörður noticed we were handcuffed, they didn't say anything. Besides, with our thick fur coats and mittens, it was hard to tell. I slipped my hand into Dark's and no one commented at all.

The thing I hate about Zemlya is not the cold—because I look cute in furs and besides, there are plenty of fun ways to warm up—it's the fact that every single person there is tall, blond, blue-eyed and beautiful. In Euskara I'm unusual. In Asiatica people touch me to see if I'm real. In Zemlya, I'm wallpaper.

Dark got plenty of attention though—from men who looked away quickly, frightened. From Kelfs who eyed him with open distrust. And from women who nearly fell panting at his feet. I tightened my hand in his and gave them all smug looks.

"Is the river passable?" Dark enquired of a man by the docks. I was amazed to hear him speaking in perfect Zemlyan—completely without accent, just as his Galatean and Anglish had been. It was almost unnerving.

"Only as far as Flodkrök," the man said, naming a town that was probably ten miles inland. "It hasn't completely thawed yet."

Not completely thawed? In Peneggan it was sweltering. Even Angeland was having warm weather. Ah well, such are the insulating properties of the Wall.

"Some summer you're having," I said, and the boatman laughed humorlessly.

"Coldest anyone can remember. Skavsta's snowed in. It's like midwinter up there."

We moved away and I bought us a munta to ride upon. Munta are bred by Kelfs, and they're found wherever Kelfs live. The Zemlyan munta walk on two or four legs, are covered with thick, triple-layered fur in shades of pale blue, and have suckers on their feet so that they don't slip on the ice of the Leac, which is their natural habitat.

We took a four-legged munta who looked like a blue camel and seemed to like Dark a hell of a lot more than the Kelf who sold him to us did.

"Where are we going?" I asked as we trotted out of the city, the munta's long shaggy neck my main view.

"South."

"How far?"

"Don't know."

I paused. "You do know where we're going?"

"Yes."

"But you don't know where it is?"

"Not yet."

"When will you know?"

"When we get there."

"How will you know when we're there?"

"*I'll know,*" Dark growled.

Silence, then I said, "Talkative, aren't you?"

He didn't seem to think that was funny.

The boatman had been right, the weather was pretty bad. Not as bad as Zemlya can get, and oddly, the farther south we went, the more inclement it got—but good weather in Zemlya usually means an absence of falling snow.

We hit a blizzard after half an hour.

About fifteen minutes into the blizzard, after I'd pulled on my thick goggles and wrapped my scarf around my face and huddled back against Dark, he suddenly stiffened.

"What?" I said, above the noise of the wind.

He didn't say anything. His body was tight, rigid, his breathing shallow as if he was in pain.

"Dark, are you all right?"

I turned to look at him but at that moment he kicked the munta on, and the sudden burst of speed cost me my balance. I wavered and fell, my arm twisting and jerking as the cuff pulled against gravity.

I hit the snow, breathless and freezing, screaming pain shooting through my shoulder as the munta galloped on, dragging me after it by one arm. One huge foot clipped my leg as it ran, and I was too winded to catch my breath and shout out. Snow filled my mouth and nose. My scarf unraveled and my goggles flew up under my hood. I was blind and helpless, flying along on my back with snow scraping inside my clothes. It felt like miles but was probably only inches. After all, how had Dark managed to stay on the munta? Catlike balance only went so far.

Then the pressure on my arm suddenly ceased and the snow stopped moving past me at such incredible speed. Dark had leapt from the moving animal and was yelling at it to stop. In perfect Kelfish.

Then he loomed over me, crouching down and clearing the snow from my face.

"Are you all right?"

I stared up at him, his dark whiskers frosted and his amber eyes hot, and managed a nod.

He felt at my arm, my shoulder, and I winced.

"Okay, that hurts."

"Badly?" His face was tense.

I moved my arm. It wasn't broken or dislocated.

"No, it's okay."

He nodded tightly and pulled me to my feet, resting me against him for a moment. A very brief, warming, confusing moment. Then he led me to the patiently waiting munta.

"Hold on," he said as he climbed behind me in the saddle. "It's not far now."

"It isn't?"

"We have to hurry."

"Why?" I asked, as the munta kicked into full speed, snow flying under its sure feet.

"There isn't much time," Dark said urgently.

"What—why?"

"I am dying."

Well, what's a girl supposed to say to that? For a few seconds I was struck mute, then I said stupidly, "But you're fine!"

"Véan is not."

I blinked behind my goggles. "Your twin?"

He said nothing, just kicked at the munta to go faster.

"If Véan dies—" I began, and didn't have the heart to go on. If his twin died, what would happen to the man behind me?

"Can I help?" I asked, and Dark's arm tightened around my waist.

"I don't know."

It seemed like hours but was probably only minutes later that the castle came into view. I figured what it was, because although I'd never been here, every Koskwim Knight knows the main residences of all the major heads of state. What I saw before me was the chilly, forbidding home of the Empress of Zemlya.

The munta sped straight for it.

"Uh," I said, "we're paying a visit to the Empress?"

Dark didn't speak. We raced toward the drawbridge that led over the high, dreadful gorge which cut below the castle.

"Is Véan here?"

"Yes."

"So...you know the Empress?"

"Yes."

We sped over the drawbridge and into the courtyard. Kelfs with spears appeared from nowhere, snarling fiercely. Dark snarled even fiercer and leapt from the munta as it was still moving, dragging me with him. Yeah—ow.

"Halt!" a Kelf in livery yelled.

"Make me," Dark growled, not stopping for a second.

The Kelf took him at his word and hurled the spear, and before I realized what I was doing my hand flew out and caught it in midair.

"Nice," was Dark's only comment as he pulled me up the stairs and into the castle.

Inside I had time only to register darkness and high, chilly walls, before a blonde woman ran toward us, dressed in velvet and fur, crying, "In here!"

We followed her through the outer chamber as she called off the Kelfs, telling them they'd done enough damage as it was. My curiosity piqued, I stumbled on frozen feet through a curtain-lined door into a room full of sudden warmth and light and people.

But I hardly saw any of them. What I saw was the huge, dark-maned lion lying on the hearth rug, ribs clear through his pelt, breathing weakly, a huge awful gash in his side.

It was Véan, and I knew that he was, indeed, dying.

What happened next was so fast and incredible it became just a blur in my memory. Dark, moving faster than I thought possible and dragging me with him, was suddenly at the side of his animal twin, and before I'd had time to register the look of pain on his face he was blurring, fading, shimmering, and the lion was wavering too, and the next second I looked there weren't two forms, just one, and it was Dark as a man, lying on his side on the ground with blood seeping through his furs.

I ripped the material away and nearly gagged when I saw the same wound inflicted on Dark's human flesh.

I could see his bare white ribs.

It was awful.

My wrist was still cuffed to Dark's, and his flurry of movement had forced me to my knees beside him. His eyes were open and he was looking at me. I took his hand and held it tightly.

"Do you think that's enough?" said the blonde woman anxiously. She was young, about my age, pale and pretty.

"I don't know," someone else replied, and I glanced up to see two more women and two men. The younger woman was the Empress Maya, and the others were her parents and brother, Menny, who was dating Jalen. On another day I might have greeted Menny more warmly—before Jalen, we had spent a few very enjoyable weekends together—but not today. Clearly they knew Dark and were his friends, and that was all I needed to know.

"What just happened?" I asked urgently. "Where did Véan go?"

"Who are you?" the Empress said sharply.

"She's cool," Menny said. "Don't worry."

"He has merged with his animal form," his mother told me, her voice tight and worried.

"Is that good?"

"They're stronger together than apart," the Empress' father said. I couldn't remember his name, not right now.

"Good, well, that's good," I babbled. "Isn't that good?"

Menny knelt down beside me, his face kind. "Chance, he's dying. Véan was pretty much dead when you guys raced in. I don't know if Tal is strong enough to carry him back."

"Then shouldn't they separate?" I cried. "At least Tal can live!"

All five of them looked horrified.

"Or not?" I ventured into the silence.

"If one form dies then the other will also," the blonde said. Obviously Menny's youngest sister, she was talking to me as if I was the one hurting Dark. "It's the worst way for a Nasc to die."

I looked down at Dark, at the terrible gash in his side, his labored breathing. "Then we have to help him," I said, and let go of Dark's hand only long enough to take the bag off my shoulder.

There was a moment's pause then Menny nodded and told his sisters to fetch blankets and bandages. They obeyed — even Maya, who was the Empress of a whole fucking Realm — without question. I didn't know whether it was because they loved Menny or because they loved Dark, but they did as they were told.

"Are you a healer?" Maya asked me, hesitating at the door.

"No," her father answered, looking at me strangely, and I knew he knew who I was. He knew Striker, and the rest didn't take much guesswork.

"I'll make him better," I said. "I need —" Shit, what did I need? All I had was basic first aid, none of Striker's props and potions. "Uh, I need silk and a needle. Sterilized. And can someone get these bloody cuffs off me?"

"I'm on it," Maya said, and left the room.

"I need privacy," I said to Menny, "but I don't think we can move him."

"We'll leave you here then," he said, as his sisters came back in with blankets and bandages.

Before they all left, Maya touched my arm and I looked up. She was holding a machete and after a second's pause, I let her swing it down surprisingly hard onto the chain of the handcuffs and set me free.

"What is he to you?" she asked as I flexed my wrist.

"It's complicated."

A second's pause, then she said, "Harm him and we will kill you."

I nodded. "I'm glad to hear it."

She gave me a strange look then left, and I was alone in the small stone room with a big fire, lots of blankets and a dying Nasc.

I hoped to fuck this would work.

Chapter Twelve

&

Striker is one of the best healers I know, but with one important proviso—he can only heal people he wants to heal. Not being the Realms' greatest philanthropist, this does narrow the field somewhat.

He's healed me plenty in the past, and he's done impressive things for Tanner and Rosie and various other people my mother is fond of. But it's Chalia he works best on—which is just as well because she does have an amazing propensity for injuring herself. When I asked her once why she heals better than anyone else Striker tries his magic on, she just said, "Because he loves me. He wants me to be well."

I poured every ounce of willpower I had into healing Dark, and after I'd stitched together the wound and slathered healing salve on it and prayed to the demigods and hungry ghosts to leave him alone, I sat there and just held him, tears in my eyes. Okay, so he wanted me dead, and I should have been more than happy to let him die but…oh, fuck. Clearly there's something wrong with me.

It got dark, and the fire burned low.

"We can't leave him here," Menny said, slipping into the silent room. "Mama had a room made up for you. It's warm and there's food and stuff for you."

"I'm not hungry." I stroked Dark's hair. His breathing was shallow, his skin waxy. He's looked better.

"You'll be no good to him at all if you're totally drained," Menny said, and I was forced to agree.

The house Kelfs were utterly devoted to Menny and they didn't bat an eyelid at the unconscious Nasc we asked them to carry for us. I was too tired to attempt it by myself, but I helped them make a sort of stretcher from the blankets, and followed Menny to the room that had been prepared for us. I didn't register much about it except that there was a big fire keeping out the chill, oil lamps chasing away the shadows left by the tightly closed shutters, and a big bed with velvet hangings and warming pans.

I gathered Dark into my arms and laid my head on his shoulder, and the last thing I remember before unconsciousness claimed me was Menny whispering goodnight as he closed the door.

My dreams were jagged and broken, full of death and blood, and I woke drenched in sweat. And alone.

The big bed was empty, the hangings open on one side. I could see the glow from the fire but the rest of the room was in shadow. My body felt heavy with exhaustion and ready to sleep again, but before I dropped off I wanted to know where Dark was.

And why he hadn't chained us back together. I was pretty sure there were more handcuffs in the castle if he wanted them.

"Dark?" I said his name on a croak, cleared my throat and tried again. "Dark!"

The shadows moved, but I couldn't see him.

I felt him out there in the darkness.

"You're awake."

His voice was smooth, low. He wasn't breathing hard. He didn't sound like he was dying.

And he was out of bed. That had to be a good sign.

"What time is it?" I asked.

"Around midnight, I think."

So I hadn't slept for long. And he hadn't healed for long. This was…unsettling.

"How are you feeling?"

"Better," he said, coming out of the shadows, into my line of vision.

I gasped.

He was glowing. What I'd taken for the light of the fire was a gentle reflection of light from Dark's own skin.

Was this a Nasc thing? Because he was now joined with his animal form? No, it couldn't be—I'd never noticed Solana glowing before. Maybe it was because he was the king?

"Chance?"

I blinked but the glow didn't fade. Dark didn't seem to be bothered by it. "You must feel a lot better," I said lamely. He was standing there naked but for the bandage I'd taped over the wound. "Does it hurt?"

He shrugged. "A little."

I sat up and reached out to touch him without hesitation. I didn't even think about what I was doing as I started pulling his pain into myself, wrapping it up and concentrating on getting rid of it.

There was so much of it.

"Liar," I gasped, as the strength of his pain nearly floored me.

"Chance, what are you—"

"Shh," I said, and concentrated hard. I needed to convince my body that, as there was no reason for it to be hurting, the pain should go away. It did, but I felt drained by it.

"That was more than 'a little'," I said accusingly, falling back against the pillows.

Dark was frowning at me. "What did you do?"

"I made it go away."

"How?"

"Would you ask a Faerie how it flies? I just did it, Dark, and a little 'thank you' wouldn't go amiss."

I had my eyes closed so I felt rather than saw Dark slide onto the bed beside me. And I felt, rather than saw, his hand caress my cheek.

"Thank you," he said, and his lips brushed mine in the gentlest of kisses.

Something had changed between us and I didn't think it was because Dark had his animal self back again. I had an idea what it was, but the idea was too tempting and too unrealistic, so I tried to ignore it and opened my eyes.

"This looks better," he said, still stroking my cheek. It still felt tender, but it wasn't horribly swollen anymore, and last time I'd looked in a mirror the bruise had faded. "And your arm, where you fell," he touched my shoulder and I realized it hardly hurt at all. I also realized I wasn't wearing anything.

"I seem to have a talent for healing," I said, because I couldn't think of anything else to say.

Dark opened his mouth as if to comment, but at the last minute changed his mind and closed his mouth. Then he reconsidered and said, "Do they teach it on the island?"

Not the way I heal. "Koskwim? Yeah—every student learns basic field medicine. You can choose to specialize in healing for the Dragon, but if you do the Phoenix then you have to learn it. You have to learn everything."

"You're a Phoenix."

I moved my foot with the intention of showing him the tattoo on the sole again, but the blanket around me was too warm and besides, it was undignified. My Association training goes too deep to allow that.

"I am."

Again that sense that he wanted to say something but changed his mind. "Why?"

I shrugged. "Because I could."

Dark nodded as if this made perfect sense. Which it did— sort of. I mean, that was the reason I'd given myself. Maybe subliminally it had to do with getting one better on Striker but officially I was doing it because, arrogantly, I could.

He was still caressing my face and I closed my eyes and arched toward him.

"You're so beautiful," he murmured, and my heart thudded a little faster. "If you were Nasc you'd be feline."

"Like you?"

"You're not a lion. You're...you'd be a wildcat."

I smiled at that and opened my eyes—and then my smile faltered, because I saw something I'd never seen before.

Dark was smiling.

It was...I mean...he was breathtaking. Mean, moody and sullen suited him like sun suits the desert, but when he smiled...my gods.

My *god*.

"Are you all right?" Dark asked, smile fading.

"Yes! I'm fine! Just don't stop smiling," I cried.

He grinned at that. An honest-to-goodness grin. I nearly passed out.

"Oh gods, that's good," I shuddered.

"It's just a smile."

"No, it's not. I've never seen you smile before. You're always glaring at me."

He sobered. "Chance—"

"Shh," I said, putting a finger over his lips. "No." I didn't want to analyze this. I didn't want him to step back and realize who he was smiling with. I didn't want to lose that smile.

So I kissed him, kissed into his smile and returned it to him, sighing at his taste, the strength of him now that he was whole again. He pulled me into his arms, against his body under the blankets, and wrapped me in his warmth.

I snuggled close, slid my fingers into his hair, his mane, and traced the line of his sharp teeth with my tongue. He felt so good.

Dark made a low sound in his throat—not quite a growl but not quite a purr either. Whatever it was, it was sexy as hell and my nipples hardened as his chest vibrated against them. He moved me to my back and kissed me, his body covering mine from lips to toes.

"You're glowing," I murmured as his subtle light filled the canopy of the bed. "Did I tell you that you glow?"

Dark looked at me like I was mildly crazy and shut me up by kissing me again, deeper this time, but still gentle, still tender. It was wonderful. Really just wonderful.

But better was to come. His hands roamed over my body, stroking me as if I was a precious pet, and his lips moved to my neck, tracing the pulse leaping there, feathering kisses over my sensitive skin. His hand found my breast, cupped and stroked the underside of it, and instead of going straight for the nipple he found places of hidden sensitivity that even I didn't know existed.

What was going on? How could anyone possibly teach me what felt good to a woman? To *me*?

But Dark did. He kissed my breast, again bypassing my tight, desperate nipple and moving down my body. My stomach contracted as his lips skimmed over my skin, kissing my hipbone, licking my thigh, finding a sweet spot at the back of my knee. His thumb tickled the Phoenix mark on my sole, making me giggle and writhe.

"Did it hurt?" he asked. "The tattoo?"

I nodded, remembering the utter foolishness of it, how it hurt so much I was hopping for weeks while the other kids laughed at me.

Dark kissed it better and the memory of the pain vanished.

His lips skimmed up my calf, my thigh—his hand on one leg and his mouth on the other. He inched my legs farther apart, wider, so that he was lying between them, and when his mouth ran out of thigh he started on the next available thing.

He licked the skin on my groin and I panted, my fingers clenching in the sheets. Then his tongue darted across the slippery folds of my pussy and I gasped.

"Sweet," he murmured, his low voice vibrating through me. "You taste sweet."

I didn't care how I tasted, so long as he liked it enough to come back for more.

And he did. Oh, how he did! His fingers parted me and delved inside while his tongue swirled around my clit, licking and sucking. He nibbled on my labia and thrust his tongue deep inside my pussy. He fed his face while I whimpered and moaned, wriggling under waves of intense pleasure, unable to think or speak or breathe unless he stopped and I lost the feeling, this incredible feeling that he—he...

Suddenly—or so it seemed—Dark curled his tongue around my clit, thrusting it forward, sucking on it, and his fingers curved inside me and I just erupted, completely mindless, my whole body convulsing. My fingers dug in his scalp. My foot kicked into his back. I swear I fully levitated off the mattress, his face firmly clamped between my legs as he feasted on my orgasm, driving heat and friction and glorious golden pleasure into me until I couldn't remember my own name.

The next thing I realized I seemed to be curled in his arms, trembling, whimpering like a child. Dark was stroking my hair, soothing me.

"Are you all right now?"

I blinked up at him. "All right?"

"You were screaming, sweetheart."

"I was just…coming." Coming really, really hard. Coming so hard, so hot, so fucking wonderfully that I had no idea I was making any noise at all.

"I know that, but for a minute there I thought you were dying."

Only a minute? I thought it lasted at least an hour.

Words failed me, so I told Dark how wonderful he'd been with a kiss. I did to his mouth what he'd done to my cunt. I feasted on it and adored it, and Dark seemed to appreciate it almost as much as I had.

More, maybe, since he slid me onto my back again and nudged inside me with his big, hard cock.

I looked up at him, felt him push home inside me and remembered the first time I'd seen his face, just the same way, his beauty so savage and overwhelming it nearly made me come there and then.

I locked my legs around him and drew him in deeper and as he thrust into me, I knew what was different. What was new.

Dark wasn't fucking me. We were making love.

Chapter Thirteen

๕๖

"So when you said your sister was mildly psychic," I said, soaping Dark's arm, "what precisely did you mean?"

He stopped nibbling on the back of my neck to say, "Don't mock her."

"Wasn't going to."

"Most people don't believe in —"

I cleared my throat, moving my arm behind my back and prodding the healing wound in his side. "You were saying?"

"Okay, I guess you'd believe it. She's not really psychic. She's a seer."

"A what?"

"A seer. She…*sees.*"

"So do most people with two functioning eyes." I tried to get my head around it. "I don't really know what a seer is," I confessed. The word conjured up wrinkled old men in Asiatica. Not lovely, slender princesses.

"She sees…things that have been…things that are…and things that may be."

I frowned as I puzzled this out. Eventually I said, "Okay, I get the seeing what may be thing, but how is it special that she sees what is and was? Don't we all?"

Dark sighed behind me. We were reclining in a large bathtub by the fire, his chest cushioning my back. "No," he said. "We don't. We…we see what our eyes present to us. We hear what our ears think they hear. Venara sees what's really there. She can see into the past — before her own birth. Places she's never been. She can look at a person and know who they really are."

I blinked as I realized what a talent that was. Bet she never got swindled by cowboy plumbers.

"And she sees the future?"

"She sees what *may* become. It's not very solid. She says it never makes sense until after it's actually happened."

"So possibly not all that useful, then?"

"It can be," Dark said enigmatically, and I felt his body tense.

And I understood.

Venara hadn't just gone on walkabout. She'd been kidnapped. Hell, a talent like that is something a lot of people would love to get their hands on. To study, even. She could have been taken by one of the universities in Angeland or Euskara. Captured by a witchhunter in Asiatica—a lot of "wise men" out there took a dim view of the paranormal.

Or she might have already been killed. A lot of people still don't understand that not everything can be explained by cutting up a body to look inside. Koskwim has plenty of files from the days when lunatics had bits of their brains hammered out to be studied.

A lot of people might think Venara was crazy.

"You think she's crazy, don't you?" Dark said, and I almost laughed at the synchronicity of it.

"No," I said. "I don't. Dark," I twisted in his arms to face him, settling myself snugly on his lap, "look at me. I'm not precisely what you might call normal, or even sane, am I? Look at this." I poked his wound again. "If I was the sort of person who didn't believe in psychics then would I have been able to do this?"

He was silent for a moment. "I didn't think you could. You said—"

"I know what I said."

"You said you had no magic," Dark persisted.

"Yeah, well, maybe that was wishful thinking," I muttered.

"Why—" he began, but I cut him off by kissing him. I didn't really want to get into this. I didn't want to remind him of who I was, of who Striker was—of what we, between us, had done to his family. I didn't want to lose the warm fuzzy feeling that had been growing inside me ever since I first saw him smile.

"Don't think you can—" Dark tried when we came up for air, but I shut him up again. "I want to know—"

"I'm trying to kiss you here," I said. "Do shut up and let me."

He appeared to consider it for a split second then did as he was told.

"Good boy," I said, and wrapped my arms around him, pressing my breasts against his chest by way of a reward for obedience. I felt that rumbling purr grow low in his chest and smiled as the sound grew, reverberating through me. I settled more snugly against him, holding his body between my thighs, trying not to squeeze too tightly and hurt the wound that was still healing.

Dark didn't seem to be complaining though. His hands roamed over my back, slick with water and the scented oils Menny's mother had sent, and his fingers lightly brushed against the sides of my breasts as I pressed myself ever closer.

"Still think the oils are girlie and pointless?" I murmured against his neck as his hands slipped under the water and stroked my bottom.

"I'm beginning to see their merits," he replied, as his hands parted my buttocks and stroked between them, right down the crack, and his finger brushed over the sensitive bundle of nerves at my back entrance. I tensed, more with anticipation of pleasure than pain. A lot of clients have used the tradesman's entrance, so to speak, and I've had more than a few who've specially requested that I pay attention to theirs.

But I'd never had anyone stroke mine like that. Never had anyone slick it with oil and slip a finger inside. Never had anyone touch me that way before.

I gasped and shuddered, and Dark stilled.

"Am I hurting you?"

"No!"

"You said…on Koskwim, you said…"

I remembered. I'd told him he could put his cock anywhere he wanted, and I'd meant it.

"I did," I said now.

Dark moved his finger and I whimpered.

"I think those oils might prove very useful," he murmured hotly in my ear, and promptly sent me into such a fit of excitement that I hardly noticed him lifting me out of the bath and carrying me to the bed.

He laid me down on my stomach then pulled me to my knees. *Just like the first time*, I thought, and braced myself on my hands.

But he wasn't going to fuck me yet. Dark stretched over me, kissing the back of my neck, fondling my breasts, slipping one hand between my legs where I was getting pretty slippery. He rolled my clit between finger and thumb then slid two fingers inside my pussy.

I started panting.

His mouth, that talented, beautiful mouth, stole down my back, a trail of hot kisses against my slick skin. The cool air chilled the water on my back but Dark heated it back up again, nibbling down my spine, making me shiver and gasp as his tongue caressed each vertebra.

Then he reached my tailbone and he didn't stop.

I realized what he was going to do as he parted my buttocks. I'd done this before, but never had it done to me, and my whole body tensed in anticipation.

His tongue flickered over my anus and I sucked in a sharp breath. "Again."

Dark obliged, and my fingers dug in the blankets on the bed. "Oh. *Again*."

He ran his tongue around my sensitive opening, and his fingers thrust slowly in and out of my cunt. Almost idly, he trailed his hand from my wet pussy to my anus and he spread the wetness around.

Then he trickled something suddenly cold and wet between my butt cheeks, and I gasped at the pleasure of it as I realized he was drizzling the bath oil over me. His finger worked it in with my own pussy juices, and his tongue lapped up the mixture.

Then without taking his mouth away, he slid his finger inside me.

I moaned as his strong digit stretched my delicate tissues.

"Tell me if it hurts," Dark said.

"It feels good," I said through clenched teeth, because it did. It really fucking did.

"How about this?" Still licking me, he carefully inserted another finger, gently stretching me.

I swallowed. Hard. "Good," I managed.

"Then how," he removed his fingers, and then his cock nudged against me, "about this?"

This time I managed a sort of squeak.

Dark drove his cock slowly into me and my muscles gently expanded around him. I knew some girls hated anal sex. I say they just aren't doing it right.

Or with the right man.

As his cock drove deep into me, Dark's hand returned to my pussy and toyed with it. He pulled back, his well-oiled cock sliding out of me and his fingers driving deep into my pussy—three of them, at the same time, so I was never empty. I was always full of him.

I came quickly, noisily, yelling out his name, and Dark stretched over me, biting the back of my neck, making me come harder. I felt him spasm inside me, felt the hot rush of his orgasm as he pumped his hot stream into me.

We fell to the bed together, sticky, oily, completely spent. I had a vague recollection of Dark fetching a cloth and cleaning me up, but I was already half asleep.

I was woken by a knock on the door. I was surprised it didn't rouse Dark, but then he'd been, um, working a lot harder than me last night. Ahem.

It was Menny at the door, although I shouldn't have known this until I opened it. He stared at me, mouth open, then said, "Um. Aren't you cold?"

I looked down at myself. Whoops…forgot to put clothes on.

"It's nothing you haven't seen before," I said.

"Yes, but it may be wise to forego discussing that in front of him." Menny nodded in Dark's direction and I glanced back to see him sprawled across the bed, lazy and magnificent. My breath quickened and my pussy dampened as I watched him sleep, so beautiful in repose. All dormant power and coiled muscle. He still glowed very gently, but Menny didn't appear to see it.

"You want me to leave you two alone?" Menny asked doubtfully.

"What?" I tore my attention to him. "Uh, what did you want?"

"To see how he's doing. He looks…" Menny frowned. "Well, he looks fine."

"He more or less is." I glanced back at Dark, then crossed to my bag and withdrew a robe. "Can I talk to you?"

Menny nodded and led me from the room. "Sure."

It was morning. Hard to tell inside the bedroom with the shutters and heavy drapes closed against the cold, but through the high windows in the stone corridor I could see sunlight streaming in.

I was glad I'd slipped my feet into embroidered slippers. The thick stone of the castle would never really warm up.

Menny led me to a small, cozy room where a low fire burned and food was set out on the table. "You must be starving," he said, "dig in."

I looked at the food and realized I wasn't hungry at all. Strange.

"Last night," I began, and Menny looked at me warily.

"Girl, I don't know what you were pulling there," he said.

"That's the thing." I ran a hand through my hair. "I don't either."

Menny eyed me suspiciously. "You always said you didn't have any of your dad's, er...talents."

I snorted. "Is that what they're calling them now?"

"But you do," Menny continued.

I shrugged hopelessly. "I don't want to," I said.

"I don't want to be this good-looking and talented. You work with what you're given."

"Liar," I said, smiling.

"Sure, add insult to injury." He grinned.

"I mean it," I said. "I never wanted…"

"You did last night."

"Well, I had a lot at stake last night."

"What is going on between you two?" Menny asked, as the door was flung open and his little sister Salya, the spoiled blonde baby of the family, sauntered in. She was precisely the same mold as Varia—only maybe a little smarter. Not that *that's* hard. There are kinds of moss smarter than Varia.

"She's shagging him madly," Salya drawled. "The whole Realm heard them at it."

I'm afraid I blushed. Yes, me. I *blushed*.

"Well, we all know that," Menny said. "But I thought—I mean…your dad—" he faltered.

"Yes," I said flatly, back down to earth again.

"Oh yes, he slaughtered millions of Talvéan's people, didn't he?" Salya said idly, flopping into a chair and picking up a magazine to flick through.

"Well, not precisely millions. I don't think there were ever millions of them," I said. "But he did kill a lot."

"Any particular reason?" she enquired.

"They looked at him funny," I said, and even Salya picked up on my tone at that.

"Remind me to stay out of his way," she said.

"Yeah."

There was a short silence. "Is that why you were handcuffed?" Menny asked. "Or was it something kinkier?"

"It wasn't kinky," I said, and thought about it. "Well, not to begin with, anyway."

"I don't think I wanted to hear that," Salya said, and we both ignored her. Then, "Oh my gods!"

"Yes?" Menny said.

"Shut *up*, Men. I've just remembered something. Didn't you kill Jonal?"

I felt my jaw stiffen. "Yes." My eyes narrowed. "How did you know?"

"Oh, darling, we're royalty. We're all connected. Plus, Daddy told me last night."

Well, that's security for you. Could've saved Dark a lot of trouble if he'd just asked his friends.

"You?" Menny stared. "His brother? Really?"

"I was contracted," I said tightly.

"By who?" Salya asked.

"You know I can't tell."

"Oh, don't be such a bore. Come on. Who am I going to tell? The Kelfs? Like they care anyway! There's no one around here for miles and miles."

"Because you bored them all away," Menny told her. He turned back to me. "Chance. Listen. I don't know how much you know about Nasc, but honor is very important to them."

"Gosh." Salya faked a yawn and picked up her magazine. "When did you learn that word, Menny?"

"What word?"

"Honor."

"Go roll in the snow. Chance, he's vowed to kill your father."

"I know."

"And the person who killed his brother."

"I know," I said, my jaw so rigid it was amazing I could get the words out.

"I heard he'd already tried," Salya said, and we both stared at her. "I have my contacts," she said, looking offended. "I am the Empress' sister, you know."

"What did you hear?" I asked.

"That he tried to rip your throat out."

"Well, that's true." I fingered the sore spot on my neck.

"And he attacked Striker."

Menny stared. "And lived?"

"Well, clearly," Salya drawled.

"But that's impossible!"

"One did think as much," she replied, letting her forehead wrinkle into a frown. "Well, possibly I heard wrong, but I did get it straight from the horse's mouth."

"Which horse?" I asked.

"Mac," she said, and I rolled my eyes. Rosie's boyfriend. Of course. I remembered he was a friend of Menny's family. Everyone I know knows everyone else I know. It was impossible to keep a secret.

"Chance," Menny asked, "how is it possible that he attacked Striker and lived?"

"Because Striker isn't used to being attacked," came a dark voice from the door, and I looked up to see my lover standing there, looking edible with his shirt unbuttoned, the healing wound pink and raw across his ribs. Apparently he didn't feel the cold. "Next time he'll be expecting it, and raw strength and surprise won't be enough."

"You've been thinking about this," I said, my heart sinking.

He closed the door and crossed the room to the sofa where I was sitting, sprawling out next to me and slinging his arm over my shoulders. A thrill of warmth ran through me.

"How are you feeling?" Salya asked him.

"Fine. Thank you," he replied, with a polite nod, and I remembered he was royalty.

"Menny helped," I said, "and Salya and the rest of the family."

"Glad to," Salya purred, smiling at Dark. I snuggled closer to him and she rolled her eyes.

"You know each other," Dark stated to Menny and I.

"We go way back," Menny said, warily. "Our...er...parents were friends. Striker, uh—" He broke off, seeing my expression.

"Can we change the subject?" Dark asked.

"Gladly," Menny and I said at the same time, and glared at each other.

"You were lovers," Dark said, looking between us, and it was worth it for the look of horror on Menny's face.

"Yeah, but it was a long time ago," he said hastily. "Really long."

"Not that long," I said, just to see him squirm.

"Long enough! Way before you came on the scene. And I swear I haven't touched her since. She's all yours, mate," Menny said.

"Is this true?" Dark turned to me.

"That I'm all yours?" I considered the prospect, and while a familiar feeling of terror washed over me at the idea of being tied to one man for eternity, somehow it wasn't as potent as usual.

"That nothing has happened between you since we met."

"Oh," I relaxed. "Yes. That's true."

"Good," Dark said, and calmly added to Menny, "otherwise I would have had to tear you limb from limb."

For a second my heart jumped like crazy, especially when I remembered him growling "my woman" when he attacked Striker.

Then I made myself calm down. It was just some Nasc possessive instinct. Well—some male possessive instinct. No man liked to share.

Chapter Fourteen

ഔ

We were on our way by midday. I gathered the trip to Zemlya had been purely to pick up Véan. Dark explained that although his animal form had been wounded while out hunting, while we were on Koskwim, it hadn't become fatal until the bleeding lion was discovered by a pack of wild Kelfs. Dark wasn't joking when he said Kelfs don't like Nasc. Maya and Salya—each with some lupine talents of their own—had rescued Dark, and we'd gotten there just in time.

Dark didn't ask again about how I'd healed him and I didn't volunteer the information. I was feeling—well, a little shaky to be really honest. I was happy, really sublimely happy, and that made me afraid. Because I didn't think it would last and I wasn't sure I deserved it, and I was pretty certain it would come back and bite me in the ass.

Also, I was having warm fuzzy feelings about a man who wanted to kill me, which couldn't be healthy.

We'd borrowed a sleigh pulled by munta, which was a lot smoother than riding the beasts and also offered plenty of opportunities for fooling around under the furs. The sleigh glided through perfect Yule card images of rugged valleys and lofty peaks, the brilliant sun sparkling off the blinding white snow coating everything like diamond dust. The sky was a perfect, unblemished blue. Dark's hand was inside my top. Everything was dandy until Dark murmured to me, "Where are we going?"

"Hmm?"

"You're steering," he gestured to the reins I had gathered around my wrist. Steering was perhaps a bit of an overstatement.

"I, uh…" My stomach sank. I had no conscious clue where we were going. But I'd still set us on this path and when I thought about our destination, I knew where it was. We were headed for the Fifth Bridge, and Angeland. And when we got there I knew we needed to go west, toward Lorekdell.

Toward Dark's sister.

"Uh, I just had a feeling we ought to go this way," I mumbled.

"A feeling?"

"Yeah. Female intuition."

"Female?"

"Are you going to keep repeating everything I say in that incredulous tone of voice?"

"I am if you're going to keep talking rubbish. Chance, you can go on pretending you don't have any of your father's abilities. But the fact that I was able to get out of bed this morning — the fact that I'm still alive at all — demonstrates that you do. And now you seem to know where we're going…"

"Angeland," I said.

"Is that where she is?"

I nodded. "At least…where part of her is. One form. Not both, I don't think."

Dark blew out a sigh. "Do you know where exactly?"

"I—I think so. At least I know the direction. I might know better when we get there."

Dark just nodded and I was grateful for his restraint. If it had been me I'd have been full of questions. Probably taunts, too. I wouldn't have left it like that without demanding to know why all of a sudden these powers were manifesting themselves.

We were halfway to Saoirsefjörd when my scryer buzzed. Dark tensed, his mouth stilling against the bite mark on my neck which he was kissing better, and I hesitated before I answered.

But I knew it wasn't Striker so I picked up, and the image cleared to reveal Menny looking up at me.

"Am I disturbing you?"

"Yes," Dark and I said at the same time.

"Okay, I'll be brief. Where are you?"

"About a hundred miles outside of Saoirsefjörd."

"What's the weather like?"

I blinked. "It's fine," I said. "Very nice."

"Yeah? It's like hell here. Only colder. Soon as you left the blizzard closed in. I just spoke to someone in Saoirsefjörd and it's the same story there."

"So there's a blizzard chasing us?" I huddled under the furs in preparation.

"I don't know," Menny said carefully. "How are you feeling?"

"Fine," I said. "Why?"

"Let me know if you get in a bad mood," Menny said. "I'll warn the Realm to put the storm shutters up."

With that he signed off, and I was left staring at the snow as Dark resumed his attentions on my neck.

"What was that about?" he mumbled, his voice hot against my skin.

"I don't know," I said, but I was lying.

Striker can affect the weather. When he's angry there are storms, when he's happy it's fine. Once when he was—I'm going to use this word because I can't think of anything more accurate—*courting* my mother, he made it snow, just because she said she liked it.

I refused to believe I was the cause of this sunny spell. But I couldn't help noticing that as my good mood dimmed, so did the sunshine.

Summer in Angeland is a lot like spring in Peneggan or Euskara. It's pleasantly warm and dry, with bright cheerful sunshine and lots of, you know, flowery things. Unfortunately it also tends to rain at a moment's notice and can often be bloody miserable. I figure this is what drove the Anglish to conquer Peneggan and parts of Asiatica so long ago. They were fed up with being damp.

I like Angeland a lot, but I can do without the drizzle. So I was both happy and cautious to discover a bright, sunny day when we crossed the Bridge. There was a train leaving in ten minutes and I treated us to first-class tickets. It was early evening in Angeland, and it would take most of the night to travel to Lorekdell, so I figured a bit of privacy wouldn't go amiss.

Dark regarded the approaching train with distrust. "It doesn't look very reliable."

"Of course not. It's Anglish."

He shot me a doubtful look.

"I thought you like Anglish efficiency?" I reminded him tartly.

"That's before I saw it up close."

"It's all right," I assured him. "My parents are Anglish. At least two of my godparents are, too." I frowned as I tried to remember which were the official godparents and which had just always been around. "Probably, anyway. But it is safe. Solid as a rock. The Anglish are amazing engineers."

We climbed aboard in a hiss of steam, and Dark commented, "I hear the Sisilian government is looking into building a railroad like this."

"Never happen," I predicted as we squeezed down the narrow corridor. "They'll make a beautiful-looking railroad and the carriages will be exquisite, but it'll never go anywhere. Sisilians are too passionate and not practical enough. The Anglish are the other way around."

"Imagine if they collaborated."

"Then everything would be ugly and broken," I grinned. "I believe Peneggan is the result of Anglish–Euskaran collaborations."

Dark grimaced. Then he said, "What authority do you have to insult the Peneggans?"

"I was born there."

"You were?"

"Yep. Elvyrn. Didn't you see my Bridge pass?"

But that question made me realize I'd never looked at Dark's documentation either. I had no idea which Realm he hailed from. If he even had an official nationality.

"Where were you born?" I asked, as we located our compartment and slid the narrow door open. Dark had to move sideways to get his shoulders through.

"Asiatica," he said, peering around the tiny cabin with interest.

"Really? You don't look Asiatic."

Dark just looked at me. Of course. Nasc wanderers.

"Whereabouts?"

"Vyiskagrad," he said, opening and shutting little doors.

"What about your sister?"

"She was born in Peneggan. Northern Province. My mother favored cold climes."

"Was your mother Zemlyan, by any chance?"

"I think she hailed from Skavsta." He replied, uncovering a tiny sink with a shower attachment. "Clever."

"Told you."

The train gave a lurch and Dark froze, catlike, all his muscles tensing. It was amazing—a normal human being just wouldn't be able to go so suddenly, completely still. I was entranced.

"Is it supposed to do that?" Dark hissed, and I came back to myself.

"Yes. It's just the engine starting up." The train gave another bone-jarring shudder, and there was a blast of steam outside the small window.

"It, er, doesn't seem very—"

"It's fine," I said, and put my hand on his arm. His muscles were rock-hard, but he relaxed a little under my touch. "Really, it's fine."

"Pieces of metal," he muttered. "Steam. Can't the Anglish use horses like normal people?"

I stroked his arm, felt him calm a little as the train moved away from the station, its rhythm easing out.

"Your sister is a horse," I said.

"Yes." He was looking out the window at the countryside, which was moving ever faster.

"Does she ever let anyone ride her?"

Dark shrugged, his attention coming vaguely back to me. "Sometimes," he said. "She rides herself."

"Interesting concept."

"Nasc like to be in close contact," he said, looking at me properly. "We can be one form, but too long and we get," he frowned, "*itchy*. It's better to be in two forms, but stay close."

"But you can separate over long distances," I said. "Like you just did."

"Stronger Nasc can," he said. "Some can't bear to cross the Wall without their twin."

"You're obviously pretty strong, then."

"I am the strongest."

He said it without conceit, without arrogance. A simple statement of fact. I ran my hand up his arm, felt the evidence of his strength right there. But I knew he wasn't just talking about physicality—he was strong of mind, of spirit.

On impulse I stretched up and kissed him. His mouth was soft, warm, his tongue gentle as it slid against mine, danced inside my mouth. I smiled against him and slid my arm around his neck, pressing closer in the confines of the tiny cabin. The heat of his body warmed me, sending a gush of wetness to my pussy, hardening my nipples.

"I've never had sex on a train before," I murmured.

"Me neither," he murmured back and we both smiled. I smoothed my hand down his back, reached under his shirt and splayed my fingers against his hot skin.

"First time for everything," I said, and Dark pulled me toward the bed.

It was tiny—a half-size bunk that pulled down from the wall. Too small to sleep on comfortably. Much too small to fuck on. But Dark didn't seem perturbed by this. He took a seat on the edge of the bed and pulled me onto his lap, facing away from him, nibbling on the back of my neck as his hands pushed my shirt up.

He bared my breasts, cupping them in his hands, running his thumbs over the puckered nipples. I felt the strength of his cock nudging me from behind and my breath quickened.

Suddenly I had an idea. Reaching out with one foot, I pushed aside the rolling door of the little closet opposite the bed. At the back of the cupboard there was a mirror.

We were facing it, and I could clearly see my own breasts in Dark's strong hands, his mouth on my neck, the insides of my thighs as I spread my legs and my skirt rode up.

"Look," I said, and Dark's eyes met mine in the mirror. His cock twitched.

I pulled my shirt off and his breath hissed against my neck. He bit into my skin, teeth nipping in a love bite, and I shivered inside. His hands slipped to my thighs, spread them farther apart and stroked up the soft skin toward my pussy.

I was naked from the waist up, but I still had on my skirt and pretty heeled sandals. The shoes I kicked off, and after a second spent persuading Dark to remove his hands for just a short while, I made fast work of the skirt, too.

That left me naked. After we'd left Zemlya and the prospect of a frostbitten pussy behind, I'd relieved myself of my underwear. Didn't seem much point for it.

I turned to Dark, watching his eyes slide over my body, his pupils dilating. My nipples stiffened and ached under his hot gaze and as he watched I ran my fingers over them.

He swallowed, and without taking his eyes off me pulled his shirt quickly off. I licked my lips and slid my hands down to my stomach, fingers just grazing the hair over my pussy. The only place on my body, apart from my head, where I allow hair to grow. Some girls shave theirs completely, but I like it. Reminds me what I am—an animal, built for hunting, surviving and fucking.

I looked at Dark, my own private lion, and had to remind myself to breathe. I moved my feet farther apart and casually drove my fingers into the blonde hair between my legs.

Dark had the rest of his clothes off faster than ought to be possible, even without the constraints of the tiny cabin. He pulled me back onto his lap, once again facing the mirror, my legs spread wide over his, and both of us watched our reflection as I settled back against him, cunt spread open to view.

His hands traveled down my body, over my ribs, my waist, making my skin jump with anticipation, my breath quicken. The folds of my pussy were pink, swollen, shiny, and I watched avidly as his hands came closer, moving with featherlight touches that had me arching to meet him.

And when I did, I saw the tall, dark column of his cock rearing up behind me, his balls swollen with wanting. And instead of waiting for his fingers, I lifted myself more and rubbed myself against his cock.

Dark's gentle touches turned into a deep grip on my thighs. Gods, it felt good. So incredibly fucking good—that hard ridge of hot, throbbing flesh sliding against the hungry folds of my pussy.

I looked into the mirror and there it was, his dark, swollen length, jerking as I pressed against it, sliding up and down, stroking it with my slick pussy lips, nearly fucking but not quite.

Dark's hands dug in my flesh, gripped my hips and moved me up and down, his body thrusting to meet me. I slid my pussy the full length of his cock, tip to base, then back to the tip again, pushing my clit against the head of his cock and feeling the hot tear of moisture seeping from the end.

I nearly closed my eyes, but I didn't want to miss the show. Instead I moved my own hands up my ribs and cupped my breasts. Dark watched the movement, riveted, as I took my nipples between my fingers and started rolling them.

I felt his groan long before I heard it, and on the next thrust he changed angles and slid up inside me.

I gasped. You'd think I'd get used to the feel of it but I couldn't. Couldn't get used to the beauty of it. I watched in the mirror as his thick, swollen cock pushed home inside me, my pussy lips spread, my clit hard and throbbing. I thrust my breasts forward, pinching the nipples tight and meeting Dark's eyes in the mirror.

His hands gripped my hips harder and he thrust a little deeper inside me.

It was the most intense thing, actually watching him fuck me. No matter how hard you try, you just can't see it the same way without a mirror. And the mirror we had was small, faded, warped—but it was there, and in full glorious color I could watch myself sliding up and down on that magnificent cock.

I felt the first tremors of my orgasm building and bit down hard on my lip. I didn't want to scream—didn't want to bring a guard or a ticket collector running. I'd had sex in front of an audience before—some men paid highly for it—but what I was doing with Dark was private. It wasn't for sharing, it wasn't for showing. Except to each other. For once in my life I was having sex for me, giving pleasure to myself and to someone I loved.

Someone I—

Oh fuck.

Fuck.

I realized what I'd just thought as my orgasm began, but by then it was too late. All other thoughts evaporated from my mind and all I knew as the beautiful heat took me was that I loved the man who was making me come so hard my vision went dark.

Dark indeed. I couldn't see anyone else.

Chapter Fifteen

Why do I always get these revelations during sex? It makes it very difficult to act on them. Not that I had a single clue about what to do now. How precisely do you go about telling a man who has vowed to kill you and your family that you're in love with him? I guess you don't. You run like hell. You don't keep shagging him.

What the fuck is wrong with me?

Sure, Dark had gotten less brutal with me. Less angry. Less urgent. He was treating me more like a lover and less like a—well, a whore. It felt good to be held in his arms, good to be close to him. As the train pulled into the station at Lorekdell, we were kissing, deep and wonderful, without a whole heap of sexual urgency. It was nice to just kiss like this, no agenda, just the pleasure of his mouth and mine, his arms around me, his heart beating against mine.

Oh shit, I'm in love. How the fucking fuck did this happen? I've never fallen in love with a client before, and there have been men I've spent weeks with. Charming, handsome, cultured men, who haven't tried to rip my throat out and vowed death on me.

Men who have fallen in love with me. They love to tell me this. And I love hearing it. It is pretty flattering. But Dark... Dark didn't love me. He enjoyed me maybe, but he didn't love me. I'd know if he did. And if he didn't love me now, after all we'd been through together, he never would.

I was screwed. Literally.

I looked at Dark as I followed him off the train. Would he really kill me? After we found Venara, would he carry through his threat? How would he kill me? Shoot me? Stab me?

Strangle me? I mean, it's been demonstrated that I'm pretty hard to kill. If I were him I'd cut my head off or something, just to be certain.

I pinched the bridge of my nose and closed my eyes as I stepped off the train. The platform was crowded and all female eyes swiveled toward Dark, his powerful body, the beauty of his face, the strength that poured off him in waves even ordinary people could feel.

I grabbed his arm, tucked my hand into his elbow and glared at them all. If Dark thought that was weird, he didn't say anything.

The Kelfish porters didn't offer to help us with our luggage or find us a taxi. Dark didn't even seem to notice. He strode through the station, reached the line of Hacken cabs outside and looked at me expectantly.

"What?" I said. "I think they're mostly driven by Kelfs. I guess we could hire something…"

"Are we going far?"

That brought me up short. I didn't actually know. I tried to think about it, but all I got was a direction. No distance.

In the end we hired a buggy and headed out to the north of the city, toward the coast. Lorekdell is built at the junction of two rivers that spill out into the sea—strangely it isn't coastal, but there are splendid beaches within easy distance. The city's elite have seaside residences there.

I drove, directing the carriage without too much thought, but it soon became apparent to me that I needed something further to go on than "north-ish". I deliberated over it as we drove out of the city center, toward the northern suburbs where dwelled the bankers and lawyers and doctors who couldn't quite afford a second home near the sea, so they bought their first home within traveling distance. Eventually, by the time the suburbs were trailing behind and the scent of the ocean was just reaching us, I caved in and called my mother.

She looked sleepy, but there was a slight blurriness to her pupils that I recognized. It didn't improve my mood. Chalia got that look when she'd been woken from a Slide.

Sliding is the one thing my mother can do that she shouldn't be able to, and that I *should* be able to but can't. Basically it's putting yourself in a sort of trance, and Sliding your mind into another reality. Chalia is something of a natural expert at it, whereas I can't do it at all. They tried and tried to teach me at Koskwim, where even the dumbest student could pick it up, but not me.

"Did I wake you?"

"No, I was just visiting somewhere cooler. It's hot on Koskwim. Are you okay?"

"Why wouldn't I be?"

"Striker beat the crap out of you."

I rolled my eyes. "He hit me once Mother, it's not the same thing. Besides, Dark beat the crap out of him." I said it with some satisfaction. Dark's hand was playing over my thigh, a casual caress.

"Yes I know, and he's furious about it. Where are you?"

"Angeland. Listen, I…" I sighed. I don't know why I called Chalia. Yes I do. Because I didn't really want to speak to Striker. I was still mad as hell at him and I wanted him to know. Wanted him to suffer. Wanted my mother to withhold every kind of favor from him, sexual or otherwise, just so he'd know I was serious.

But at the end of the day, Chalia was a damp squib where magic was concerned. She had the psychic abilities of a biscuit. Sliding was the only thing she could do, and it was strongly suspected she could only do that because Striker was involved.

"I need to locate someone," I said, "and I can't get an exact lock."

"Who?"

I winced. "Dark's sister."

"He doesn't know where she is?"

"No. She's missing. I've gotten as far as Lorekdell, but now I'm getting a little bit lost."

Chalia blinked. "How did you know she was in Lorekdell?"

"I, uh, just sort of felt it."

There was a pause. Chalia let out her breath in one long sigh. "I'll get your father," she said.

The scryer went blank and I turned to Dark.

"Sorry I can't find her by myself," I said. "I haven't exactly had much practice at this. Well—any, in fact."

"You said you didn't have any of your father's power."

"I..." I didn't know what to say. The truth was I'd never wanted any of them. I'd seen what it had made him and I damn sure didn't want to end up like that.

"I used to have accidents when I was little," I told Dark, looking down at my lap. "When I got angry or upset, things just got...broken. And one time I threw a tantrum and this building fell down, and it hurt Chalia. And I realized I'd let it happen, I'd hurt my mother, the only person who actually liked me in any way, and I..."

"You didn't want to end up like your father," Dark said softly.

"Well, no." I looked up at him. "I was only seven. I made myself work so hard at not using this power I seemed to have, and after a while I talked myself into believing I didn't have it at all. I mean, occasionally it leaked out, like when I was hurt and should have died, but I don't use it on purpose. And I especially don't use it by accident."

My scryer buzzed then, preventing me from any more verbal vomiting, and I grabbed it. To my relief, it was Chalia, not Striker.

"He says go to his old house," she said. "That's all he said. I don't know if that's because Dark's sister is actually there or what, but that's what he said."

"He's still pissed off at me," I said.

"Yep. But I told him what an arse he was being and I—well. You don't need to know the details."

"No," I agreed firmly, "details are bad. What does he mean by 'his old house'? Am I supposed to know where that is?"

Chalia rolled her eyes. "Chance, sweetheart, I know that most of the time it doesn't seem like it, but once upon a time your father was very nearly a normal person. He went to school and drank in pubs and everything."

"At the same time?"

"Usually. Now—tell me what his name was before he became Striker."

I smirked. I couldn't help it. "Ganymedes."

Dark turned his face away, his shoulders shaking.

"I mean his surname."

"Lorek—oh." We were in Lorekdell. How could I have not figured this out before? "Will it be obvious?"

"I can give you directions. I don't know who'll be living there—Striker was an only child and his parents died a long time ago. Probably it will be strangers." She paused, looking sad for a moment. Memories of the handsome young cavalry officer she fell in love with twenty years before I was born.

"Mum?"

"Where are you? I'll give you directions."

She did, and I turned the buggy around. We drove in silence for a while before Dark finally spoke up.

"Ganymedes?"

I couldn't help smiling. "According to legend, the most beautiful boy in existence. He was personal servant to Great Renex, head of the Peneggan pantheon."

"I thought your father was Anglish?"

"He is, but his family was the sort to travel widely."

Silence again then Dark asked, "What was he, before he…before…"

"Before he became him? He was normal." I thought about that. "Well, not normal exactly. But he was born and he grew up and he had no magic until after he disappeared."

"Disappeared?"

"He left school and joined the army. I think his father bought him a commission. Anyway, the army sent him on some cock-and-bull mission to the New Realm, the Mundus Nova."

"I thought that was a myth."

"There's a reason for that. Within days of crossing the Wall, his whole troop was slaughtered. Including the mage who'd been sent to protect them. The story goes that the mage transferred his magic to Striker before he died and that's how he survived."

"How long was he there?"

"Twelve years. Most of it alone."

"Twelve *years*?"

"Yeah. And people wonder why he's insane. Then Menny's parents banished a sorceress out there who was even more wacko than Striker. She was the first person he'd seen in twelve years. Being Striker, he shagged her, stole all her power, and used it to come home and find the woman he fell in love with before he left."

"Chalia?"

"Chalia. Who by this time was making her own life and falling in love all by herself. Striker is not just destructive in a physical sense."

Dark frowned. "The guy on the dragon flight. The captain."

That was pretty perceptive, considering Dark had only been in a room with them once. "Tanner. Chalia was engaged to him once. It got messy."

"I see," Dark said, but I could tell it was a lie.

"Look," I glanced at him, "I'm not trying to excuse him. There is no excuse."

"No, there isn't."

"There isn't really much of an explanation. He's too crazy and too powerful. But that's how it happened."

Dark was silent a while longer. "Why does your mother —
"

"I don't know," I said shortly, because I truly didn't. She was an intelligent, compassionate woman. What in the name of fuck was she doing with a maniac like Striker? How could she possibly have left the nice, handsome, *sane* Captain Tanner for the most evil man in history? No one knew. I sure as hell didn't. Chalia said she wasn't even sure herself.

It didn't make me feel particularly warm and fuzzy, I can tell you that.

The sky clouded over as we drove back into town and I didn't think that was a coincidence. By the time we pulled up outside the tall iron gates of the former Lorek residence, it was decidedly chilly.

The house was pretty grand. I'd known both my parents came from moneyed backgrounds, but I hadn't known Striker's had been this wealthy. I wondered where old man Lorek's money had ended up. Probably Striker made a firework out of it or something.

The house had become a hospice. A home for the terminally ill. In a way, it kind of figured. We rang the bell and spoke to the Kelf on duty, who regarded Dark with suspicion but allowed us entrance.

We were greeted in the grand marble lobby by a woman in a cape and starched hat. Matron. She was substantial in build and didn't look like she'd take shit from anyone. She smelled of disinfectant. The whole place did.

"It's about Ara," I said, twisting my hands and trying to look distressed. "My sister's horse. She ran away and we've been trying desperately to find her. My sister is a little," I paused for effect, "fragile. She's not been the same since Ara went."

"I understand completely," Matron said. "And you think this horse may have wandered into our grounds?"

"Yes," I said. "Yes. She's tall—fifteen hands would you say, darling?"

"Fifteen-five," Dark said. He'd wisely kept silent until now.

"Yes. And the most beautiful pure white, her coat and her mane."

"Well, I'm sure I'd have been notified if she'd turned up here," Matron said. "Our grounds are extensive, but the Kelfs are very well organized."

"She may be hiding," Dark said. "She's nervous around Kelfs."

Matron looked doubtful, so I added, "It makes it so difficult to get good stabling. It's why she ran away. We were visiting friends, and a strange stable Kelf got too close and off she went. Just bolted. My sister is beside herself…"

"Well, I suppose she could be in the woods," Matron said.

Woods? This place had freaking *woods*? It was in the middle of a city!

"I suppose she could be," I agreed solemnly. "Do you think we might go and look?"

I put on my most appealing face, widened my eyes and tried to look sad. It's never failed me yet. Today was no exception.

"Of course," Matron said. "Do let us know if you find her."

"Oh, we will," I promised with a suitably grateful smile, and off we trotted.

"That was mildly scary," Dark murmured as we went back into the cool summer air.

"I know. It's so sad to think that used to be a home and now it just smells of disinfectant."

"It smells of death," Dark said, "but that's not what I meant. It's scary how you just became this whole other person."

"It's called acting," I said.

"You're good at it."

"Thank you."

"Too good."

He looked uneasy and it dawned on me why. "You think I'm acting with you?"

"Well, you do seem to be the perfect woman."

That stopped me in my tracks. I mean, I know I'm perfect. I've worked hard to be perfect. I get paid a lot of money to be perfect. But it was something else entirely to hear it from the lips of the man I was falling very rapidly and deeply in love with.

"I suppose that's part of your profession," Dark said, and he didn't look particularly happy about it.

He thought I was *pretending*? My heart plummeted.

"Yes, it is," I said, and walked on quickly, passing him.

He caught up with me as I rounded the corner of the house. "I didn't mean—"

"You meant am I pretending to be your perfect woman so you might not want to kill me anymore?" Ha bloody ha. Yes, I'd been planning on it—but I haven't had a chance. So far I haven't gotten around to being anything other than myself. He didn't let me.

"Well—yes."

"Fuck off, Dark. The only way I could be perfect for you is if I wasn't who I am." I stopped again and faced him, suddenly furious. "I can't change who my father is or what he did. And I can't change that I chose to go to Koskwim and learn how to take a natural ability for killing people and channel it into something that wasn't horribly destructive. And I can't help that it was me who got commissioned to kill your brother. That is who I am. I haven't pretended to be anything else with you, Dark."

He stared at me. "You—"

I knew what was coming. I just knew it. "Don't you *dare* say I tricked you! I never tricked you. And I never lied to you, either." I took a deep breath. "I'll find your sister, and then you can stick a sword in my neck and then I guess I'll be perfect."

With that dramatic if not terribly wise little speech, I stormed off into the gardens, not really caring if he might be following or not.

The woods began at the edge of the lawn. The Anglish belief that they could tame nature by creating a perfect vista in their back gardens—such hubris.

Pretty, though.

I stomped through the dark woods, clouds gathering overhead. I'd probably have walked past the white horse if I hadn't nearly tripped over her.

She lay on the ground, legs folded beneath her, looking tired and hurt. For a moment I stared at her, realizing that this had to be Ara—there was a sort of energy about her that I realized I'd felt coming from Dark and Solana. She was Nasc, even if she was incredibly weak.

"Ara?" I asked, and she raised her head. But she was looking at something behind me and when I felt Dark rush past me I understood what. He fell to his knees, throwing his arms around the horse's neck. She whickered softly and he held her tight to him.

"Ara, Ara! I thought I'd never see you again!"

"Or I you, Dark."

I blinked. I'd heard the horse make a horsey noise, but a human voice arrived in my head. The voice of a young woman, slightly faded as if she was tired and weak. As well she might be.

"How long has it been?" Dark asked.

"Too long," Ara replied, and again I heard her words inside my head and her horsey voice outside of it. Strange indeed. "Months. I…I can't tell."

He stroked her mane. "I've been searching for you. We'll find Ven," he said, "and then you'll be stronger."

"We?"

"Chance found you in the first place." He glanced back at me and his face was unreadable. "She's good at that sort of thing."

"You found me by chance," Ara said, and there was the faintest suggestion of a giggle inside my head. "I know where Ven is."

"You do? Is she in Angeland?"

"No." The horse shook her head and the movement looked strange. "She is far away. Far, far away…"

I frowned. Ara sounded mildly nuts. But then, she had been stuck in a horse's body with half her soul missing for months.

"How far? Which Realm?"

"It's warm there. She sees the sun but she can't feel it."

"Ara," Dark said gently. "Where is she?"

"It's…It's…"

"Yes? Take your time."

"South," she said, and turned her head in exactly that direction. "South of here. And west. A little bit west."

Dark frowned. "South and west of here is the sea, sweetheart."

"And the Wall," I said.

"And Euskara," Dark said thoughtfully. "She's in Euskara?"

Ara nodded again. "A hot place. In the west."

"Iberia," I said. "Maybe even Carthage."

"Ara," Dark said, "if we kept in touch with you, by scryer—"

"Can't use a scryer with hooves," I said.

"—or by Faerie," Dark went on smoothly, "could you tell us when we're getting near?"

Ara nodded again, her lashes descending sleepily over her big brown eyes.

"Um." I raised my hand. "What's with the 'us'? Faeries won't come near me."

"Why not?"

"Striker killed one. Years ago, but they've never forgiven him for it."

"You can't kill the—"

"Striker doesn't believe in 'can't'," I said quietly. It was like a nursery mantra gone horribly wrong.

"Dark," Ara said. Her eyes were opening again. "Who are you talking to?"

"Chance," Dark said. "I told you, she helped me find you."

I glared at him.

"Okay, she found you. With some help from her—"

"It's nice to meet you," I broke in, pointedly.

Ara looked left, then right. Then she looked right at me.

No, not at me. Through me.

"There's no one there," she said.

I looked at myself. Dark looked at me.

"She's standing a foot away," he said. I waved.

"I don't see her." Ara sounded panicked.

I frowned. "Can you hear me?"

There was no response.

"She can't see you," Dark said, looking confused.

"Or hear me, apparently." I went to my knees, reached out a hand and touched her neck.

Ara jumped, muscles tensing under pelt, her nostrils flaring, her eyes rolling. Dark stroked her mane, murmuring soothing things, but Ara didn't look soothed.

"What was that?" her voice whispered in my head.

"That was me," I said.

"You can hear her?" Dark stared at me.

"Of course I can hear her."

"She can hear me, but I can't hear her?" Ara asked.

"Okay, this is getting a little weird even for me," I said. "Am I not supposed to be able to hear her?"

"No other human has," Dark said. "They hear the horse sound, not the human words."

"Well, I hear human words," I said. "And I hear that she can't see me. Or hear me. Which is freaking me out a little." I touched Dark's arm, taking his hand and running it over my wrist. "Do I feel solid to you?"

"Yes."

We both looked at Ara, whose flanks were heaving.

"Oo-kay," I said.

"Dark," Ara said, and she sounded frightened. "What is she?"

"She's—" Dark looked at me, and I wondered how he'd answer. "She's here to help," he said finally.

Smooth.

"But what is she? Make her touch me again."

I reached out and touched the horse's neck again. I felt her jump, but then she calmed a little. Breathing fast. Thinking fast.

"She feels…" Ara's eyes darted about. "She's not Fae…"

"Most definitely not."

"She's not…I've never felt… Show yourself!"

"I would if I could," I said. "Look. Dark said you could see what's really there. I'm really here! See me."

Her eyes flickered over me, rested on me.

"Blonde," she said, and Dark and I looked at each other.

"Yes, she's blonde," Dark said. "Can you see her?"

"Not with my eyes," Ara said, and I knew exactly what she meant.

"What else?" Dark asked.

"Keep touching me," Ara said. "I can feel you stronger now… There's power."

"Yes."

"It's…blue eyes. Strong, strong…" She flinched suddenly. "Sin," she whispered inside my head.

Dark's eyes pinned me. I almost drew back, but kept my hand on her neck. Felt the warmth of her coat, her skin. Grounded myself.

"I'm not a sinner," I said. "I don't hurt or lie or—"

"The Original Sinner," Ara whispered, and I froze, because that was one of Striker's nicknames.

"Chance?" Dark said. "Are you all right?"

"How did you know that?" I breathed.

Ara didn't answer. Her flanks heaved with panic.

"How did she know?" I demanded.

"She sees," Dark said. "I told you, she sees what's really there."

"Then why doesn't she see me!"

"You're not there," Ara said.

We both stared at her.

"You heard me?" I asked.

Nothing.

"Ara, did you hear her?"

"I didn't hear...I saw."

I knew she didn't mean with her eyes this time, either.

"What does she mean, I'm not here?" I asked. Dark repeated the question.

"She doesn't..." Ara broke off, looking distressed. Dark stroked her mane, making soothing noises. But I was too impatient.

"I don't what?"

"Chance. Shut up."

"She isn't meant to be here," Ara said.

"Here? As in these woods? Angeland?"

"She walks...leaves a trail..." Ara's eyes were darting from side to side. "But she doesn't belong. Original Sin," she murmured.

"Original Sin. Something Striker did?" I asked.

"What is this 'original sin' stuff?" Dark asked.

"Anglish religion," I said. "Striker's nickname. What does it have to do with him?"

He frowned, but relayed the question.

Ara looked distressed. She shook and trembled. "He changed...everything changed... The stitching went wrong and now there's a hitch. I didn't mean it to happen but now I can't undo it. Everything's changed, the fabric's wrong, I have to change the pattern…" Her head fell against Dark's arm, her eyes closing. Her flanks rose and fell.

I looked at Dark. "What the hell is that supposed to mean?"

"It means she's tired and she can't see clearly."

"But—"

"Leave it, Chance. She'll explain when she's feeling stronger."

"But—"

Ara's eyes suddenly snapped open. She looked right at me.

"You should not exist in this world," she said, and then her eyes closed and she seemed to pass out.

I stared at her a while, at Dark who was kneeling there holding her, stroking her, murmuring soft things to her, and I saw them move into the distance. I didn't really realize I was backing up until my foot hit a branch and I lost my balance, and then I turned and ran. I ran out of the woods, out of the garden, away from the house that was once Striker's but never his, and when I was far away from the creature that said I shouldn't exist, I grabbed my scryer and concentrated furiously on the source of all this trouble.

"See you've forgiven me then, pet."

I glared at Striker, looking sleepy and smug. I hated him for that smugness. He was always smug. I hated him. "Why shouldn't I be here?"

"Dunno, love. You trespassing somewhere?"

"Yes. This universe," I said.

For a moment nothing moved.

"Ah."

"Ah? Ah?! What the fuck is that supposed to mean?" I squawked. "*Ah?*"

"Shut up, love, you sound like a seagull. It means what it means, Chance. You're not supposed to be here."

I stared at him. He calmly lit up a cigarette and blew the smoke away at an angle. I was standing on a bridge in the middle of Lorekdell, thousands of miles away across the Wall, and I smelled the scent of his roll-up.

"Explain," I said coldly.

Striker blew out another stream of smoke. Then he said, "Your mother ever tell you about the first time she got pregnant?"

I stared. "No."

"She was eighteen. First time we..." He trailed off, his face softening a little. But only a little. "I was getting seven kinds of hell beaten out of me by a bunch of murderous Kelfs in the New Realm, and she fell down some stairs and miscarried." He frowned. "Still not sure how that one's my fault, but you know your mother."

Did I? I just stared at him.

"Mucked her up inside," Striker said. "By the time I found out about it there wasn't anything I could do. Besides, who wants babies? Nasty little smelly buggers, noisy, demanding. Fuck off."

"Is this going anywhere?" I asked.

"Yeah. You know when she was killed?"

"I don't personally recall the event, but yes. She got cut across the stomach, died, and you brought her back." Just another normal day for Striker.

"I put her soul back in her body, pet. Different thing. But anyway—all that damage made it worse. Didn't figure it was a problem, she was never the kid type. But then things changed. Everyone, all her friends, started having kids. Tanner, and then Nuala—I mean, look at your bloody uncle, pet, all parental. He used to be a bloody good womanizer, he did." Striker looked sad.

"I'm still not seeing how this is relevant," I said."

"It's relevant, love. All your mother's friends started having babies and she wanted one too."

So I was the result of Chalia's one and only adherence to a trend? Fan-fucking-tastic.

"Only it wasn't easy. I mean, we tried," he smirked, "but nothing was happening. I can mess with a lot of things, pet, but this wasn't working. And then I had one of my strokes of genius..."

If that's what you called them.

"Do I want to hear all the details?" I said.

He smirked. "Probably not. You know us Anglish are great engineers pet. But I only worked it out last year. By which time everyone's kids were all grown up, going out and shagging their little hearts away and, well, it wasn't right. The timing. She wouldn't want a kid now."

I was starting to realize where this was going and I didn't like it one bit.

"So I went back in time and did it. Came back to the here and now, and presto, there you are."

He looked very smug. I stared at him some more.

"Just like that. You just time-traveled and impregnated her and that was it?"

"Pretty much."

I stared some more. "You *time-traveled*?"

"What, like it's hard?"

"Yes! It's hard! No one else can do it!"

"Not the same thing, love."

You're telling me.

"Besides, I don't do it often. Got to find a portal. Sometimes they're not even in this reality, and I have to Slide out. Don't get much choice over when I land up, either."

"So you couldn't have gone back and, say, undone the damage caused by the miscarriage?"

"Me turning up after my own memorial service? You don't think that might have done her more damage?"

"How about going back to the point where she was killed and undoing that?"

"Because there wasn't a portal there, love. It's not that easy. Besides," he tapped fag ash all over the scryer and swiped it casually away, "some things are meant to happen."

"Like me?" I shrieked. "Was I meant to happen?"

He shrugged. "Were to me. Not to the gods, though. They were a little bit pissed off. Don't like their plans getting changed."

"*What plans?*" So I'm getting hysterical. I think I'm entitled.

"Plans that meant someone like me should never be allowed to procreate. If I'd gone back and changed the damage done to your mother, they'd have figured it. They never saw this coming."

I stared, and was about to tell him that if the gods were so desperate for him to not have children then they could have killed me off already. Or done something to Chalia so I wouldn't have been born. But then it occurred to me that they'd probably tried. Striker was more powerful than a lot of gods.

"So," I said, and my voice came out suddenly small, "you just created me. Knowing I wasn't supposed to exist."

"Pretty much." He lit another cigarette off the end of this one.

"Why? Because you could?"

"To make her happy," Striker said. He looked right at me when he said it and I knew he meant it. He'd do anything to make her happy.

Part of me wondered what it must be like to be sleeping with a man who would change the course of history just to make you smile, instead of a man who wanted to kill you when you'd outlived your usefulness.

The rest of me wondered what the fuck I was doing here.

"That's why I can't Slide," I realized out loud. "If I shouldn't exist here…"

"There are no alternative worlds where you exist," Striker said. "Clever bunny."

"Nowhere? Not one?"

"Never had a kid in another world," Striker said. "Never had a kid at all until last year when I got back from my trip."

"Your time-trip?"

"Yeah. Things were different."

"How different? It's not like you were around much last year. In fact, since you shipped me off to Koskwim—"

He pointed his glowing cig at me. "Hey, you *chose* to go there, madam. We didn't ship you off anywhere." He muttered something like "headstrong little bitch" that I chose to ignore.

"How was it different?" I asked.

He shrugged. "Oh, you know."

"Funnily enough," I ground out, "no."

"Everything was different." He made a face. "Everything was shit."

I just stared. I was getting really good at it.

"The world is a worse place for having me in it?"

He shrugged, blew out a smoke ring and nodded.

I gathered enough energy to say, "Fuck you." Then the scryer rolled out of my hand and off the bridge, into the wide, deep river below.

Chapter Sixteen

හ

The rain was hard enough to make dents in the river, but it was the thunder that was really impressive. The clouds were so dark they made the sky black, but there was almost constant lightning to brighten things up a bit.

I didn't feel bright.

The storm had arrived all on its own. I hadn't called it. But it was damn angry. Like me.

I had whirled through Lorekdell, screamed and ripped at buildings, threw carriages across the streets, grabbed at the river like it was a malleable thing and threw it downtown. I took hold of a few people and hurled them after it. Rage and pain tore out of me in a huge destructive surge and it was only now, still and cold on the edge of the bridge again, that I saw the holes in the cityscape and the palls of gray smoke and realized distantly that I'd done it. I wanted to hurt and tear and wound, because I was hurt. I felt it like a huge jagged scar inside me.

I wasn't supposed to be here. I was never meant to exist.

The bridge swayed in the wind. It was closed to traffic, possibly because I'd thrown one of its huge stone towers into the river. No one tried to get me to move. Maybe they couldn't see me either.

It all came tumbling down on me. Every little thing. Chalia's sword—the Deirfiúr, famous Kelf killer. It had killed Chalia once when the wrong person got hold of it. Even Striker couldn't wield it with any grace. It was Chalia's—it had been forged for her, meant for her. A couple years ago there'd been some fuss with some renegade Kelfs who'd tried to find the Heir of the Deirfiúr, to take her out, to lead some glorious bullshit revolution. I was the one who stopped it, but you know what? They weren't interested in me. They were after Rosie. Said it was Rosie whose blood they wanted. Not mine. I wasn't the Heir.

The sword knew. Rosie could use it and she was crap at swordplay. But the sword knew her. It clattered out of my hands and left me bleeding. Why Rosie? Why not me? I'm Chalia's fucking flesh and blood. One of those god things. Trying to change destiny. They'd already decided what should have happened—that Chalia should have settled down with Tanner and Rosie should have been hers. Striker shouldn't have been there. I shouldn't be here.

And why I couldn't Slide? There was nowhere to Slide to. No other reality in which I existed. I'm just flesh—no soul to Slide around. Maybe that's why I'm so good at selling my body and using it to kill people. No soul. Chalia said once that in every reality she'd been to, she'd ended up with Striker. It was meant to be.

I wasn't.

The thunder crashed in a marvelous symphony of discord. I wasn't meant to be here, I wasn't meant to exist. Everything I did changed history, jarred, stuck in the fabric of time. That was what Ara had been babbling on about. A stitch in time, and now the fabric was wrong.

I was wrong.

I don't know how long I sat there, feet dangling over the river, looking at the churning water far below. It wasn't that I was thinking of jumping. I doubted drowning would kill me. It hadn't before.

The sky began to darken with night, the rain lashed at me. My skin stung, but it didn't really hurt. How could it? I wasn't even really here.

No one had tried to cross the bridge in what amounted to hours. It was swaying with the storm, not safe, not safe at all. I didn't hear the footsteps padding behind me, didn't see the shadow falling, didn't know there was anyone there until I felt the sudden warmth at my back and the presence of a huge creature behind me.

And the glow. Dark's glow.

If I hadn't known the lion was Dark I might have been afraid, but I was past being scared anyway. He nuzzled my neck then licked my face with his raspy lion tongue.

"You're frozen," he said, his deep voice arriving straight into my head to the background of his lion growl.

"I'm fine," I murmured.

"We have a hotel room," he said. "Tal is stabling Ara. We found a vet."

I tore my gaze to him. "Is she okay?"

The lion nodded, an odd movement for a cat. "She needs a tranquilizer to help her sleep. She was worried about you."

"She thinks I don't exist."

"That's not true. She's confused, distressed." His soft muzzle nudged me. "We were both worried about you."

I stared at the choppy water of the river, watched the rain pounding into it.

"Chance," Dark said. "You're soaked through. Come back to the hotel and warm up. Eat something. Feel better."

I wanted to tell him that nothing in the Realm could make me feel better, but I found myself standing up, steadying myself against his heavy mane as my stiff legs gave out, walking alongside him with my head resting against his shoulder. He was so big, as tall as a horse, his paws as big as my head. His thick dark mane was soaked into dreadlocks with the rain, his fur pelted into patterns, but he didn't complain. He padded beside me, huge feet soundless on the cobblestones. We walked back into town and toward the big hotel where he'd apparently secured a room for us.

Just as I started to wonder how the hotel staff would react to a bedraggled woman with an eight-foot mountain lion, Dark's human form emerged from the gloom and came over to us. Without a sound he and Véan merged back into one form, and he took my hand and led me into the hotel foyer.

With that one gesture, strangely, I did begin to feel a little better. Or maybe it was just being out of the driving rain. Hard to say.

He'd rented a suite, and still without words he led me to it, left me in the opulent sitting room and vanished into the bedroom.

I started to shiver.

Sounds of running water came to me, and Dark came back, started gently tugging the wet clothes from my body. I held on to them and started to tell him that right now, for once, I really just didn't want sex, but he didn't seem to want it either. He led me into the beautiful bathroom where the big tub was filling up with water.

"There's some bubbly stuff," he said, looking at the little bottles the hotel provided. "I don't know which one's for the bath."

I shook my head. "It's all right."

Dark frowned at me for a second then he touched my cheek and stepped back.

"I'll be right out here," he said, and left me in the spacious, warm, steamy bathroom. I stood for a second then methodically started to remove my clothes. My body was cold, I needed heat surrounding me. Hot water. I could do with cleaning up, too, since the storm had blown all kinds of crap into my face.

I stared at the water and without any trigger at all, what had been sleeping inside me since Dark found me on the bridge suddenly welled up inside and poured forth as hot tears. They scalded my eyes, blinding me, wiping the strength from my body and leaving me to fall to the floor, naked and wretched. There was nothing left inside me but this bitter misery, this pitying hate, this anger, this uselessness. What was I? What the fuck was the point of me?

I curled on the floor by the tub, sobs shaking my body, torn from me, ugly sounds of loathsome misery that filled me up to bursting and escaped from my mouth, my eyes, leaking into the room, sweeping despair into the very air until I didn't know if I was crying because I was so angry or so angry because I was crying.

It was like this that Dark found me, huddled on the floor with my eyes swollen full and my throat closed with misery.

"*Chance,*" he said, and swept me into his arms. My wet skin and dripping hair soaked into his clothes but he didn't seem to notice. He held me close, the heat of his body seeping into mine, his quiet strength and the beat of his heart slowing my sobs and soothing them.

"I heard the rain," he murmured, gently stroking my hair. "The thunder calmed a little but the rain got so much harder. I knew it was you."

I gulped in a breath. "I'm not doing it on purpose."

"I know." He kissed my temple. "I know."

I shivered in his arms, and he lifted me up and deposited me in the tub. The water was hot enough to make me gasp but it felt good, warming me, working through the deep chill of my skin. Dark held up the little bottles and asked me which one made the bubbles in the bath.

"The one that says 'bubble bath'," I said, wrapping my arms around my knees.

"Well, if it was that simple I'd have figured it out," he said, and his sarcasm broke the tension a little. "None of them say that. They say things like 'arome de camille' and 'for softness and shine'."

His helplessness made me laugh. "The camille one is for the bath," I said. "The other one sounds like shampoo."

He nodded and tipped the stuff into the water. I swirled it around and watched the bubbles rise, popping one or two that floated near me.

Dark slid his arm around my shoulders and kissed me, pouring his warmth into me, taking some of the chill that seemed to have slid into my soul. Okay, so maybe I do have a soul. With his arms around me and his lips on mine, I didn't feel so bleak anymore.

"Want me to wash your hair?"

I blinked at him, then nodded, and let him wash my hair like I was a child.

I pretended it was soap getting into my eyes, but the tears that leaked out were because I remembered Chalia washing my hair when I was a little girl. She remembered it too, I was sure—but Striker didn't. Striker had only known me as a daughter for a year. I had only been his child for a year.

I'm sure a lot of parents would beg for children who arrived fully grown with not only one, but two highly lucrative careers—but there's a reason we're born as infants. We're supposed to grow up and experience things and learn about life all by ourselves. We're supposed to have a childhood.

Although I remembered mine, I hadn't really had one at all.

Dark's gentle hands made it impossible to be properly angry, but the sadness remained. He probably didn't wash my hair very well and I think he put the conditioner on before the shampoo, but that wasn't the point. When he was done he wrapped me in a warm towel and laid me down on the bed in the next room. He didn't say much, but he stripped off all his clothes and held me close against him.

No sex, just holding, and as his heat melted the frozen horror inside me, my humanity returned. I kissed Dark's whiskered cheek and he offered me a smile.

"I went crazy, didn't I?"

"Little bit," Dark said.

"I have to fix it."

His fingers combed aimlessly through my hair. "It's not that bad. Some flooding. A few buildings. Nothing a really bad storm wouldn't do."

"But the storm is my fault," I said. "It's not an act of the gods."

I winced as I said it, because what was Striker if not a self-made god? And what was I?

"Everything will be fine," Dark said. "I promise."

I wished I could believe him.

I slept. Not well, but I slept, and in my dreams I walked a pale shore. Beaches are rarely perfect in life, but this one had the white sand, the palm fringe, everything. Moonlight fell cool and strong upon the waves as I sat by the shore and dug my toes into the soft sand.

A woman walked along the shoreline toward me. She wore white, long layers that shifted in the breeze. Her hair was long, dark and unbound. She was exotic, beautiful.

She was my mother.

Chalia took a seat beside me on the sand and didn't say anything for a while. The waves crashed gently upon the sand and there was no other noise. We sat there identically, knees up, toes in the sand, looking out at the sea.

"Striker always said he wasn't one for family," Chalia remarked, still gazing at the dark water. "Of course, this was mostly because his family thought he was dead."

"He could have gone back to them," I said.

"I told him that."

"What did he say?"

"He said that he couldn't."

"Loser."

"I told him that, too."

Silence a while longer. The beach was incredibly peaceful.

"We had a big fight," Chalia said without prompting. "Just before you were born. He kept referring to you as mine. Like you were a gift he'd given me. He didn't want anything to do with you."

"Nice to see times have changed."

"Then when you came along, I nearly died—again—and Striker made a heroic reappearance just in time to save the day." She blew out a sigh that was faint against the sound of the waves. "He doesn't like to think of you as his," she said.

"*Really?*"

"If you were like Striker, would you want to pass that on to anyone?"

"Probably."

"Okay, bad question. Listen Chance, I know it might not seem this way but he does care for you."

"Bollocks."

"Hasn't he always come to your aid?"

"Because you make him."

"No, because he wants you to be well."

"Well, thanks to his screwy genetics, I always will be. Very hard to kill someone who isn't supposed to be here."

A longer silence. I stared determinedly at my feet.

"I should have told you," she said.

"You think?"

"At least I could have gotten it right. What did Striker say?"

I looked at her then. I stared at my mother who had been in her thirties when I was born but who could have been my sister for all the years that showed on her face. I had a feeling Striker was actually reversing the aging process now. She was bloody well getting younger.

"He told me he implanted me in history and when he came back, everything was — different."

"Different how?"

"Not in a good way."

Chalia sighed. "You know that Striker's concept of goodness is lots of explosions, plagues, violent death, that sort of thing? His idea of a perfect world isn't likely to be full of flowers and puppies."

"Well, duh."

"When he said things got worse, he meant they got better for everyone but him. Did he tell you about Jalen?"

I blinked. "What about her?"

"Before you came along to save the day, Jalen lost a leg to torturers. Also there was some mix-up with Menny that caused him to fall for this mute girl. Jalen was devastated. Broke off the engagement."

"They're engaged?"

"They were in that world."

"You're making this up."

"No, Striker swore it was true. And you know your father."

Unfortunately, yes. I know that while he's a filthy rotten bastard right down to the core, he doesn't lie and he doesn't break promises. He is awfully fond of bending the truth, though.

"And Rosie," Chalia said. "That Heir of the Deirfiúr thing came to a pretty nasty conclusion without you."

"How nasty?"

"Rosie died."

I stared out at the waves. "If you're trying to make me feel better…"

"Is it working?"

I glared at her. "Yes. Stop it. I was enjoying being miserable."

Chalia grinned at me. "Ah, you're your father's daughter, all right. Listen—the hurricane in Lorekdell, did you get caught up in that?"

"You know full well I did."

"Destroy much?"

I winced. "Dark seems to think not."

"I like Dark."

"I like him too." It was the most I'd admitted out loud.

"Well, we can all tell that." She stood up, one graceful movement, and brushed off her skirts. "He likes you too."

"No he doesn't." I said it wearily. I'd resigned myself to it already.

"Chance, don't be dense. He's crazy about you."

"No, he's just crazy. You weren't there when he tried to rip my throat out."

"Oh, Striker's always fatally injuring me," Chalia said cheerfully. "Works out okay in the end."

"Well, not for me. Dark really wants to see me dead."

To my horror, tears came to my eyes again. I was in love with this man, horribly, deeply, crazy in love with him, and he was going to kill me. And I'd let him. I'd just let him because, at the end of the day, I knew he was right and someone had to pay for what had been done to his people.

"Oh, love." Chalia plopped down beside me again and wrapped her arms around me. "Come on sweetheart, it's not that bad."

I stared at her.

"Striker once accepted a contract on me." She showed me the scar on her arm.

"Your arm? Not a very good hit," I said.

"He says I startled him."

No kidding. "Was this before he fell madly—and I use that in its strictest sense—in love with you, or after?"

She frowned. "Hard to say. 'When' is a fluid thing with Striker."

"You don't say."

"Once he realized exactly who he was supposed to be killing, he gave up," she said. "So probably after."

Probably.

"Dark is serious, Mum. He hates me. He hates Striker even more, but he can't kill Striker so he'll kill me instead."

Chalia sighed. She stroked my hair like Dark had done earlier. "I'm sorry Chance," she said. "I really am. I chose Striker—you didn't."

"Damn straight." I wiped my tears away with the back of my hand.

"I'll talk to him," she promised.

"What good will that do?"

"Maybe he'll apologize."

I snorted.

"Well, anything's possible," Chalia protested.

"Don't get sucked into this Mum."

"I got sucked in a long time before you came along," Chalia said, and it was one of those rare occasions when she actually sounded like a parent. "Now, I think it's time for you to go back to Dark. He's probably lying there all naked and delicious, waiting for you…"

And there goes the parental image.

"And I've got a man of my own to try and talk 'round." She stood up again and pulled me to my feet. "Nice beach, isn't it?"

"Lovely," I said, and frowned at her. "Is it my dream or yours?"

She grinned. "What do you think?"

I debated the issue. "Mine," I said finally, "and you Slid into it."

"Prize for the blonde," she said. She kissed my cheek and stepped away. "Bye, Chance. Sweet dreams."

"Bye Mum," I said, feeling sad as I watched her go.

"It'll all work out okay," she called as she went. "I promise. Well, reasonably okay…"

I woke in Dark's arms, the night still strong around us. Moonlight silvered his skin the way it had bleached the dream shore. He was beautiful, so amazingly beautiful. Dark lashes casting shadows on his strong, high cheekbones, dark whiskers, hair curling against the pillow. I moved back, the better to appreciate the long lines of his body, his tight pecs, long narrow waist—the line of dark hair that led down to his thick, strong cock. He'd kicked the sheet away and I gazed in wonder at the perfect curve from buttock to thigh. Even his feet were beautiful.

I wanted to devour him. I wanted to bite that gorgeous ass, run my tongue along the inside of his hard thigh, lick his stomach and feast upon his cock.

I looked at the hardness of his body, all coiled energy like a cat, relaxed in sleep with a moment's notice to be ready, and the thought of that body over mine, his rough chest hair brushing my nipples, his teeth biting my collarbone, the heat of him between my thighs and his thick, throbbing cock driving deep into me, the *memory* of it, made me lose my breath, and all I could do was stare at him, mindless with desire, a hot desperate need inside me.

I loved this man. I loved him completely, despite his anger and his hatred. Maybe because of it. He loved his family and fiercely protected his people. How could I fail to love a man who had his sense of honor? Who wanted to avenge his slaughtered family, his murdered brother, his missing sister?

Asleep, he was calm, but when he was awake the pain pulsed through him. He was alone, and Striker and I were the cause.

I was probably the only person alive who knew how to kill Striker. And right then, my hatred for him and my love for Dark were so strong I'd have passed that secret on if Dark had asked for it.

I lay on my stomach, chin propped on fist, just staring at him. Beautiful, beautiful man. I'd seen his beast and I wasn't afraid. I wasn't afraid at all of Dark. So he wanted me dead? To die by his hand and avenge his family didn't seem as awful to me as it once had.

I didn't care about it anymore. I just didn't care.

I reached out a hand and traced the beautiful line of his chest. He was perfect, an avatar of male beauty. His skin was smooth, surprisingly soft, like silk over hard metal. Every muscle in his body was hard with use—there wasn't a single ounce of spare fat on him anywhere. Bone and muscle, in such beautiful combination.

I leaned closer and ran my tongue around his nipple. It hardened under my mouth, puckering into a luscious little bud that begged to be sucked, tasted, maybe even nibbled a little.

Dark stirred under me and his warm hand covered the fingers I had splayed on his chest.

"A man could get used to being woken like this," he said, his voice deliciously husky with sleep.

"Could he now?"

"Mmm." He pulled me up his body and kissed me thoroughly. His mouth was hot and soft and I savored the taste of him, his own perfect taste. And that reminded me— there was something of him I'd yet to taste. Something I couldn't believe I'd been so remiss in leaving untasted.

I licked my lips as I moved away from him, and smiled. Had I wanted to kiss him all over? Right now there was only one bit of him I really wanted to wrap my lips around.

His cock was already getting hard and I caressed it—silk over steel again—before slipping my hand down and fondling his balls. The weight of them was perfect in my hand and the little shudder Dark gave was wonderful. His thighs parted and I settled between them, licking my lips.

Then I licked his cock.

"Did I ever tell you," I blew gently on the patch of skin I'd just moistened, "how delicious you taste?"

Dark swallowed. "I don't think so."

"Mmm." I swirled my tongue around the head of his cock. "You taste," I licked right down to the base, "really," a little flick on his balls, "really," another long lick, upward this time, "gorgeous."

"Really?" Dark panted.

"Mmm," I said again, any other words being a little difficult in light of the big mouthful of cock I'd just swallowed.

"Oh gods, Chance…"

He grew thicker and harder in my mouth and I relished it. Delicious…incredibly so. Delicately I nibbled around the edge of the crown, ran my tongue in long licks up and down. Dark started breathing faster.

I dropped down to his balls, licked around them, opened wide and sucked. Dark moaned, and I smiled with his flesh in my mouth. My hands slid up his thighs, stroking, trying to calm the rock-hard muscles under the surface. I wasn't successful. Every muscle in his body was tense.

As I let go of his balls and moved back up his cock I let my hands wander, stroking the wicked curve of his hipbone, the line of soft hair on his belly, counting up his stomach muscles like a ladder. I fondled his nipples, stroked down his arms and took his hands as he thrust his cock into my mouth, deep and hard, the fat head hitting the back of my throat.

Now this is where I come into my own. Plenty of girls with great promise get no further than the rank of Filly because of this. A fat cock hits the back of your throat and what happens? You gag. You want it out.

Not me. I'm a natural. They couldn't believe just how natural. I taught classes on how to deep-throat because, believe me, I'm good at it.

I took nearly all of Dark's huge, swollen cock into my mouth and he moaned my name, taking my head in his hands, thrusting slowly into my mouth. I wrapped one hand around the base of his cock and stroked his balls with the other, letting him thrust, content to let him control the pace.

When he started to quicken I braced myself. This was what I'd been waiting for, after all. The taste of him. I'd sipped the pre-cum that seeped out of his cock, but I wanted to feel him come in my mouth, the endless jet of orgasm pumping into the back of my throat. I wanted to taste his cum.

"Chance," Dark gasped. He started to tug me away, but I sucked closer. He bucked and thrust hard against the back of my throat, but I carried on womanfully. My lips were stretched as wide as they'd go—I felt like my jaw was dislocated. He was so thick and meaty, this huge hot cock just filling my mouth. The heavy weight of him against my tongue was almost more than I could stand.

"Chance, I'm going to—"

I squeezed his tight balls and he never got to finish. Well, finish the sentence, anyway. His cock erupted in my mouth and the force of it nearly blew my head off. He came with a loud yell, on and on, a thick, hot jet of semen pumping into my mouth in hard spurts, shooting down my throat, filling me up.

I drank it all down. Dark's cum tasted as good as the rest of him.

I carried on stroking him, sucking as I swallowed, milking him for every drop. His cock jerked and spurted more cum into my mouth, and then I felt him soften, his whole body relaxing, going heavy.

I suckled on him a bit longer, enjoying the taste of him. I licked every bit of his cock and his balls clean, and went over certain bits twice, just to be sure.

Dark groaned as I flicked my tongue over the slit in the head of his cock.

"Stop it," he moaned, "you're going to kill me."

"Can't have that," I mumbled around a mouthful of cock, and let him slide from my lips, wet and shiny. My mouth felt stretched but in a good way, like my cunt after a really good, hard fuck. Speaking of which, a good hard fuck sounded like just what I needed. My pussy was dripping, throbbing with need. I could feel my pulse thudding inside my swollen flesh.

I licked my lips, tasting Dark on them, and wondered how soon I could get him up to heat again. I'd milked him pretty dry. He was amazingly resilient, but I wasn't sure I could last long enough for him to fuck me. Not the way I wanted, anyway.

When I stretched up to kiss him though, Dark had other ideas. He kissed my mouth, slowly, cleaning from it the last drops of his own cum, and his hands moved languidly to my breasts.

Then one hand slid between my legs, and as his fingers touched my fevered flesh I started breathing faster.

"Chance," he breathed against my neck, the sensitive healing tissue where he'd first bitten me. It seemed so long ago.

"Don't stop," I whispered, and he laughed softly against me, his finger seeking my clit and pressing gently. I whimpered and pressed against him, and his mouth moved to my breasts, taking one aching nipple between his teeth and flicking his tongue over it.

I came, and the release was wonderful.

When I came to, Dark had me on my back and had taken up residence between my thighs. He slowly licked me all over, sliding his talented tongue deep into my pussy, swirling it around my clit.

"Fuck, you're good at that," I gasped.

"Mmm," he said, and I'm not sure if it was agreement or he really liked the taste. I wasn't complaining—the vibration of his voice did glorious things to me. Shivers raced up and down my spine and I moaned, grabbing his head and hauling him back up to me.

"I want you inside me," I said fiercely. "I want you hard and deep inside me."

As I spoke my hand snaked down to his cock. He was hard again. Oh, glory be, he was hard again!

Dark licked into my mouth, a wicked promise of things to come, and his cock slipped easily inside me, sheathing deep in my cunt, resting for a moment. Home.

Right then I didn't doubt that I was exactly where I should be. Here in Dark's arms, his cock inside me, his lips on mine. If I wasn't meant to be here, then how could this feel so right?

Thankfully, all thoughts of an introspective nature were driven out of me by the first deep stroke of Dark's miracle cock. I was lost for words, cheated of breath as he pushed so deep my very soul wrapped around him. With each stroke I fell a little deeper, into pleasure, into love, and as the first golden wave stole over me and my pussy contracted around him, I grabbed Dark's face in my hands and kissed him, hard, brutal, branding him with my mouth.

I wanted to shout out that I loved him but I didn't dare. Not yet.

Dark took my orgasm and pumped his own back into me. He bit down on my lip hard enough to cause pain and I relished it, my eyes on his, watching the amber glow as he came.

He was glowing again, just as he had in Zemlya. He was glowing, this magnificent man who plowed his cock into me with such force the pleasure made me weep.

We lay together a long while, sticky and messy and too fucking knackered to move, and when Dark nuzzled my neck it was all I could do to manage a weak moan of appreciation.

"You can't be sated," Dark murmured. "So easily?"

"Easily?" I yawned. "You can't move either."

"Mmm. No." He snuggled me into his arms. "I suppose we'll just have to stay like this, then."

"Oh no."

He smiled at me, a lazy smile that stole my breath.

"Thank you," I said.

"Anytime."

"No," I smiled, "I don't mean the sex. Although…well, you know. Thanks for that too."

"Are you blushing?" Dark grinned at me.

"Associées don't blush," I told him.

"You do."

"Well, maybe I'm in the wrong profession." I didn't want to think about that. Didn't want to continue the thought that my job entailed sleeping with other men, lots of them. And I didn't want to do that anymore.

I only wanted to sleep with Dark.

Oh hell.

"What?" Dark asked, seeing my smile fade.

"Nothing."

He frowned. "Is this about last night? Ara explained it to me," he said.

"She did?"

"About your father. What he did."

"She knows what he did?"

He nodded. "She wants to talk to you. She's worried about you." He stroked my hair, silent for a second, then added quietly, "I'm worried about you."

I looked up at him, and the concern in his eyes stole my breath.

"Ever felt like you don't belong somewhere?" I said.

"I belong everywhere."

"I don't. I shouldn't even be here."

"I shouldn't be in love with you," Dark said. "Don't worry so much about should and shouldn't. You are here and you can't change that."

I blinked, not sure if I'd heard him correctly. His tone was so very matter-of-fact and what he'd said after it was so ordinary, but…

No, it just wasn't possible. I was becoming delusional on top of everything else.

Chapter Seventeen

🙠

I left Dark sleeping and stole from the room. It was nearly dawn and there was no one about as I made my way to the hotel's stables. Dark had chosen well—they were roomy and clean. Not what you might imagine for a princess, but then Ara wasn't your usual princess.

I found her lying in the largest stall under a snug blanket. The hotel staff had suited and booted her, and there were fresh vegetables in her feed basket. Not bad, really.

Her head came up as I closed the stall door. "Someone there?"

"It's me. Chance. Can you see me?"

Her eyes darted around and I sighed, stepping forward and touching her neck.

The muscles under her white coat jumped then she said, "Chance?"

"Yes, it's me. Can you hear me?"

"Yes." She paused, stared hard then said, "I can just see you, too."

"Improvement."

"Indeed." She lay her head back down, murmuring, "I'm sorry, I'm tired. Not well. Keep touching me, I'm more aware of you if you do."

I sat down beside her, keeping one hand on her neck as I did. "Dark said he'd brought in a vet for you."

"Yes. He wasn't much help. I need to be reunited with Ven. We've been apart too long, that's all."

"You must be pretty strong to be this far away from her."

"We're often separated. But not for so long."

I stroked her soft coat. "Ara, can you really see the future?"

"I see things that may happen," she said. "I can't tell you for certain how everything will turn out."

"No gambling certainties then?"

She laughed softly. "There's no such thing."

"I suppose not." I paused. "You know that we'll find your twin? Dark and I. We'll go to Euskara and bring back Ven."

"Yes," she said. "I know. Dark has been searching for me for so long."

"Why?" I asked. "Why have you been lost? Why can't Ven come to you?"

"She's being held," Ara said, her voice distant in my head. "They want to know…what she is. What we are. How we can see things."

"Are they mistreating her?"

"Define that," she said wearily. "Keeping her against her will is mistreatment."

"I mean, are they hurting her? Physically?"

"No. They run tests, but they don't hurt. They treat her like a rat in a laboratory."

I stroked her neck and wondered how much of this Ara saw as a seer, and how much she felt as a Nasc.

"We'll find her," I promised, "and give them what they deserve."

"I know you will," Ara said. "I don't need second sight for that." Another pause, then she added, "You're looking for them anyway. Your people are."

"My people?"

"The Order."

I frowned. "How do you—what do you mean?"

"I see them. Young people with the tattoos. They've been trying to infiltrate but they're all dead. *They* keep finding them and killing them. No Knights. They're trying to win, but they're so brutal."

I was confused. Which "they" was she talking about now?

"So many of them," she said. "You'll stop them Chance, but…"

"But? But what?"

Her eyes rolled to look at me. "But be careful. I can't see you Chance…I can't see you at all."

"I'm right here."

"In the future," Ara said. "I can't see anything of you. Just Dark. He's so sad."

"Sad? Well, he's sad now. Sad for your brother and your parents." Although that wasn't the word I'd have chosen. Grieving, angry, vengeful—those were the words I'd have picked.

"No," Ara said. "The sadness of losing his mate."

I blinked at her. Whoa. This was news I should have had before. "I'm sorry?" I said. "His what?"

"His mate."

I swallowed several times, rapidly. Dark had a mate. Nasc mated for life.

The ratfink had a mate and he hadn't ever told me!

"Your brother is such a fuckwit," I exclaimed.

"A what?" Ara giggled inside my head.

"I mean it's not the first time I… I get paid for this, for fuck's sake—but a girl has her ethics, you know? I wouldn't just—I fell in *love* with him and he has a fucking *mate*."

"Yes," Ara said, laughing now. "You."

I opened my mouth, shut it, then opened it again.

"No, I can't be his mate. One, we only just met, and two, I'm human. Well, almost human. And three—"

"You're in love with him. And four, a Nasc can't cheat on his mate. It's physically impossible." She hesitated a second then added, "You see it, don't you? You're special. You see him glow?"

I opened my mouth but no sound came out.

"I see it sometimes, between new mates. When it's strong. They don't always…but you see it, don't you?"

I stared at her. "I'm not his mate!"

"Nasc mate for life," Ara said. "We can only have children with our mates."

"Children?" I was hyperventilating now. "I take really strict precautions on that matter. And what would they be? Half Nasc? You're talking crazy, Ara."

At that her giggle disappeared and I knew I'd hit a sore spot. Dammit. That was pretty stupid of me.

"I mean—I don't think *you're* crazy," I backpedaled. "But I can't be Dark's mate. It's not…I can't be."

"He loves you," Ara said, and Dark's words replayed in my head.

"He wants to kill me," I said uncertainly.

"There's been enough blood spilt."

"I can't be his mate. He's the Nasc king and I'm a whore."

"No you're not."

"Well no, I'm a little more than that, but still. It's not…I think your visions are going wonky, girl. You said yourself you couldn't see me," I said, voice stronger now. "How can you see I'm Dark's mate?"

"I feel it," she said. "I feel his love for you now and I see his grief in the future."

"Grief?" I asked. "Over what?"

"I don't know," she said, her voice distant. "But you must be careful. It could never come to pass. I don't see anything certain."

"So…" I frowned. "So I'm his mate."

"Yes."

"Nice of him to tell me."

"I don't think he knows."

"And I'm going to die, is that what you're telling me?"

Her eyes closed. "After Ven is rescued. Yes. Maybe. Dark's grief is strong in my head."

Ha. And she thought Dark didn't want to kill me. But he was going to, just like he'd said, after we'd rescued his sister.

He was going to kill me. At least I knew he'd be sad about it.

I stood up to go. I'd heard all I needed to.

Well, nearly. I turned back at the stall door. "Ara?"

Her ears twitched. I sighed, went back over and touched her long, soft white nose. "Ara. I have to ask you something."

"I don't know who will win the Treegan cup."

I laughed at that. "The Elvyrn Lyons, I know that. They're like lightning this year. That wasn't what I wanted to know."

"Then what?"

I chewed my lip. This wasn't going to be easy, so I might as well just go ahead and ask.

"Why did you commission me to kill Jonal?"

She went so still I thought for a moment she'd died. Or that I'd read the file wrong and it was another Princess Venara who'd paid for the assassination. Yeah.

"Does Dark know?"

"Of course not," I said.

"Will you tell him?"

"It's not my secret to tell," I said.

Another long pause. "He wants to know, doesn't he?"

"Yes."

"So he can kill the person responsible?"

"Probably. But if it's you he might reconsider. Especially if you explain why," I hinted.

"You're so sure I had a reason? That I didn't just dislike him?"

I frowned. "I don't think so. You're a seer. What did you see?"

Venara sighed and but for the soft movement of her flanks as she breathed, she was still again, and silent.

"Jonal was the middle of us three," she said. "Dark was the heir, I was the princess. He was just a spare. That was the way he saw it. He was jealous and resentful of our power and position."

"Power?"

"Nasc don't settle on one form until puberty. As children, Dark and I would take to the skies as eagles or go hunting as cheetahs. Jonal was jealous, not just of our strength as Nasc but of our bond as siblings. We tried to take him with us, but the truth is…" She sighed a little. "The truth is we were children, and children don't care about other people's feelings so much. Dark and I wanted to fly as eagles and we did it, and because Jonal could only manage a sparrow hawk, we left him behind."

She hung her head. It's hard for me to understand because I never had siblings. Gods, can you imagine? But all the kids I grew up with—Rosie and Menny and Jalen, Nuala's kids and my classmates at Koskwim—they weren't weak. They all had their own strengths. I don't know what to do with people who get left behind.

It was never a problem for me.

"His adult form was a razorback hog," she said. "Not the most noble of beasts but quite fearsome, nonetheless. And that about summed him up. Humans are hard to understand for us, because there's no animal twin to indicate personality. With Dark, you know he's strong, sensual, graceful, intelligent, proud—you can see it in Véan. I'm strong, I'm clever, but I'm a little unstable. There's grace and there's dependability — Dark has both and I just went for the former."

"And a hog has neither?"

"No. Jonal was smart, but brutish and crude. He got worse and worse as he grew up. My parents could control him to an extent, but after they died…"

I didn't need to ask if she knew Striker had done that. Of course she knew.

"I saw the future, Chance. I saw what would happen if Jonal was left unchecked."

"What would happen?"

"I saw my own death," she said. "Not at Jonal's hand, but he didn't do anything to stop it. He killed Dark though, out of spite and jealousy and greed. His followers were like him, we lost our diplomatic links with humanity. Became a hunted species. It wasn't just your father killing Nasc in the visions I saw, Chance. It was everyone. Hunted like animals, hunted for sport. Nasc heads on plaques. It was awful."

"You really saw that?"

"Saw the monster my brother could become? I saw it. I tried to stop it. Tried to include him. My parents, and now Dark, have worked hard to harmonize with humans. We have good relationships with most major governments. Nasc are allowed free passage in Angeland, Peneggan and Zemlya, and most parts of Euskara. Dark was working on Asiatica when Ven was…"

She trailed off and was silent for a while.

"I saw the future," she repeated eventually, raising her pretty white head to me. "I saw it and I had to stop it. My shame, my weakness, is that I couldn't kill him myself. For all I knew about him, all I hated about him, he was still my brother. I went to the Order for help and they recommended you. I'm glad they did, Chance. I saw his death, and it was clean."

I closed my eyes. I didn't want to think about Jonal, but I couldn't help it. I'd known that the easiest way to kill a brute like him would have been to fuck him and stab him while he slept. But I couldn't. Jonal wasn't unattractive, but I did have ethics. He was a prince and he was a person. He deserved to die with a little dignity.

I'd introduced myself, told him my intention—then fired my crossbow before he'd had time to run.

"Now what do you see for the future?" I asked. "The future of your people?"

"Harmony," she said, her voice dreamy, peaceful. "We are fractured and decimated, but Dark is a good leader. He can make things right again. His children will be strong and kind. The Nasc will be strong again."

Her eyes were fluttering closed and I knew I wasn't going to get much more out of her.

"Do you want me to go?"

Her head lolled. "I'm so tired. I have no energy since… Please rescue Ven."

"I will," I said. "We will. I promise."

Dark was awake when I returned, out of bed and in his lion's body. He looked me in the eye—yes, he was that tall— and rumbled, "Where did you go? I was going to come and find you."

"I needed to talk to your sister."

"Oh." He relaxed a little. "About?"

"You know. Girl things."

Guaranteed to put any man off. Didn't fail this time.

Dark turned and padded into the bedroom. I followed and found him lounging on the bed like a big kitty-cat. Like a really big kitty-cat. His paws touched one end of the bed and his tail the other—and that was no small bed, I'm telling you.

"Ara said that your animal form indicates your personality," I said, slipping out of my shoes and sitting on the edge of the bed. Dark nuzzled my hand and I stroked him, feeling the velvet of the fur on his face, the deep thickness of his mane.

"It does," he said. "I knew she'd become a horse. Strong and delicate at the same time. Beauty, grace, intelligence."

"You have all those qualities too."

"You think I'm delicate?"

His paws were bigger than my head. "Okay, maybe not delicate. But you're graceful."

"Cats usually are."

"Strong, sensual." I followed the line of long, dark mane down to his back. It covered his shoulders completely. "Powerful. Intimidating."

Dark's rich laugh sounded in my head. "I find it hard to believe you're intimidated by anyone."

"Hey, I get scared. Big freaking lion coming at me and I'd be intimidated."

"If a lion attacked you, it'd come off worse."

"Well, of course it would." I lifted my chin, Phoenix pride coming to the surface. "Not much attacks me and gets away with it."

Dark's heavy muzzle nudged my neck and his raspy tongue licked the sensitive place where he'd bitten me.

"Apart from you," I sighed.

"Striker made sure I didn't go unpunished." He paused then added quietly, "He does care for you, you know."

"Funny way of showing it." I frowned sulkily and fiddled with the hair of his mane. It ought to have seemed odd, talking to my lover while he lay there gently swishing his tail, but it wasn't. Dark was so hugely feline anyway that it just seemed natural to see him this way.

"Your mother intervened," Dark said. "Otherwise he would have killed me."

"Not on my behalf," I said. "He just likes hurting people."

"Oh, I know that."

Silence for a while, then I blurted, "I know how to kill him."

Dark didn't say anything immediately. He lay there with his big head in my lap, purring gently, and eventually his voice sounded in my head.

"I thought you said it was impossible."

"Nothing's impossible," I said. "That's one thing I learned from him."

"No blade or bow will do it. I don't think he'd drown or burn. Poison wouldn't have much effect."

"No," I said. "You're thinking too literally. Don't ask *how* he's immortal. Ask *why*."

"All right, why?"

"Chalia. He lives for her, and only her. Take away his reason for living and he will die."

Another long silence. Part of me couldn't believe I was saying this. Then part of me remembered Striker telling me I'd made the world a worse place and I wasn't sorry at all.

"I couldn't kill her," Dark said. "I'd never get close. Besides, I have no quarrel with her."

"She could have stopped Striker from killing your people," I said. "He listens to her. But she didn't stop him, she just yelled at him and sulked a bit and then he apologized and carried on doing it."

"Do you want me to kill your parents?" Dark asked, and pain stung my throat. My eyes prickled. Not my mother. I loved her. But Striker?

"Two people to save a whole race?" I said. "Isn't it worth it?"

Another silence. I worked to control my tears.

"You really hate him, don't you?" Dark said softly.

"He's an evil man and he doesn't love me," I said. "What else can I do?"

My thoughts might have continued in this nihilistic vein had Dark not morphed into a naked human man and fucked me senseless. I fell asleep in his arms, breathing in his scent, knowing I loved him enough to kill myself and my parents. And that thought scared me more than a little.

In the morning we arranged livery for Ara and left Lorekdell to cross Angeland, then Peneggan and finally into Euskara. The journey took days, and I spent as much of it as possible naked in Dark's arms. Who knew how long we had left together?

Whatever doubts had been planted by Dark's strange declaration in Lorekdell had been quickly dismissed by Ara's prophecy. She wasn't the only one with mildly psychic powers. However much I fought it, my intuition had always been unnaturally strong, and I knew that something bad awaited us in Iberia. Something very bad.

We docked in the port of Colacochea, inland a little and at the foot of the mountains. I smiled as I thought to myself that the other side of those mountains was where Dark and I had first met. Before I knew who he was. Before he knew what I'd done.

I'd had time to think during our journey and two things had become apparent to me. The first was that if Dark found out who'd ordered his brother's death, he might not want to kill me so much. After all, I was just the tool. It'd be like destroying the crossbow that killed Jonal. Or so I told myself.

But the second thing that occurred to me negated that thought entirely, and I'll tell you why. Venara was all Dark had left for family. His parents had been murdered and his brother assassinated. I'm sure Dark wasn't blind to his brother's faults, but as I understood it, the sibling bond is strong and family is family.

In most cases, anyway.

If I told him Venara had ordered Jonal's death, he'd lose the only family he had left. I didn't want to be the cause of that. I didn't want it to happen at all. There was more at stake than the happiness of one man. Destroying Dark would destroy the Nasc, and Striker had already done enough damage in that direction.

Speaking of Striker, I had an uncanny feeling he was near. I'd never intuited things so strongly before, but now it seemed I was coming into my powers. I guess magic is like a muscle—the more you use it, the stronger it gets. Locating Ara, healing Dark, even causing that storm, all of it had strengthened a natural tendency toward magic. I knew from watching Striker what could happen if you let such a thing carry on without discipline, and I was determined not to let it happen to me. Control was the answer. I am a Phoenix, I am good at control.

Except where Dark is concerned.

I knew where we were headed. Since meeting Ara, my connection with her was even stronger. I knew where Ven was without having to think about it. Crazy thing, though—the more I did think about it, the less I could feel it. Magic's a slippery little bugger.

We'd hired munta and were starting up the mountain when my scryer buzzed. I answered it and saw a pair of huge Kelfish eyes staring up at me. It took a moment to recognize Varnus, the Kelf who'd been so devoted to me since he'd driven my coach over the cliff.

"Lady," he said. "Are you well?"

"Yes," I said. "Thanks. You?" Stupid question, because Kelfs don't get sick. Or rather, they do—and then they very suddenly die. There's no recovery, not even from a common cold. But on the plus side, their skin is impenetrable and their bones can't be broken. Which is why the fall in Galatea hadn't even bruised Varnus.

"Yes, lady. Thank you. I have a message for you from the Association."

"I'm not really available for work now, Varnus."

"It's not work, lady. Lady Solana has news for you."

I frowned. "Solana?" Then I remembered. She was working for the Iberian ambassador. "Did she say what about?"

"The Federacion, lady. She said you would know what that means."

"Yes, I know."

"She wishes to meet with you, if you are close to Iberia."

I glanced at Dark. "Can we make a detour?"

"How far?"

I asked Varnus, who replied, "Colacochea."

Well, that's intuition for you. Fate. Whatever you want to call it.

When I asked Varnus for a meeting place, he gave me the name of the Gata Bonita club. Translated, it means Pretty Pussy. Go figure.

I didn't tell Dark we were going to a bordello. He probably guessed. I mean, his language skills were as good as mine, maybe even better. And he knew Solana was an Associée. But still. Neither of us said anything about it as we turned around and rode back into town.

We'd left our luggage at a hotel. No one wants to be dragging around a suitcase during a rescue attempt. I mentioned to Dark that we ought to change, and he just nodded and went along with me.

I showered, too, and while Dark was washing I picked out my clothes. In Euskara, certain things are expected of an Associée. Beautiful clothes are one of them. Not just stylish, chic, pretty—but beautiful. Chalia wears a lot of beautiful things, rich fabrics, exquisite details. She taught me about clothes, makeup and hair, and a lot of it's ingrained.

I selected a long green gown—ladylike being the current fashion—with gold brocade accents. The dress was velvet, heavy and sensual, and split at the front to reveal either a colored kirtle or nothing at all. Since a Lady is expected to act with decorum, I chose a kirtle to go under the dress. In deference to the situation, I picked a sheer one.

The dress covered all pertinent areas, which was just as well since my underwear didn't. While Dark was in the bathroom I dressed in a deep gold corset, with matching garters and sheer knickers. The corset, custom-made, just brushed the tips of my nipples. When I put the dress on, the fabric slid sensuously against my exposed skin.

I added delicate embroidered slippers, fastened my hair in a series of loops and was applying makeup when Dark came out of the bathroom.

"I wasn't aware there was a dress code," he said.

"I'm an Associée. People have expectations," I said.

He didn't say anything to that, but started putting on the clothes the hotel Kelfs had pressed while we were out.

"Does an Associée usually arrive with a companion?" he asked eventually.

"Of course," I said with a laugh, putting on earrings. "Only usually," I looked him over in his tight, Euskaran-cut breeches, soft white shirt and thigh-high boots, "he doesn't outshine her."

We hired a carriage to take us to the club. One of the things you have to love about Euskara is the relaxed attitude toward sex. Short of actually stripping off and doing it in the street, no one really cares what you get up to. Or with whom. Only a Realm as sensual as this could have come up with an organization like the Association that's not only perfectly legal, but highly respected.

The Gata Bonita looked like a luxurious hotel. Past the liveried door Kelf, there was a modern, spacious lobby with a couple of very pretty girls on reception. Sofas, ferns and magazines decorated the room. It was only when you looked closely you realized that the magazines were portfolios and the pictures on the walls were of naked women and fornicating couples.

Sometimes the couples had friends.

"*Belle jour,*" I greeted the brunette receptionist, the traditional Associée greeting. She was attired in a beautiful red satin dress, the sort of thing one might wear to a cocktail party.

"*Belle jour,*" she replied, clocking the Associée mark artfully displayed by my gown. "What is your desire?"

"I believe Solana is here."

No need for a last name. She was a Lady—if the girl didn't know who I was talking about she shouldn't be working here.

"Yes, she's in the ten o'clock show."

I raised my eyebrows. "Is she, now?"

"Yes." The girl beamed. "Cover fee has gone up, attendance has doubled. It's not often we have an Associée of such ranking join us."

"No," I mused, although I'd done it once or twice. "Is Roco Rico still here?"

Her lips curved in a very satisfied sort of way. "Oh yes. My lady," she added, checking a logbook on the desk, "we still have one room free."

I didn't have a mirror, but I'm quite sure my eyes sparkled at that. I glanced at Dark, then back at the receptionist.

"Charge it," I said.

She smiled and handed me a key. The fob was a carved wooden representation of a couple fucking. Each fob was different—corresponding to a symbol on each door. There were no numbers. We were in the fucking-from-behind-while-standing room.

As we moved away down the corridor, Dark said to me, "Okay, what did we just sign up for?"

I smiled. "You'll see."

"Tell me," he said patiently. "I thought we were coming to see Solana."

"Oh, we'll see her all right," I said.

"You're talking in riddles."

"All will become clear," I said, spying our door and turning the key. "I promise."

Each room was different, but they all had the same features. A chaise, a chair and a bed, a painted screen and a shower. Oh, and a big curtain covering the far wall. Our room was green, which was nice because it coordinated with my dress. Not that I'd be wearing it for long.

"Uh," Dark looked around. "I am confused. We already have a hotel room."

"We're not staying here." I took off my gloves.

"Then…?" He gestured to the bed.

"Dark, what sort of place is this?"

"I thought it was a bordello."

"And so it is."

"But—a show? I'm guessing we're talking more than dancing girls."

"Well, sometimes they dance."

"But mostly they fuck?"

I smiled. "Now you're getting it."

He looked around the room again and his eye fell on the curtain. "And we watch."

"Prize for the Nasc."

He looked at the furniture. There were more pictures on the walls of people having sex, in all kinds of positions. Inspiration, I guess, in case the show didn't do it for you. One could hire a room and get one of the club's employees to…entertain, but it was pretty popular with couples, too. The clever thing about the arrangement was that each room had smoked glass that allowed the occupants to see out, but not to be seen. There was a cheap gallery, too, where the poorer—and less inhibited—could be tended to. Or tend to themselves. The gallery usually turned into an orgy by about half past ten.

I started taking the pins out of my hair. "The show started ten minutes ago."

"How many, uh, people are in this show?"

"It varies. Usually four or more."

"Four." Dark swallowed. "Huh."

"Not one for group sex?"

"It's not something that's ever occurred to me." His eyes fell on a picture of a woman sitting on one man's cock while she held another between her lips like fat cigar. "We don't… Nasc believe in fidelity."

"So I'm told," I said softly, letting my hair fall loose and running my fingers through it to check there were no stray pins.

"Actually, it's less of a belief and more of a biological," his eyes hit the next picture, which was a rather spectacular sixty-nine performed standing, "thing. We, uh, mate for life and…" He licked his lips. I could see a familiar bulge appearing in his deliciously tight breeches. "Um. Once mated, there's no possibility of infidelity."

"What about before you're mated?" I reached for the edge of the curtain.

"Well, I…I don't know. I never really—" His attention was caught by the swish of heavy fabric and the glow of candles spilling into the room. His voice just died. I tied the curtain back, and Dark stood and stared.

Solana wasn't there yet. Currently the stage—covered with mattresses at varying levels—was occupied by a swarthy-skinned man lying on his back. It was hard to see what his facial features were like though, because a brunette woman was sitting on his face. His hands caressed her hips as his lips and tongue pleasured her shining, bare pussy lips. Everyone who worked at the club was shaved. Made things easier to see.

A second woman, her curly hair spilling down her bare back, rode the man's cock. She rotated slowly then rose up and down. His legs were wide apart so the audience could see how her pussy lips brushed his balls.

The two women leaned together and caressed each other's breasts. The curly-haired woman had small, high tits, but the one bouncing on the guy's face had plentiful round boobs. They bobbed and swayed, heavy pink nipples thrusting out. The women kissed each other with plenty of tongue, stroking and moaning as they fucked the swarthy man.

"Well?" I said, standing behind Dark as he pressed one hand to the smoked glass and stared. His cock was getting so big and hard, if released it would have pressed against the glass, too.

He swallowed hard, but eventually said, "There are only three of them."

"They add people one at a time." I started unfastening my dress.

"Are they—are they, uh, employees or…?"

"Probably," I said. "Or enthusiastic amateurs. The club has plenty of regulars who pay for the privilege. The Association recruits from places like this."

"How can you tell which is which?"

"You can't. If the women are Association, they'll have the mark on their breasts. Probably not more than one or two lines, though. Solana's a bit of a star attraction. But the regular girls—and boys—here won't have anything to identify them. It's a sort of leveler. Rich men and whores are equal on that stage."

I removed the dress and soundlessly laid it over the chair. Standing in stockings, sheer panties and velvet corset, I stood behind Dark and slid one hand around to his crotch. His cock twitched through the fabric of his clothes.

"Aren't they beautiful?" I murmured.

He nodded wordlessly and I unfastened the front of his breeches. His cock sprang into my hand, hard and heavy, and I caressed the soft velvet of it, forgetting about pleasing Dark and thinking only of how wonderful it felt in my hand.

As we watched, the big-breasted woman started shaking and convulsing. Through the glass we heard her moan, her head thrown back, as the other woman sucked on her tits and the man gobbled up her pussy.

My own pussy was getting plenty wet watching the show. Dark's cock leapt in my hand and I absently soothed it with my fingers.

The big-breasted woman made a meal of her orgasm, bucking and writhing, but eventually she calmed down, rose up on her knees and slid away. We watched as the other woman leaned forward, licking into the man's mouth, tasting the first woman's cum there. He was a handsome devil, but not anyone I recognized. As they kissed, he continued to thrust into her. From this angle, we had a prime view of her ass as she arched her back, pressing her small breasts into his chest.

A tear of moisture seeped from Dark's cock and I decided it was time for a treat. I turned him by the shoulder and stood there in my lingerie, hard nipples poking over the top of my corset, crotch damp with moisture. I was breathing hard, bosom heaving without intention. My cheeks felt flushed and my eyes glazed.

Dark's mouth met mine before any other part of him touched me. His hands cupped my face, grabbing me to him, and his cock pressed hard against me as his tongue slid against mine.

I pushed his jacket away without breaking the kiss and his cravat quickly followed. But the shirt, alas, had to be taken off over his head, which was annoying as hell, because it meant that for a few moments that glorious mouth of his wasn't on mine.

Then he was bare-chested, and as we kissed harder, deeper, the light hair on his chest abrading my nipples to the point where I thought they might burst.

"Okay," I drew back, breathing really hard.

Dark fingered a lock of my hair, still curly from the fancy style I'd worn it in. His knuckles brushed my heaving breast.

"You are so beautiful," he said hoarsely, and I just smiled at him, smiled in delight to hear the man I loved say such a thing.

I peeled his boots off, then his trousers and then he was naked before me, cock dark and throbbing, and I dropped to my knees, taking him into my mouth as he watched the show. Gods, how I loved that cock in my mouth. It was so big I could hardly fit my lips around it—so long it seemed to be pushing right down my throat. I brought up my hands and caressed his balls, and Dark started thrusting gently into my mouth.

"Chance," he moaned softly. "Oh gods, that's good."

I licked around his cock as I sucked, and he groaned. I could never get tired of this. Never.

"Oh fuck," he breathed, as my hands clasped his tight buttocks, drawing him in deeper, "you have to see this."

I was pretty sure I'd seen it before. Hell, I'd probably done it before. But I withdrew Dark's fat, pulsing cock from my mouth and dutifully turned my head to watch.

The small-breasted woman had turned around to face the guy's feet, and his hands dug in her ass as she bounced up and down on his balls. Between their legs kneeled the other woman, her head down, licking. From the looks on their faces I'd guess she was giving both of them a tongue-job.

A curtain shifted on the far side of the stage and another naked man came out. I smiled as I recognized him—Roco Rico, hardest cock in the west. This guy could fuck for hours without coming. He was a regular for the live shows.

Without preamble, he sauntered up to the kneeling woman and thrust that ever-hard cock of his into her pussy. She moaned. He moaned. Everyone moaned. Catching her large breasts in his hands, he fucked her slowly, and the four of them settled into a rhythm.

I felt Dark's hands on my shoulders, pulling me to my feet. He kissed me long and slow, tonguing my mouth until my knees went weak. His hands worked the hook-and-eye fastenings on my corset, reaching in and rubbing his thumbs over my nipples.

I whimpered against his mouth and he smiled against mine.

I lost all strength in my body then, but it didn't matter because Dark lifted me in his arms, carried me to the bed and continued to undress me. I'd thought he might want to leave the stockings on, but he stripped me naked and ran his hands all over me. His lips caressed my skin, sucking my nipple into his mouth and tonguing it delicately.

"Don't you want to watch the show?" I asked rather breathlessly as he kissed down my stomach and started licking my clit.

"I've got my own show right here," he said, and slid his tongue into my pussy.

And hell, I gave him a show. I writhed and screamed and moaned and begged him to never, ever stop fucking me. When he finally raised his head — leaving me limp and exhausted — and kissed me, I tasted myself on his lips and curled my leg around his waist.

As he slid inside me, filling me deliciously, that incredible cock of his stretching my cunt to its limits, I looked up at him and knew I'd never been with anyone quite like him before. I'd never love anyone quite like him again.

After tonight I might never see him again.

This could be the last time we ever made love. Tonight we'd leave the club and go after Ven. And when we found her…

When we found her…

When we found her, Dark was going to kill me.

His whiskers nuzzling my neck brought me back to myself. He glided deeper into me, that incredible feeling of fullness. I was so wet for him and he fit so well. The slide of his body against mine, the roughness of his chest, the heaviness of his thighs—it was all heaven.

I'd never known completeness like this.

He looked at me before he came, the darkness in his eyes lightening for just a moment, his skin glowing, and I held him to me, kissing him as he shuddered inside me, an endless stream of hot pleasure. I came too, eyes open, memorizing every breath of him. I probably told him I loved him. I know I cried.

And Dark held me in his arms, wrapped me in his warmth, tucked my head under his chin and murmured, "Are you all right?"

I nodded, blinking my eyes dry. "That was beautiful." I raised my head and brushed my lips over his. "It was…"

Dark smiled at me and I smiled back helplessly.

I was so helpless. If he drew a sword and killed me right then, I wouldn't have stopped him. I'd never felt so damn complete in all my life. Screw what Striker said. I belonged right here.

Chapter Eighteen

ဢ

We lay together long enough that a Kelf had to come and politely mention that Solana was waiting for us. Apparently the ten o'clock show was over and we'd missed her. I was starting to think it might be weird to watch my friend fucking a load of strangers anyway—and Dark hadn't seemed too keen on the idea of watching one of his subjects. We dressed, and at Dark's insistence I left my hair loose. His fingers played with it as we walked along the velvet corridor to Solana's dressing room.

Misnomer. Mostly it was used for undressing.

She was seated at a dressing table lit by gas lamps, wearing a silk robe, brushing her hair and looking exquisite. If she'd joined the orgy out there it didn't show. She even smelled sweet, like vanilla.

Sign of a Lady.

"Your Majesty." She swept to her feet and into a graceful curtsey.

"Solana."

She rose again and smiled at me. "Chance. So good to see you."

"You too," I said, as if it hadn't only been days since the last time we saw each other. "Taking holiday time?"

She smiled. "My contract with the ambassador included this."

"It did?" Some contract.

"He's taken one of the private rooms. Did you enjoy the show?" she asked, like an actress or an opera singer.

"We only caught the beginning of it," I said. "It was good to see Roco's still here."

"Ah, yes. Roco." She smiled and fussed with some roses on her dresser. "He's the highest-paid man here."

"As high as us?"

She flashed that pretty dimple again. "It's a pity there's no Association for men."

"I've often thought that. Solana, I hate to cut into the chitchat, but my Kelf said you had a message?"

Her eyes flickered to Dark, just for a second, and I hesitated. "Dark, I… Could you give us a minute?"

He frowned a little, but nodded and kissed my temple. "I'll be outside."

Solana curtseyed again as he left and gave me a knowing look.

"There's a flush in your cheeks I haven't seen in a long time," she said.

"Your king is quite the lover."

"I've no doubt. Are you…" She paused, searching for what to say.

"It's complicated," I said. "About the Federacion?"

"The ambassador mentioned it. He was dictating to a Kelf. A letter, most of it made no sense to me. He told the Kelf to take the message to the Castillo de la Montaña."

"Imaginative name," I murmured.

"It's in the hills about thirty miles from here."

Of course it was. What was I saying about fate? And what had Ara said to me? "Your people are already there."

The Federacion had Ven.

"I read the message," Solana went on. "The Kelf took money for it. It was a short note saying he was going to speak to the Senadoro about the Federacion."

"Which Senadoro?"

Her eyes closed for a moment, then opened again. "César Aparicio Pérez."

I tried to remember the name. Then I bit my lip and said, "Solana, I need to ask another favor."

"Of course."

"If you don't hear from me after tomorrow, I need you to contact this person." I wrote down the name of a Phoenix Knight based in Puerta Nueva, the capital city. "Tell her what you've told me. If you're worried you're in danger go to her, she'll take care of you."

Solana took the name, looking a little unsettled. "What is this Federacion?"

"I don't know exactly. But I'm pretty sure they have your princess."

Her hand went to her mouth. "They're holding her? Is she all right?"

"I don't know yet. I think so. Dark and I are going in tonight to rescue her."

She nodded.

"If I don't come back, do what I said."

"Don't come back? How dangerous will this be?"

Ordinarily I'd have said "not very". But even aside from Ara's warning I knew it. Knew that there was a very strong possibility I wouldn't come back down that mountain.

I pulled Solana to me and hugged her. I was never one for close friends, but we had a lot of common experience and I was fond of her.

"Thank you for helping me," I said, and she pulled back, frowning worriedly, but smart enough not to ask questions. "You're a good friend."

"I will see you tomorrow," Solana said slowly, looking at me strangely. "I have an engagement with the ambassador at the Casa Flores. Come there."

I looked at her for a long moment.

"If I don't see you, I will go to your friend in Puerta Nueva," she said finally.

"Thank you." I kissed her cheek and she kissed mine. "I have to go. Goodbye Solana."

"Goodbye Chance."

I left her dressing room and found Dark standing outside, glowering at a pretty young man who appeared to be quite interested in the contents of my lover's pants. I gave him a sweet smile, linked my arm through Dark's and led him toward the exit.

"We're leaving so soon?"

"How much heat are you packing?"

Dark gave me a smoldering look.

"I meant weapon-wise."

The smokiness in his eyes faded when he heard my tone. "An eight-foot lion with claws bigger than your head."

"Not enough," I said.

"For what?"

"For rescuing your sister."

That pulled him up short. "You want to go in tonight?"

I nodded.

"Will it be so dangerous?"

I bit my lip and tried to think how much to tell him. "The people who have her are known to the Order. Known mostly for killing us on sight."

"What quarrel do they have?"

"No one's gotten close enough to find out." As I spoke, I wondered if Kett and Striker had made their move on the Federacion yet. Don't ask me how I knew they were on the job. "But they're vicious Dark—really vicious."

He paled a little. "And they have my sister."

"They do. My guess is they're interested in her psychic powers. The more she weakens, the more they'll find her to be…disposable."

A muscle worked in Dark's jaw. "We go tonight."

"We go get changed first. I am not getting blood on this dress. And you need more weapons Dark. Véan isn't enough."

In a nihilistic frame of mind, I dressed to impress. If I was going to die, I was going to have a damn pretty corpse. Eyeliner. Lipstick. Hair fastened back—because despite the romantic image, it's just not practical to go in fighting with hair flying in your eyes. I slid into my old faithful leathers, perfectly conditioned with enough give to let me move. A proper bra and a shirt that let me stretch. I fastened on holsters absolutely fucking everywhere—waist, thighs, ankles, wrists, back. I had plenty of practice moving with this much hardware, or I'd have clinked when I walked.

Low-heeled boots and a long coat finished the outfit. I was ready to rumble.

My scryer buzzed as I was fastening back my hair and some instinct made me take it out of the bedroom, out of Dark's range of hearing.

It was Striker. Damn instincts.

"What the fuck are you doing here?" he demanded, not looking happy.

"Existing without reason," I said. "You?"

"I mean in Iberia," he snarled.

"Rescuing Dark's sister."

Irritation flashed in his cold eyes. I peered into the background, saw the silhouette of a castle over his shoulder.

"You're at the Castillo," I said.

"Smart girl."

"With Kett?"

He nodded. "And your mother. Quite the team we make."

"You've infiltrated the Federacion?"

"Intelligence gathered. They want us dead," Striker said. "New orders."

Horror swelled in me. I knew what those orders were going to be. And I knew Striker would be more than happy to carry them out.

"Dark's sister is in there."

He blinked at me. "Better tell him to get a move on then."

"We're on our way."

Something flashed across his face.

"No pet," he said, and his tone was quite different. "Not you."

"Yes," I said, "me. My fight."

"Your death, love. Don't come up here." His voice was soft, his eyes intense.

"What is this, prophecy day?"

"I mean it," Striker said. "You come up here, bad things will happen to you."

"I know," I said.

"Very bad things," he repeated. "Look. Your mother's with me, she'll meet you, stay with her—"

"Striker, no," I said. "No. I know what's—"

"Listen to your fucking father," he snarled suddenly, startling me. "You come up here, you die. The Nasc girl isn't the only one who can see the future."

"No and neither are you," I said. "I know."

We stared each other down.

"I'm not joking Chance," Striker said. "You've had two warnings now. You know it's true."

"I know."

"You want to die?"

"Can I avoid it?" I asked.

"Stay where you are."

"No. I made a promise."

A longer silence. I could see it weighing on him. It was a curious dichotomy that Striker didn't lie or break promises. It wasn't honor. It was just the way he was.

"Don't say I didn't warn you," he said eventually, and the scryer went black.

Dark had changed into dark jeans and a sleeveless T-shirt that showed off beautiful muscles. I ached to touch them, kiss them, rub my naked body all over them. But we had work to do.

"Armed?" I asked.

He fastened on baldrics holding sword and crossbow, then thigh and wrist braces for knives.

"Véan will make an appearance when we get there," he said.

"Good," I said. "Another pair of claws is always handy." I slipped one final dagger into a special sheath between my breasts and went for the door. "Let's go kill things."

Dark's hand on my shoulder pulled me back.

"Chance," he said, and as his eyes searched mine he seemed to run out of things to say. "After tonight…"

I willed my face to stay neutral. No tears. No anger.

"I will take Ven back to Angeland. She and Ara need to merge."

I nodded. "Contact the Order. They might help you with transport."

His hand caressed my face. "I'm going alone," he said.

"I know." If he didn't shut up soon I was going to lose my battle against the tears behind my eyes.

"It has to be this way," Dark said fiercely. "If I could change it, I would—"

"Stop," I said, my voice breaking. "Don't say that. Don't make it harder."

He looked at me, really looked at me, for a long moment. "You would be a good Nasc queen," he said finally.

"I'd be a fucking great Nasc queen," I snapped, and the barest hint of a smile crossed his face. "Now, can we go?"

Thirty miles have never been covered so fast. The munta were used to traveling uphill, but not at the speed we rode them. I couldn't guarantee Striker wouldn't start his assault on the Castillo before we got there.

The place was in darkness. Well—there were torches burning and guards patrolling, but no signs of untoward activity. No obvious slaughter. Just the wind, singing lightly through dark trees. The castle had no moat, but it did have high spiked walls and a lot of people with weapons.

We left the munta tethered in the forest and crept closer in the darkness.

"Ideas?" I whispered.

"Shoot them all and climb over their corpses?"

"We'll call that Plan B."

"One of us has to get in there."

"What do you think their reaction to a lion would be?"

"I think they'd fill it with arrows."

"I think so too."

"You could use your feminine wiles," came a voice from behind us, and we whirled to see Chalia leaning against a tree. I fought a mad impulse to rush over and hide under her skirts like a five-year-old.

"Or you could just walk in," Striker suggested, materializing behind her.

"I can't go invisible," I snapped.

"Neither can I," Chalia said, "and I did it. Kett's on the inside," she explained. "These castles have hundreds of secret passages."

I looked at Dark and he nodded.

"Show us."

Kett met us at the mouth of a cave. The passageway was low, pitch-dark and filled with locked doors to which there were no keys. But Striker didn't need keys, and, I discovered, neither did I.

"Impressive," Dark murmured as I pushed open the last one.

"You ain't seen nothing yet."

My heart was beating fast. Adrenaline filled me up so high I was amazed I didn't squish as I walked.

The passageway came out into a cellar. It was dark and slimy and water splashed underfoot. Things scurried over the walls as we followed Kett toward the stairs.

"Goes into the kitchen," she said, stopping on the lowest step. "Should be quiet this time of night but once you're out into the main part of the castle there's no telling who'll be around."

I nodded. "Okay."

"They're like the Order, Chance," she said. "Only they have purpose. Officially, like an army. Government links. They won't ask questions," she said plainly, "they'll just kill you."

"Got that," I said, and clicked the safety off my crossbow.

"Big doors from the kitchen to the main hall. Offices and training rooms downstairs, dormitories upstairs. Dungeons reached through the east wing, ground floor. There are turrets but I don't know how to access them. Do you want me with you?"

"No," I said. "Don't get involved."

She nodded and melted into the shadows. "I'd say good luck," her voice floated after us, "but you of all people won't need it."

Hah.

The castle was huge. I could tell that from the kitchens. Cavernous. Dark. Old. Empty.

Dark took the downstairs rooms and I headed up the main stairs. He'd wanted to check the dungeons, but I knew Ven wasn't there. She was upstairs. Curving stairs. In a turret.

Intuition led me on, getting stronger as I moved. I knew when there were people behind the doors I passed, I knew when a guard approached. I knew which doors were unlocked. I started scaring myself when the turret door opened and I ducked left, then down, then left again as spikes shot out of the wall toward me. Another one flew up from the ground and I somersaulted over it without thinking.

Shame I'm going to die. I'm getting good at this shit.

Ven was waiting for me, a shadowed waif whose white hair was actually darker than her translucent skin. Her big soft eyes were haunted and she threw her slender arms around me as soon as she saw me.

"Chance," she said.

"You can see me? Ara couldn't."

"Ara sees more in abstract forms," she said. "I can see you." Her eyes flickered. "Dark is here?"

"Yeah. We need to get out."

But before we reached the turret door I knew something was wrong. Then I heard the shouts, the clank of weapons, and my heart plummeted.

They'd found Dark.

I glanced at Ven and I knew she knew.

"Run," she said, and I did, grabbing onto her hand and tugging her after me. She tripped after a few feet and I swung back and hauled her into my arms without breaking stride. We were on the third floor and there was no one around, but I had to go help Dark. There were dozens of people here, all armed, apparently all trained. And even without training a heavily armed person can be pretty fucking lethal.

We reached a window and it overlooked the courtyard, and when I saw what was happening in the flickering torchlight my heart leapt into my mouth.

Striker was there, and Dark in his lion form, and a whirling dervish of a thing that I thought might have been a gryphon. Kett. And there were hundreds of people with swords and bows.

"Oh gods," Ven whispered.

My eyes were fixed on Véan and I hardly heard her. He moved so fast I could barely keep up, a blur of grace and speed, leaving behind a trail of blood, exposed bones, screams and bodies. But they still kept coming.

"I have to help him," I said, and without even recalling the journey I was flying through the main hall, out into the amber-lit courtyard, Ven in my arms.

Federacion warriors fell on me, men and women, some of them not more than teenagers, all armed to the teeth. I let Ven slide to her feet and fired the single-shot crossbows on my wrists, taking down two of them instantly. A sword came to my hand and I sliced through two more.

Then Ven was moving, being tugged away, and as I whirled to defend her I saw Chalia blur before my eyes and felt the hilt of her sword in my hand.

"I've got her," she said, and then they were gone, and I stood there holding the most lethal weapon in all the Realms.

I smiled. These guys were dust.

Whatever my thoughts on inheritance and fate, they were quickly skewered by the Deirfiúr's insane maneuverability. Last time I'd held it I'd been as clumsy as a child, but now it felt like my own body, the sharpest blade in existence, scything through the air so sharply it broke a droplet of blood in half and splattered it on my face.

This was meant to be. Fuck knows if acknowledging my magical heritage had anything to do with it. I was on fire.

I swung that sword from hand to hand, and a swath of bodies fell before me. However many of them there were, they were no match for me. Hail Chance—lover, fighter, survivor.

I danced toward Véan in an orgy of death, whirling in circles, clearing my path like a harvester. I felt a fleeting flash of pride and knew it was Striker's.

I felt them falling back. Victory was mine.

And then it happened. I hadn't even been aware of Dark's human form arriving in the courtyard, but in the back of my mind I knew it was hubris to think the retreat was entirely my own doing. They'd fallen on him, fresh meat, and as my eye followed the surge of metal toward the door I saw, almost slowly, an arrow fly toward his chest.

The Deirfiúr sliced through a woman's throat. I hardly noticed.

Another arrow pierced Tal's shoulder and the sword fell from my grasp.

"*Dark!*"

Véan paused, his teeth tearing through someone's midsection, and his head snapped in Tal's direction. I heard his "*No,*" in my head, and then he was bounding toward the castle steps, blood flying from his mane in a deep red shower. A man leapt toward him and Véan broke his neck with one swipe.

My feet turned me in Tal's direction and I ran to him. I couldn't even see him now. He'd vanished under men with swords, women with bows, a flashing mêlée of steel and blood.

I heard Striker's bellow echo around the courtyard but I didn't stop. Didn't stop until I felt the cold slice of the Deirfiúr slash upward through my back, waist to shoulder, and my spine snapped in two as my ribs gave way.

For a second I swung there, spun by the force of the blow, and through a deep red mist I saw a man raise the Deirfiúr again, ready to take another blow.

He burst into flame, a Striker specialty, but I didn't live to see him burn. Pain slashed through me, bright and hard, and my mind floated free.

Death wasn't the way I'd expected. There were less of the pretty angels playing harps and more of the steel and blood. There wasn't even a white light. There was no fucking difference at all.

For a second I was confused. I'd felt the sword slice through my body, effortlessly deep, opening up my heart and lungs and stomach and everything else. I saw my body lie there, saw Striker just incinerate everyone around it and drag it from the courtyard, and then I saw Dark, in one form again, bleeding badly, staggering, chasing after Striker.

Then I—whatever the hell I currently was—swooshed toward him faster than light, and in that instant I understood.

This was how one Slid.

Chapter Nineteen
Dark

&

In the firelight everything looked hellish. Nasc don't like fire any more than any other animal, but right now I had more important things to worry about.

Ven's safety flew from my mind, and Chance's death consumed me.

Striker had Chance's body outside the castle. The gryphon fluttered down beside us, wings torn, beak stained with blood. Striker aimed one hand at the castle and the whole place erupted in flames.

None of us looked back.

"Is she dead?" the shapeshifter had become human again, a naked bloody woman, big eyes concerned.

"I warned her," Striker muttered, hands probing the horrible slash in Chance's perfect smooth back. Somehow the smoothness of her skin made the red, fleshy, oozing wound even harder to bear. "I fucking warned her."

"I didn't see it happen," I said urgently. "What happened?"

"Her sword," the shifter said. I couldn't remember her name. I didn't care. "Chalia's sword. She dropped it."

"It's not fucking meant for her," Striker cursed. There was something like pain on his face. Tears in his eyes.

"She can't die," I said. "She said herself she can't die."

"Does she look bloody alive to you?" Striker snarled. He grabbed her wrist. Her arm swung grotesquely. "Feel a pulse there? See her breathe? She can't survive this."

"She can't be dead," I repeated numbly.

"You were the one who was going to kill her," Striker flung back at me.

"I wasn't. I mean, *I meant* to but I…not for a long time…" I trailed off. I hadn't meant it for a long time. Not since…hell, I don't know. Somewhere between her wrapping her mouth around my cock and her saving my life. I could never kill Chance. I couldn't even hurt her. I love her.

I love her, and now she is dead.

I didn't know what was worse, my grief for her or my anger that I'd gotten her into this. Waves of violence rose in me, pain that had nothing to do with broken bones and bleeding cuts, and the beast inside me let out a roar that shook the mountain.

There were tears rolling down my face. I reached for Chance's body, that sweet, perfect body that could make me so dizzy with desire I could hardly stand. The body that could make me painfully hard in seconds. The body I'd been thrusting into only hours ago.

Her cold, broken, bloody body.

Striker wrapped his arms around her and yanked her possessively away from me. Her head lolled like a rag doll.

"She's mine," I snapped.

"Fuck off," he said. "My kid. My blood."

"Mine," I snarled, lashing out at him, and Striker caught my wrist.

And he stared.

"Let go," I said.

"Shut up." Something like wonder came over his face. "How did you do it?"

"Do what?" I tugged but his grip was like iron.

"She's there, how did you—?"

"What the fuck are you talking about?"

Striker looked down at the broken body of his only child, then back at me. Then he laughed.

"Whatever it is, it's not funny," I said.

"It's fucking brilliant," he replied. He gathered Chance's body into his arms and stood. "You and me," he said, "we got work to do."

Chapter Twenty
Chance

ဆ

My sojourn in Dark's head was enlightening, to say the least. For one thing, I finally understood how my mother had come back from the dead when her corpse was three days cold. I watched through Dark's eyes as Striker mended the damage to my body, sewing organs together and fusing vertebrae whole again. It looked damn painful. I wasn't looking forward to waking up.

I was still bloody amazed I'd done it. All my life I thought there was something wrong with me that I couldn't Slide. When the truth is that I *could*—just not into another dimension. I could Slide into another person, and to my knowledge that had never been done before.

Dark had a strong mind, and I could do little more than take a backseat and watch what he was doing without influence. I was just trapped there, a spectator. If it hadn't been for Striker calling me back, I might have stayed there forever. Could think of worse places.

Although, being stuck in Dark's head would make sex with him rather difficult.

I came back to myself in a room, a hotel I guessed, lying facedown with a truly horrifying amount of pain searing through me. In case you aren't aware, a sword through the back really fucking hurts.

I was alone, but I heard voices in the next room.

"So you're just leaving, then?"

That was Striker, and he sounded like he was sneering.

"I have things to do."

Dark, his voice quiet. An ache started inside me that had nothing to do with physical pain.

"Right. And all these things, they're more important than the woman who died helping you and yours?"

"She didn't die."

"Her body did. I felt it, mate. Felt her soul depart." There was a thud, like Striker's heavy boot kicking something. "Never wanted to feel that again."

"That's what happened with Chalia?"

"Like mother, like daughter." The cockiness returned to Striker's voice. "We got a bargain, then?"

My ears pricked up. Bargain?

"I don't hurt Chance and you don't hurt Nasc."

"Man's gotta protect what's his," Striker agreed.

"She's not yours," Dark said.

"Blood is blood, mate." Another pause, then his voice became gentler. "You love her, don't you?"

I held my breath.

"About as much as you do."

"Gods help you then, mate. She's awake now. Sure you don't want to see her?"

A short pause, then Dark said quietly, "There's nothing I could say that wouldn't sound like goodbye."

I didn't hear footsteps, but I still knew when he was gone.

I stayed where I was. Hell, I couldn't move. I knew I had to let him go anyway. So he wasn't going to kill me. We still had the same chances at a future together — none.

A pernicious little voice at the back of my head whispered, "You big fat liar, you knew he wasn't going to kill you. That was just an excuse not to get involved with him."

"Shut up," I said.

"Otherwise you'd have had to face the fact that you could never be what he wanted. All the training in the Realm, all the hot sex, all the screaming orgasms couldn't make you into what he really wants."

"I said shut up."

"He wants a Nasc woman. A nice queen to give him little Nasc babies. If you had children they'd probably have horns and tails."

"Please shut the fuck up."

"Besides. You murdered his brother. Were you really stupid enough to think he was going to forgive you for that?"

"Shut. The. Fuck. Up!"

The door opened. "Talking to me, love?"

I turned my head, painfully, to see Striker smirking at me.

"Just the voices in my head."

He nodded as if this was perfectly normal. "How you feeling?"

"Peachy. Remind me if it's five hundred and thirty-five stitches in my back or five hundred and thirty-six?"

"Oh, at least twice that." He closed the door and came in. "Your mother's sleeping. Want me to wake her?"

"No, it's okay." I paused, wanting to ask about Dark but quite unable to find the words.

"Take you a while to heal," Striker said, coming over and running his hand down the stitches on my back. The cut ran diagonally from right buttock to left shoulder, effectively taking in most major organs, plus my spine and several ribs.

"Really? I thought I'd be up and about in a day or two."

"Don't be flippant. Take you at least a week."

I met his eyes and we both smiled.

"Your mother's going to give you some bollocks about it being her fault 'cause she gave you the sword," he said, shrugging off the moment.

"I didn't have to use it."

"You didn't have to be there, pet. I warned you, and so did the girl."

"Ven? Is she okay?"

"Yeah. Your bloke's taking her back to herself."

He watched me carefully and I womanfully managed not to say, "He's not my bloke."

Silence stretched.

"You know, your mother still manages to maintain the illusion that she needs me," Striker said, apropos of nothing. He took a seat on the edge of the bed, and I winced as the mattress dipped. "She's always fucking up in some direction or other. Keeps a man on his toes. Makes him feel needed."

"Oh," I said, not sure what my response should be.

"But you…" Striker's eyes narrowed and he idly played with the stitches on my shoulder blade. "You beat me at swordplay when you were seven. You've made it clear all your life you don't want anything to do with me. You don't bloody *need* me. You never did."

I stared at him. "I thought you didn't remember anything past last year?"

He shrugged, made a small moue of chagrin. "I may have bent the truth a little there."

"You remember everything?"

"First word—'fuck'. First sentence—'shut the fuck up'. Fourth birthday present—punch bag. Yeah pet, I remember it all."

I stared some more. Since I could hardly move, it seemed like the best thing to do. "You bastard! Do you know how much this is going to cost me in therapy?"

"Do you know how much the Order is going to pay you for helping destroy the Federacion foothold?"

"I didn't—"

Striker put his finger to his lips. "Call it compensation," he said with a grin and stood up. "Right, before I forget, some bimbo from your whore club left a load of messages. Seems to be under the impression you were supposed to be somewhere while you were dead."

My hand would have flown to my mouth if I'd been able to move it. How the fucking-fuck was I going to explain this to Solana?

As he opened the door, Striker paused and said over his shoulder, "He loves you, you know."

I grimaced into the pillow. "About as much as you do."

Striker gave a snort. "Yeah, well, that's a bloody lot then, isn't it, love? I ain't gonna tell you to go after him, mostly because you can't get up off that bed. But you know it's not over, don't you pet?"

For the first time in my life, I really wanted to believe him.

Epilogue
Several months later

ɛɔ

The vampire had a hot, silky mouth. He licked at my breast—his tongue skillful, his every move exuding sensuality. His hand smoothed over my thigh, slipping between my legs to caress my pussy.

I winced as his fingers encountered dry flesh. *Again.* Come on, what the fuck is wrong with me? I'd been back on the job a week now and I'd been taking clients every day. Clients that were far below my ranking. I just wanted to get laid. To get the memory of Dark out of my head.

But every client had been the same. No matter how sexy the man, how skilled his mouth and hands and cock had been, I'd been as dry as a bone for each one. I was getting desperate now. I'd have to resort to lubricant if I ever wanted to get laid again.

The other Associées had started asking me if I was well. I hadn't been able to satisfy a client since I came back. I was going to lose my ranking over this.

The vampire raised his beautiful head. "You are like a desert, *ma cherie.*"

I tried not to visibly wince. "You're pretty hot, too."

He chuckled sensually. "That's not what I meant." He flicked his tongue over my flat nipple. "I can hardly get a response out of you."

"I'm sorry," I said. "My mind is on other things."

"I can't fuck you if you're so dry."

"I know," I said. "I'm sorry. Look, just do that thing with my clit again, I'm sure—"

The door slammed open so hard it banged back on its hinges and I heard the wood splinter. Over the vampire's shoulder I couldn't see who'd come in, but I felt the deep fury filling the room in waves.

"Get the fuck away from my woman!"

Well, that gave me an answer. I didn't need the vamp to scurry away to know who was there, but he did anyway, giving me a prime view of Dark standing there in the doorway, big and hot and angry and sexy as hell.

I felt a flood of moisture in my pussy just at the sight of him.

"Hey," the vampire regained his feet, "I paid—"

"I don't care," Dark said, grabbing him by the shoulder and throwing him bodily from the room. The vamp was naked, but he had enough sense not to come back in for his clothes.

Dark slammed the door shut, threw the bolt which was of course broken, and rammed a chair under the handle. The chair rattled and slid around and finally Dark just grabbed the dresser and shoved that across the doorway as a barrier.

I lay there watching him, hotter than I could believe, my nipples hardening, pussy wet for the first time since we'd parted, and tried hard to breathe through my sudden, crippling lust.

"Hello, lover."

He turned and glared at me. "You were about to fuck him."

"I was about to try," I said. "He's going to be some kind of angry that you chucked him out."

"Don't care." Dark stalked toward me like the big cat he was, and a thrill of excitement fluttered through my pussy. I licked my lips.

"You know, you can't just barge in here like that after not coming near me for months—" I began, but Dark effectively shut me up by yanking me into his arms and kissing me so hard I saw stars.

"And…never calling or…anything," I panted as he let me go.

"You didn't call *me*."

"I didn't leave. In case you'd forgotten, I was lying there with my body nearly cut in half."

Dark flinched. He turned me gently in his arms and looked at the long scar on my back. Striker could have healed it completely, but he said some scars were useful for remembering.

Like I could ever forget.

"It's healed?" he said, running his fingers over the line.

"Pretty much."

"Does it hurt?"

I turned back, looking up at him. I saw the same pain in his eyes that burned behind my own.

"Not anymore," I said, and he kissed me again, gentler this time. My sweet Dark. Probably I ought to be angry with him for buggering off like that, but I was far too glad to have him back.

Speaking of… "Why are you here?"

"Is it not obvious?"

"Last I heard you needed a queen and I was just the whore who killed your brother."

Dark winced. "Ah. Yes. Well."

I raised my eyebrows.

"I don't…you're not a whore. And Venara told me about Jonal."

"She did?" I asked guardedly.

He sighed. "I haven't quite forgiven her, but I understand. I'm working on understanding."

I smiled at him. "Progress."

"I wouldn't have killed you."

I kissed his temple. "I know."

Laying his cheek against mine, Dark asked in a reluctant voice, "Did you fuck him?"

"The vampire? Didn't get a chance. No pun intended."

"But you've been working? There've been others?"

He looked at me anxiously and I thought about teasing him, but instead told him the truth. "There have *nearly* been others. I haven't been able to fuck anyone since I came back to work. I was thinking about taking on women clients but I couldn't get very excited about that, either."

"Excited?" His hand brushed my breast and my nipple leapt to attention.

"I've been like the desert since you left," I said, taking his hand and kissing the fingers. "So dry it's impossible. I think there's something wrong with me."

Dark's other hand slipped between my legs, where my pussy was bubbling happily with moisture for him. "Feels fine to me."

Oh, me too.

"For the first time since you left."

"Let me get this straight." His fingers idly stroked my wet labia. "You haven't had sex with anyone since me."

"Nope."

"Haven't been able to get wet for anyone since me."

"Not even a nipple erection."

Dark suddenly grinned, took my hand and slid it over his crotch. He was hard as anything.

"Remember how I told you infidelity is impossible for Nasc?"

I stared at him.

"But I'm not Nasc."

"You're mated to one."

I stared some more. It's becoming like my trademark now.

"I've been traveling the Realms looking for a mate," Dark told me. "Every Nasc woman I could find. Do you know how beautiful Nasc women are?"

"Is this going somewhere?" I asked grumpily.

"Couldn't get hard for any of them. It was ludicrous. Solana pointed it out to me."

"You tried to fuck Solana?"

"She comes highly recommended." He stroked my cheek. "She was surprised I asked for her. She thought you were my mate."

"I can't be," I said. I know his sister had told me the same thing—but let's face it, if I went around listening to psychic horses I'd have to ask myself some serious questions about my sanity. "Your mate needs to be Nasc. Your queen, remember? Giving you lots of little Nasclets?"

He nuzzled my neck, which made thinking a bit harder. Certainly it took the fight out of my protestations.

"I mean, I don't even know if I can have Nasclets."

"Are you willing to try?"

Right then I'd have happily birthed a full-grown munta if it'd make him happy.

"Yes," I said, and he kissed me. "But Dark, I'm only human. Well, almost human."

"I'm almost human too," he said, playing with my nipple.

"No, you're—"

"Your mate," Dark said. "It's a love bond."

My breath caught in my throat. "You love me?"

"I love you."

I didn't know what to say. Well, actually I did, but my mouth wasn't working.

Dark tilted my face up to his with two fingers. "Be my queen?"

I did my goldfish impression. Maybe that's my Nasc form.

"Venara says our children will be strong. Blonde like you." He kissed me. "Nasc like me."

"Did she say what animals?"

"She couldn't see that."

"How about their favorite foods?"

Realizing I was teasing him, he bit my lip. "Is that a yes?"

"Yes." I started unfastening his fly.

"Do you love me?"

Happily, I wrapped my hand around his cock. "I love you."

"My cock or me?"

"Hard to say. Your cock, mostly, but since it comes attached to you, I guess I have some residual affection for—eee!" I yelped as he wrestled me onto my back.

"Did that hurt?"

"Will you kiss me better if I say yes?"

"Yes."

"Then it hurt dreadfully. I may never recover."

Dark's mouth met mine, his tongue sliding against my lips, tasting me as I pushed his shirt off his shoulders. His body was twice as delicious as I remembered, big broad shoulders and the hardest, hottest abs I've ever had the privilege of rubbing up against.

"Two things," he said when he came up for air.

I concentrated on taking his trousers off.

"One, you're giving up this Association stuff, right?"

"Well, duh." I squeezed his buttocks.

"Just checking." He licked my neck.

"And the other thing?"

"Mmm. I'm the king."

"I know that, honey."

"Which means you'll be the queen."

"Boy, you must've taken a class in this."

"So you have to do what I tell you to."

I withdrew my hands from his pinchable backside. "The hell I will."

"At least in public."

"Do you even know me at all?"

"Or maybe you could just pretend to." Dark looked at me pleadingly.

"Hey, I'm a woman of independent means. I don't need a man to tell me what to do. I beat my father in a swordfight when I was seven," I told him for emphasis. "I—"

Dark kissed me again and swallowed my argument. His hand caressed my breast. I'm afraid I moaned.

"You can't win every argument by kissing me," I told him.

"Well, no," he played with my clitoris, and my eyes glazed over, "but I figure you can't be too angry with me for it. Besides, I can always progress to full sex."

"Oh, I can be angry and still want sex." When it came to Dark, I could be *dying* and still want sex.

"I am the king," he said, not very convincingly, "you have to obey me. Deal with it."

"I don't have to—" His finger slid inside me. "*Ohhhh…*"

"How about this," Dark suggested, nibbling on my nipple. "You pretend to do what I say and afterward I fuck you into oblivion."

I can deal with that.

Why an electronic book?

We live in the Information Age—an exciting time in the history of human civilization, in which technology rules supreme and continues to progress in leaps and bounds every minute of every day. For a multitude of reasons, more and more avid literary fans are opting to purchase e-books instead of paper books. The question from those not yet initiated into the world of electronic reading is simply: *Why?*

1. *Price.* An electronic title at Ellora's Cave Publishing and Cerridwen Press runs anywhere from 40% to 75% less than the cover price of the exact same title in paperback format. Why? Basic mathematics and cost. It is less expensive to publish an e-book (no paper and printing, no warehousing and shipping) than it is to publish a paperback, so the savings are passed along to the consumer.

2. *Space.* Running out of room in your house for your books? That is one worry you will never have with electronic books. For a low one-time cost, you can purchase a handheld device specifically designed for e-reading. Many e-readers have large, convenient screens for viewing. Better yet, hundreds of titles can be stored within your new library—on a single microchip. There are a variety of e-readers from different manufacturers. You can also read e-books on your PC or laptop computer. (Please note that Ellora's Cave does not endorse any specific brands.

You can check our websites at www.ellorascave.com or www.cerridwenpress.com for information we make available to new consumers.)

3. *Mobility.* Because your new e-library consists of only a microchip within a small, easily transportable e-reader, your entire cache of books can be taken with you wherever you go.

4. *Personal Viewing Preferences.* Are the words you are currently reading too small? Too large? Too… ANNOYING? Paperback books cannot be modified according to personal preferences, but e-books can.

5. *Instant Gratification.* Is it the middle of the night and all the bookstores near you are closed? Are you tired of waiting days, sometimes weeks, for bookstores to ship the novels you bought? Ellora's Cave Publishing sells instantaneous downloads twenty-four hours a day, seven days a week, every day of the year. Our webstore is never closed. Our e-book delivery system is 100% automated, meaning your order is filled as soon as you pay for it.

Those are a few of the top reasons why electronic books are replacing paperbacks for many avid readers.

As always, Ellora's Cave and Cerridwen Press welcome your questions and comments. We invite you to email us at Comments@ellorascave.com or write to us directly at Ellora's Cave Publishing Inc., 1056 Home Avenue, Akron, OH 44310-3502.

erridwen, the Celtic Goddess of wisdom, was the muse who brought inspiration to storytellers and those in the creative arts. Cerridwen Press encompasses the best and most innovative stories in all genres of today's fiction. Visit our site and discover the newest titles by talented authors who still get inspired - much like the ancient storytellers did, once upon a time.

Cerridwen Press

www.cerridwenpress.com

Discover for yourself why readers can't get enough of the multiple award-winning publisher Ellora's Cave.

Whether you prefer e-books or paperbacks, be sure to visit EC on the web at www.ellorascave.com

for an erotic reading experience that will leave you breathless.